Presents

Tony Sewell's

JAMAICA INC.

Published by THE X PRESS, 55 BROADWAY MARKET, LONDON E8 4PH. TEL: 081 985 0797

Distributed by Turnaround, 27 Horsell Road N5 1XL
Tel: 071 609 7863

Printed by Cox & Wyman Ltd, Reading, Berks.

To Adèle

BOOK ONE

At the sound of gun shots, the deejay abandoned his microphone on stage, followed by the backing band who dropped their guitars and left the scene with their shirt-backs full of wind and knocking a stack of speakers over in the process. The boxes fell crashing down off the stage, sending the tightly-packed crowd into a panic — nobody needed to be told that it was every man for himself. This was meant to be a happy event, but the shooting had turned everything sour. The stadium, normally alive with the charged adrenaline of athletes, had become an arena of fear, with men, women and children scattering in all directions trying to dodge the stray bullets.

David Cooper lay flat on his back, his light brown suit covered in blood. He had worn his best for the occasion — Jamaican people loved to see their leaders dress in style. His eyes opened in time to see a large white cloud drift by in the bright blue afternoon sky. It looked peaceful. Cooper listened to the noisy panic, trying to figure out what had happened. He was neither in heaven nor in hell, but at the National Stadium in Kingston, Jamaica, where the sound of screaming women accompanied loud shotgun blasts which echoed to the slopes of the Blue Mountains in the distance.

"Lawd have mercy, dem kill David!" cried one voice.

"Mek me go fe me M16, is time fe war!" cried another.

Cooper struggled to remember who he was. The pain in the back of his head, and another in his side, jolted his memory. The Prime Minister of Jamaica had been shot as he stood on stage at the Peace Concert which aimed to end the gun war paralysing the nation's capital, by bringing together the warlords to shake hands on stage. Cooper turned his head slightly to see that he was lying in a pool of his own blood — so much for the truce.

Along the sides of the stage, hastily erected posters advertised Jamaica's best musicians who had consented to appear at the concert to help bring unity to the island. It was a virtual who's who of reggae music. From where he lay, Cooper noticed one heavily breasted woman running back and forth on the stage during a break in the shooting.

"Fire and judgement to all gunmen!" she screamed. "God in his heaven will judge the whole of Jamaica for this wickedness!"

She fell to the ground, rolling over and shaking as if possessed by some tempestuous spirit. Two soldiers tried to carry her off the stage. When she resisted, one of them shoved his pistol into her mouth.

"Lady, yuh have ten seconds fe come off de stage!"

1

The command was enough to revive her senses and she sprinted off, cussing the soldiers' insensitivity.

Could this really be the end? If so, death was spectacularly pathetic and terrifyingly banal. Close by, Cooper saw his pregnant wife Marva. Thank God she was with him. The familiar scent of her favourite perfume wafted across the stage, despite the madness surrounding it. Was he really living his worst horror Cooper wondered, or was he just imagining everything?

"Marva," he groaned, beckoning his wife, "what happened? Tell me, please..."

"Don't worry yourself David." Marva spoke softly, caressing his hand reassuringly. "The helicopter will soon come to carry you to the hospital. I'm sure you're going to be alright."

"I've been shot, haven't I?"

"Yes darling, but you're going to be fine, don't stress yourself." Under pressure, Cooper's wife was ice cool. "Will someone make haste with the water!" she ordered the security personnel, who had taken tentative steps to the flanks of the stage once the shooting had subsided.

Cooper was grateful for his wife's calm. Had it not been for her, he would probably have been trampled underfoot in the pandemonium which followed the first gun shots. Marva leant over her husband, her face close to his. Cooper blinked rapidly as a warm tear dropped into his eye from above. He looked up and admired the features which had secured her the title of Miss Jamaica World. She was still the most stunning woman in the island — black and beautiful.

But where the hell was the helicopter? It seemed to be taking forever. The pain in his head was unbearable. Everybody had to die one day, but not like this — slaughtered at a peace concert, the Prime Minister of Jamaica.

"Heavenly Father," he prayed silently, "I don't want to die, not now, not this way. I want to live, please God allow me to live. I don't want to die, no, not like this... dear Lord, please..."

Once the shooting had stopped, a trio of the island's big shots braved the stage. These were the warlords, the power players who would fight over the spoils of the David Cooper legacy. But he wasn't dead yet. Ken Williams — the young Brigadier General, Rodrigues Cooper — the PM's brother and leader of the opposition, and Trinity — Jamaica's most notorious gunman gathered in a semi-circle above David, peering down with concerned faces which gave little away of their real interest. They really needed to give a thumbs up or a thumbs down, but no-one dared make the move lest the finger of guilt be pointed in their direction. There was little love lost in Jamaican politics, David Cooper was simply a casualty of war. The power struggle for control of the island and its billion dollar drugs industry would begin the moment the Prime Minister had breathed his last.

Cooper resolved to cling to life like white on rice. If it really was his day for leaving this world, his departure would be a dignified one. Nobody would see David Cooper racked with pain.

"I'm feeling fine boys, I'll soon be up and running the country as usual. A few little gun shots can't stop David Cooper," he said with fake bravado. The expression on the faces of Rodrigues, Williams and Trinity told a different story. David wouldn't be up running anything for a good while — if ever.

Marva smiled and tearfully assured him that she didn't doubt he would be "back at work first thing on Monday morning."

"Does anyone know who shot me?" David asked. There was an embarrassed silence, each of the assembled powerbrokers looking at the others for the answer.

"Now don't worry yourself David. There'll be an investigation, don't you worry," said Marva firmly, wiping sweat from her husband's brow.

"I don't know who shot you yet," Ken Williams offered, "but my men have sealed off all the roads to the stadium. Rest assured Sir, we will find those responsible."

Trinity denied that it was a Yardie hit. "My boys were under manners," he insisted. Rodrigues suggested the theory that it could have been a mad man seeking revenge on society. It was a plausible theory Williams felt and Trinity agreed. David listened with fear and pain twisting his insides. He wasn't convinced that the mad men who traipsed the streets of Kingston, dicks hanging out of ragged pants could be such accurate shots. He wondered why, that amongst the brace of 'pretenders' to his throne assembled around him, none thought to mention the possibility of the gunman being an ambitious politician.

The stadium was still noisy as scuffles broke out between the army and groups of distressed people, who dispersed temporarily only when warning shots were fired in the air by a trigger happy young military officer. Out of this chaos came the booming voice of the deejay, who had previously warmed up the crowd with the deafening roar of ragga music.

"Will everyone leave the stadium in an orderly manner, the Prime Minister has been shot, but the latest report is that he will make a full recovery. So please, in the name of Jah and unity, let us not show the world that we are an ignorant people. Go home in peace and and leave the rest to the security forces. I beg you, please."

His pleading fell on deaf ears. In fact the crowd grew more restless and two Red Stripe bottles came sailing through the air in his direction. He left the stage hurriedly under army escort.

"Is who you ah call ignorant? Come off the stage, nuh man! Unity me backside!! We want raas claat justice, we want revenge!" cried one woman who sported a blonde wig and tight batty riders.

David was the poor people's champion — a latter day version of his biblical namesake. Armed with little more than a sling and a stone he had slain the corporate Goliaths that held the country to ransom and had put food in the ghetto children's hungry bellies. This Peace Concert was intended to end the violence that had left hundreds dead in Kingston's shanty towns. But fear in the eyes of frantic mothers desperately seeking children lost in the melée was indication that many more would die this day.

David Cooper refused to believe that it was all over, that he would never again rally the Party faithful, never again lead the people of Jamaica. Then came the pain — like a hot iron piercing his side and burning his brain, a reminder that he had a hole in his head. The masses had elected him with the biggest majority since his uncle Oliver Cooper. Whether he would get the opportunity to exercise that mandate was now down to the gods.

Then, as if a ghost had appeared before him, an old man, dressed in white and holding a long rod in one hand, stood above him preaching into the deejay's abandoned microphone.

"In the name of Jesus, I say rise! As our Lord went to Lazarus and told him rise from the dead, come alive David Cooper, come alive!"

The crowd erupted. Virtually every man, woman and child cussed the old man and a number of soldiers ran onto the platform and beating him, dragged him off stage.

Cooper winced. Far from dignity, a tragi-comedy of commotion surrounded these desperate moments as he struggled for life. The peanut and ganja sellers were doing brisk business, because no one wanted to miss the next act.

"Sensi! Get yuh lovely sensimilla... Sensi...!" Cooper heard one vendor cry. "Everyone knows that sensimilla was grown on Solomon's grave, so come now fe the weed of wisdom!"

It was madness, but David Cooper could do nothing about it. He was feeling weaker and weaker, but still there was no sign of the helicopter that was his only life line. He felt Marva squeeze his hand and as his eyes began to close he saw her smile nervously, unable to hide her fear.

"David, my sweet, when they get you to the hospital and you're better, I'm going to make sure that you teach me how to do the latest reggae dance."

Those around her laughed an uneasy laugh. Cooper looked up faintly and flashed a false smile.

Suddenly more gunshots exploded in the auditorium and the crowd

4

went mad. A ring of armed soldiers surrounded the fallen leader their backs to him, in a shoot to kill stance. There were cries from the crowd:

"Kill the babylon, kill dem!"

Rival gunmen were shooting at each other, and both sides were exchanging shots with the troops. A quartet of new recruits dragged Cooper roughly to a safer corner of the stage. A spotlight illuminated the huge bloodstain which marked the spot where he was shot. The Prime Minister's role was over. The action now was being acted out within the audience as people ran screaming, and bullets cut through the air.

It was clearly too dangerous to get David Cooper out of the stadium, so he lay with his head propped on Marva's lap as she tried to stem the flow of blood. Even if the helicopter arrived now, she wondered if it would do any good; the Angel of Death was knocking at her husband's door.

David Cooper felt his life flash before him. He thought of his mother, his father Gladstone and his father's father Lionel, who established the Cooper dynasty in Jamaica. He recalled how, as a small boy, his father had told him about the destiny of the Cooper family. He saw his father looking down at him as he played in the garden, telling him that one day he would be an important man in Jamaica. His father was a strong believer in destiny and the Cooper family's role among the great and powerful. He remembered the story his father told him about his grandmother, the story that had passed down from his grandfather Lionel Cooper. It was the story of a poor woman, who grew up in the countryside a hundred years ago. Her name was Mary...

She lived at Eden Park Estate, St Catherine, Jamaica, the British West Indies in the beautiful Caribbean sea when the queen was Queen Victoria. Eden Park was a sugar estate found near Ewarton. To reach the hamlet, a man had to take the road from Ewarton which climbed for about five miles winding like a snake. It was dangerous and you had to be careful in case a branch took off your head. You kept climbing the forested mountain track and minded the hole near the coconut tree. At this point you had to catch your breath before reaching the final ridge which was and still is, the scene of one of the wonders of creation. You were then looking at a big valley called the Vale of Lluidas.

The sugar cane was spread out for miles and the stalks bent slowly in the wind like a child holding its run belly, while the orange trees favoured a pretty lady with earrings of emerald and gold. That was where Mary called home, where she would often be the only woman among the men as they climbed from below to reach the ridge. It was here like 'Bucky Massa' that they took stock of the feast of lush green spread out before them.

The valley stretched for miles, and was completely surrounded by blue-green mountains. In the right corner, standing like the Tower of Babel was a huge chimney belching out smoke. Working in the cane piece, Eden Park men would look up to see the smoke from the chimney in the skyline and know that sugar was cooking. These men were the same as the palm trees in whose shadow they worked. Both were strong and no matter what calamity they met, whether hurricane or drought, remained attached to the earth. Backs bent, the men would begin their daily toil, their faces shining from the scorching early morning sun. After a hard day's work, their bare feet would be sore from stepping on wild bush for fourteen hours and treading down on the dirt track, but 'them nuh bother fuss'. They would wash their feet at home later in cool river water and bay leaves, to the rhythm of crickets scratching tiredlessly outside. These hard working poor men had long since lost their memories and abandoned their aspirations. No matter how hard life found them, they were umbilically tied to creation and awoke automatically when the cock crowed every morning.

It was in these cane fields that Mary discovered the difference between men and women and decided that what she needed out of life lay beyond the mountainous confines of the valley that had held her mother captive and her mother's mother and her mother before that. The men in Eden Park would look down on Massa Henry, whose daddy used to own their daddies during slavery times. Seen in the distance from the cane piece, Massa Henry was the size of a toy in their hands and they would 'pick him up' with their thumb and second finger, while they strutted around pretending to be lords. The women on the other hand were fearless and came down and stood so firmly in front of Massa Henry's mighty house, they could feel his hot breath on their cheeks as they looked him straight in the eye. Eden Park women knew the limits of Massa Henry's power and acted accordingly. For them, dreams and reality were one and the same, that is the way of women. Unlike their men, Eden Park women could never be content with the pretence that the valley equalled paradise, for they yearned for a world beyond. When the women worked the land they would dig deep, searching under the cotton tree to find the rusted anklets buried by a slave or the cruel neck brace that held together the innocent blood of Africa who arrived on Jamaica's shores, their families 'mash-up' and lost. The men would plant their yams in shallow earth but the women would dig deep until they found the wretched of the earth, the devil and his wicked angels. These women had stared the devil 'inna him eye' many times, and knew as the good book says, that Eden Park was no abiding city.

To Mary, Eden Park was nothing less than hell on earth, dripping with the blood of bondage. There were no accounts of a settlement in Eden Park before her great-grandmother's generation and all of them were slaves. One story says Eden Park Estate was once a big volcano until one day when its head blew off and created this valley. The estate was now bankrupt, completely 'bruk'. It used to annoy Mary when all the 'fool-fool' negro people talked about their parents winning their freedom when she understood that the English planters couldn't wait to give it up, now that sugar was worth no more than sand. Still the men in Eden Park would claim victory, pushing out their chests all 'boasy' and tell you how their fathers fought the redcoats with their bare hands, how they caught a bullet in their batty and then fired it back again. They would boast of how they burned down the cane and forced the Englishman to free them from bondage. Mary knew the truth however. Eden Park closed down when it stopped making money and everyone was given notice. With the Estate out of commission, Mary's mother ran with her grandmother to the bottom of the hills to make a new home; soon everyone was living on the edge of the valley with the huge clearing of neglected wild cane in the middle a permanent reminder that the world no longer needed it. The Eden Park Estate workers were left high and dry after its closure, with no money, no machinery and no direction. All Mary's generation inherited were hands that needed work and a picture of Jesus to bow down to.

At sixteen Mary got pregnant for a cane-cutter named Horsemouth and after she had the baby and Mama had tired of cussing her, she was instructed to only talk to church men in future. Yet she still liked

7

Horsemouth, he was full of jokes and always made her laugh. He was the blackest man in Eden Park — they say his grandparents were Maroons — and would wait for Mary after Sunday service when they would go into the thick bush behind the big Anglican church. He would slowly cut down the plantain leaves and spread them carefully on the ground for their makeshift bed. He did this with such care and serious attention that Mary found herself laughing when with the same care, he took off her frock and wrapped it in a bundle next to his things. He certainly knew how to make her feel good. She rested her long skinny legs on his shoulders as he came between them, the dew laden leaves making a squelching rhythm as their bodies moved up and down. Horsemouth pressed his large hands into the earth as if the ground was giving him pleasure and then when his time came, would grip the plantain leaves tight as if he was squeezing them for juice and then let go, his touch becoming gentle like a child. People said that he was the ugliest man in the valley but to Mary he was strong and handsome. He did have a stutter which made him seem like a fool, but if you took time to listen to him you'd discover that he talked sense. Mary would talk to him on any subject and find him an interested listener, though his habit of agreeing with everything she said would annoy her. That was the problem with Horsemouth, nothing worried him.

The two illicit lovers had no entertainment but themselves, so Mary called upon Horsemouth to crack jokes and act the jackass. If he wasn't amusing her by riding backwards on a donkey, he would allow small children to mimic his stutter; "All f..f..f..f..fe yuh, Mary," he would reassure her. But the children were ruthless and even the smallest pickney would gather to follow him and shout in a loud chorus: "Me...Me... Me... seh...seh...seh... How...How... de..de..do... do-do, do-do. Horsemouth fava do-do."

Instead of getting vexed as they expected, Horsemouth would burst out laughing, leaving the children to walk away uneasy, confused and not sure who the jackass was — him or them.

As they sat there, their naked bodies cool in the shade of the bush, Mary said "Horsemouth, you nevah wonder what's beyond the Vale?"

"Sometimes, but I don't think it's any bet..tter."

"How yuh mean, yuh nuh want to go Kingston? Walk tall down King Street with all the big people dem. Drive downtown in a horse and buggy, eat the best fish and drink foreign wine from France?"

"Yes I s..s..suppose I would like that."

"Wha' do you Horsemouth, you going to be a fool all your life? Things can't remain the same, they must change but if you jus' sit down on your foolish black batty and not even hope for change, then yuh is no better than a dead man."

8

Horsemouth grabbed Mary's thin arms and pushed her roughly to the ground. She was glad the man was vexed for once in his life.

"Everybody ah call me f..f..fool. But you d..d..don't understand do you? Me auntie say, you have to play fool fe catch wise. People look at me and call me Horsemouth 'cause me mouth big an' ugly an' 'cause me is black. Well as far as I...a..a..a..am concerned, them is right. But me n..n..n..no care."

"Is that it?" Mary asked surprised. She laughed loudly expecting him to mention how handsome he really was and how he was really wiser than everybody else. But no, he just simply agreed. She looked at him again, this time with suspicion. He returned a smile of wisdom. Shortly after, they raced to the beginning of the mountain slope, weaving through the long grass skillfully, his naked back awash with sweat. He was not a fool at all, Mary decided. Acting the fool was his way of survival and it kept him from going mad.

Horsemouth returned with the old men to work for Massa Henry. This was to prove a wise move, because freedom on the hillside was lonely and hungry while with Massa Henry, Horsemouth had a rent-free cottage and money in his pocket. Mary never planned to stop seeing him, but she soon felt she had outgrown him even though at eighteen, he was two years older. The last time he came around, she remained seated inside watching him as he waited behind the house — she was now too old to come out to play.

As a child Mary slept with a clothes-peg on her nose, tired of her mother telling her that it was too flat and that she looked like "salt-water African." Most people said she looked like her mother however, so Mary concluded that she too must be beautiful, because her mother was tall and proud and black as the night sky. Her face was perfectly carved and her head rested carefully on her neck.

Mary had never known her father. Mama said that he was a gentleman who was now living in England, but no one knew of any Negro gentleman who went to England from Eden Park. In search of the truth, curiosity took the young girl to the cock pit below the mountains where the old men regularly assembled to huddle around the fighting cocks. Mary would sit for hours studying every crevice of the worn faces of the old men, for any hint of similarity with hers. The men ignored the young girl, their only interest was in being the victorious winners of a cock-fight, standing proudly waving their winnings in the air, a moment of satisfaction in a day full of hunger and pain. Mary was certain none of them could be her father, for they were all so ugly it was a shame. She resolved to never tell her own daughter who her real father was. Like Mama, she would say he was a gentleman who had returned to England. It wasn't because she was ashamed of Horsemouth, but explaining why he wasn't around anymore would be

9

difficult. Eden Park women had come up with some wild stories in explaining the identities of absent fathers to their children and no one was surprised to hear that sister had married brother in the valley without them knowing.

Mary's four brothers died at birth and Mama was told that she was now barren. From that moment she was marked as a mule and no man would have her. People whispered that someone had lit a candle on her head and cursed her to remain without any more children. No man would have her, that is except for Blind Joe, who Mama would feed and then lead to the corner of the shack where she made him feel good. They would sit together until they thought Mary was asleep and then Mama would take off his shirt, to reveal two long scars on his back like a pair of snakes. Mama would gently rub it for him like she was Martha at the feet of Christ and then he would groan as he felt her bosom and thighs. Blind Joe was about 67 but was still muscular, his strong frame having been over-used like any workhorse in half a century of hard labour. His veins were tight and like swollen rivers, ran down his arms searching for the sea. He himself had spread the story that he had been a runaway and when he was brought back the overseer had dug out his eyes. That was a lie. The true story was that his woman caught him in bed with a sweetheart and when he reached home one night, she waited until he was fast asleep... She was fat like any cow, so when she sat on him he couldn't move. She then peppered his eyes with a blinding mixture given to her by the Obeah woman. Anyway this didn't stop Mama from giving him some loving. She used to joke and say that even if no-one else would look at her again, at least a blind man could see she was worth something.

Mama died before Mary was 20; her heart gave up, but Mary felt she had given up living a long time before. At 50 she still should have had so many years to live. She had always secretly been lonely and hated Eden Park for making her feel she was no good to anyone.

More than anything Mama had wanted to see her daughter get married, so when the time came Mary wasted no time in following her instructions. Yes she was married, but when her husband tried to make her look like a fool, she decided it couldn't go so.

Mama's instructions were, "Find yuhself a Christian man," and "mek sure him brownskin, you must bring up the colour." According to Mama, childish things like Horsemouth had to be put aside in favour of a serious man.

Mary married Orville Dean Johnson. He was brown in complexion but not mulatto and he was better than a Christian. In fact he was a preacher. Their wedding day was the envy of Eden Park. A real wedding in the valley was as rare as sweet mango out of season. To Orville it went without question but with little excitement and no fuss.

10

Mary's seven-year-old daughter Stella, looked on throughout the ceremony, not knowing what to make of her new father, while Horsemouth played his wooden flute, occasionally winking at the bride as if to remind her that he had been first.

Orville was a man who regularly travelled to Kingston, a name that was legendary in Eden Park and a place which most of its simple country folk had only heard of. Even before they married, he had promised to teach his new wife how to read and write but once the wedding was over with, he somehow never had time.

Initially, Mary was surprised that a man of 35 had not been married, but she could soon testify to how the local women would spoil Orville rotten. He had so many places to go come dinner time, that women openly fought each other to have him at their home for a meal. He lived on one of the estate houses and his clothes were washed and pressed without him asking, while his house was spring-cleaned every day. As for Mary, she had never really paid him any mind previously and that made him look at her more keenly. He wanted to break down the girl with the hardest heart. From the outset there was no courting. The only hint of his desires came in Church when, from ever since, he used to hold onto her hands for a long time when he greeted her. Also, at the altar call, he would pray over her the longest, rubbing his hands gently on her head and shoulders. It had been like that even before Mama died. Mary remembered her getting vexed and cussing how Pastor Johnson "ah feel my pickney up" in church. "Is Jesus fe wash sin, not the rubbing hands of a preacher," Mama used to say.

It was after one Sunday service that Orville asked Mary to marry him. His hands had remained on her head for such a length of time that he must have thought she was the Devil himself. He told her that the Lord knew who the right woman was for him and he had had a vision that they should get married. Mary didn't argue. After all he was a prize choice. He had been to Kingston, Mama would have approved of him as a husband and he could teach her how to read and write and that was her 'vision'. Best of all, he had a good waistline.

Orville was a storekeeper on the sugar estate. He got the job because he could pass as a mulatto. All the same, he grudged the white vicar at the Anglican church who was able to be a preacher full-time, while Orville had to go out to work. He was however, considered a fine preacher. He stood at the pulpit with his long side-burns, looking like an English planter and his reading was excellent. But for Mary, the fact that Orville was more learned than Horsemouth made him no bigger in spirit. And while the women of Eden Park admired his authority and his sweet English, he needed his wife to remind him of his greatness every day. She would take his pride and allow it to suckle her breasts. It didn't take long for her to get fed up with reassuring her naked king that he was dressed in beautiful robes.

It was after church, just two Sundays after they married.

"Well, did you like my sermon, Mary? It sound sweet, don't it?" said Orville vainly. For spite, she never answered him. So he got vexed.

"What wrong wid you? You jealous of me. Look how you eyes them turn red. When me did meet you, you never have farthing to rub together. You was jus' a negga gal with a pickney for that idiot Horsemouth."

She was too upset to bother answering him. She just fixed her gaze on the small bookshelf in the corner. He was half right. She never completely grudged him, but her eyes were red for his book-learning and the way he was able to stand there on a Sunday and read the Bible without making one mistake. Forgetting that he was vexed, she said, "Orville, please could you teach me a few things 'bout reading?"

"Fe what?"

"So that I will be able to read the Bible."

"Don't me read to you every evening?"

"Yes but..."

"Well, argument done!"

"But Orville, I would like to read for myself."

"Look, me don't have time, I got me work fe do and you have yours. Anyway a woman with too much knowledge is a trouble to a man."

"How can my learning to read be trouble to you?" Mary asked pleading. "Don't you want someone you can be proud of?"

"Trouble yes, don't you know the scriptures? When Eve ate of the fruit of the tree of knowledge and gave it to Adam, death and destruction come to Paradise. It was then that they became naked and realise good from evil and God haffe run them out! You be content with what you know and allow me to keep us safe, for who knows what evil will come upon us."

What hurt Mary most about this self-righteous little sermon was that Orville didn't really believe what he said, but because she was a woman, he took her for a fool.

"Anyway, you know why Eve took that fruit?" Mary said confidently. "It was becáuse Eden turn sour, everything in the Garden dry up. She wanted to get out and join the rest of the world. She wanted to know 'bout Spanish Town, Kingston, London and all of them big places, she wanted to get a ladder and climb to the moon."

"Gal yuh mad," said Orville scornfully.

"No, ah you mad," Mary said vexed, but still afraid to cross the head of the house. "How can you endure it here? Your grandfather was a slave fe Massa Henry's father. Then some big boss in London says slavery done. Surely if we are free men and women then we must be like the rest of the world. But no, we all just ah go round like we don't know what to do with we freedom."

"I'll tell you," he said, "to reap eternity we must labour full-time for the Lord."

"That's right, you just go and dance straight back into slavery..."

"But wait...!?" Orville cut in, unable to believe his ears. "Woman, it look like a screw loose in yuh head."

With her hands on her hips and looking him straight in his eyes, Mary continued undaunted. "You know, what me love 'bout Eve is that she bring in some of that good, good, devil business. And she catch some knowledge. While Adam ah sit 'pon him batty."

"I'm not staying here to listen to such blasphemy!" Orville shouted as he stormed out, slamming the door behind him.

"Well go on then, preacher bwoy, I'll teach myself how to read!" Mary shouted after him, once he was too far away to hear. It would be a disgrace if people heard you cuss your man, especially a preacher. Mary picked up the large Bible with tears of frustration streaming down her face as she looked at the beautiful words before her, without recognising a single one.

By the time Mary was 32, she had given birth to two boys, Dudley and Richard, half-brothers to Stella who was now 16. Sundays at Eden Park were always hot and the congregation were forced to pull out their paper fans in the packed church as Orville, a shower of perspiration, turned up the heat as the spirit worked within him.

Massa Henry, his family and friends adorned in hats and parasols, rode home together from the Anglican church. Mrs. Henry always looked vexed and when she was ready she could indeed 'cuss bad word' like any market woman. The women were obsessed with her. She was the living example of the dreams of their lives, her life the Bible that inspired them. But these women were hypocrites for in the same song of praise they would say that she was a mule. They would laugh as her husband rode every woman he saw while his wife marked time in the stable.

Orville soon turned flabby with his belly hanging over his trousers and had developed breasts as big as Mary's. After their second child he stopped any love business. It suited Mary, because the man was a fool. He shaped his life around Massa Henry, down to his wide-brimmed white hat which made him look like an Englishman. Sometimes Mary wondered why he didn't just marry Massa Henry and done. Then Orville asked a carpenter to make him a planter's chair, which he polished every day, nobody was allowed to sit in. The children saw this as pure *puppy-show*. Before Orville came home from work, Dudley, the eldest son, would sit in the chair with a pipe in his mouth and a piece of cane in his hand. He would then stick out his tiny belly and puff his

13

cheeks, pretending to be his father, prancing up and down like a bull-frog. His mother and siblings all laughed at this mimicry. But they all knew their place once father returned.

One evening when Dudley was entertaining his brother and sister in the usual way, Orville arrived early. There was a sudden silence. Orville grabbed Dudley by his 'neck-back' and dragged him to the sour-sop tree. He tied him up and horse whipped his son's tiny backside until his arm was weary. As her little baby cried out Mary was tempted to take away the switch and lash her husband, but that was the way you beat unruly pickney in Eden Park so there wasn't a thing she could do about it. Orville was not vexed because of the mimicry, he was too fool to see that. He beat his son for the small transgression of daring to sit in his sacred planter's chair.

The more Orville tried to be the high and mighty preacher in the house, the more his wife scorned him. In the end he became no more to her than someone sharing her shelter. When she was feeling generous, she thought of him as still growing up innocently, trying to find himself in the world. She was prepared to put up with this, but deep down she was never satisfied. What use was he to her? She longed for a change. This soon came and it was then that Mary realised that Orville was no innocent fool but really a wolf in sheep's clothing — but wait a little.

These were troubled times for Jamaica's planters and not many were left. Most of those that surrounded Eden Park were in bad debt. The valley once had nineteen sugar estates in full operation, with the usual white managers. By now, all except Eden Park had ceased cultivation. Trees were growing out of roofs and walls could not be found because of the bush. Massa Henry, with a quick eye for business, was able to purchase these lands cheap and soon almost the whole area of Lluidas Vale had become Eden Park. Slowly the men started to see that Massa Henry needed them. Anyway, it hurt everybody's 'soul case' to work for Massa Henry and so some would work when they felt like it, but others would go capture land and plant for themselves. Even faithful Orville had forsaken his master and joined his wife on her land. They had built a small board house and grew yams and cocoa.

On Saturdays Mary and the boys would travel the five miles to Ewarton market, loaded with two donkey carts of produce. Stella and Orville stayed at home to guard the property from thieves. "Eden Park people teef," Mary would remind Orville constantly. "...Dem teef...dem teef so 'til dem would tek Christ off from de cross. If ever I catch any one of them I jus' woulda chop off dem hand!"

It was the last Saturday before Christmas and Orville was over-eager to pack Mary off to market.

"Come nuh, you people must get weh yuh going quick a clock, cause 'nuff crowd deh ah market," he urged

"Easy nuh man," Mary said climbing onto the cart. "Is why you hurrying us these last Satdeys? I hope you nuh have no woman ah come inna me home."

"You love run too much joke woman, gwan ah market," said Orville, smiling as he returned to the house.

The boys wore their white hats and Mary tied her head as the sun was trying to crick its neck over the mountains. Soon it would rise like a burning torch. Dudley sat quietly in the first cart. He was only nine, but he behaved older, especially after his new job as head donkey cart driver. His mother often called him 'Big Man' as he would never play with boys his age but loved to go to the village and act like a big man, leaning back on one foot with the other pushed forward, his little arms folded.

The journey to Ewarton first took the two carts through the estate. It was crop time and the canefields were full of colour, ranging from the rich browns of fresh ploughed land to the full bronze of dead, cut trash, and from the tender green of young cane shoots to the emerald with a little dash of gold, which told the workers that the cane was fit. The few left working on the estate were mostly old and infirm — they felt a loyalty to Massa Henry and didn't know what to do with their lives.

The donkeys didn't need driving. They knew the complicated route through the narrow paths that separated the rows of cane. They would start to strain as they began the long struggle up to the ridge. The view from up there was always a surprise no matter how often Mary made that journey. When they reached the top it was early in the morning for the sun had still not completely risen. After resting on the ridge Mary noticed that Dudley was asleep inside his cart ahead.

"Wake up, nuh man," she demanded.

"Me tired Mama, me never sleep last night."

"Is how come?"

"It was Stella, she jus' ah bawl all night. A man can't get no rest."

"Crying, why? Wha' do her?"

"Me nuh know. It happen every night. She jus' ah lie down an' crying 'Dada, leave me please'."

As Mary heard that she just turned the donkey's head and pointed it towards their house. The journey home seemed longer — like a vigil in slow motion.

"That's why the one Orville ah hurry we fe go ah market," Mary seethed to herself. "That nasty son of a bitch ah feel-up me pickney. I kept thinking of my baby Stella. Of him on top of my daughter, holding her, caressing her, him ah push himself inside of her..." Her blood was boiling. Then her mind flashed to Stella and she wondered if her daughter had looked at Orville as if he were an obeah man who had marked her. Her vengeance soon turned on Stella. Did she call him over

15

to take something out of her eye and then cling onto him and rub her young body against his weak flesh? Mary thought of them both naked, lying on her bed, talking about her and laughing. Then her mind saw Orville again and her poor baby fighting to get away as her step-father held her down and Stella screaming, "Mama! Mama!." Then she saw them naked again, holding each other and he had a Bible in his hand, teaching her to read and they were chanting, "Mary can't read, what a fool, Mary can't read." Mary felt helpless as hot tears scalded her cheeks.

The donkey hadn't stopped when Mary jumped out running like a bull towards the house. It all seemed to happen in one movement — the door crashing open, the two of them lying in the small bed, Mary reaching for the machete and the blood which covered her, Stella and the bed. Orville had jumped through the window holding his injured arm. It was lucky for him he moved so fast.

"He made me, he made me do it!" screamed Stella.

"So why you didn't tell me chile?!" Mary wanted to push her daughter out of the house and shake the life out of her, but the look in Stella's eyes made her stop. Stella was the same image as her mother at 16 — tall and slim with eyes that looked like they saw more than what was in front of them. Now Mary held her tight as if she were a jewel. The boys came in screaming and wanted to know what had happened. That night, Mary and her children held onto each other tight-tight.

Stella kept crying. "Mama, me sorry. Him threaten fe kill me if me talk."

"I understand, me love, we'll go ah river and bathe."

"What about Dada?" said Dudley.

"Him will have fe go find s'maddy else, fe him wounds too deep fe we. But as me make ten on this ground, Father God mek sure that me don't set eyes 'pon him again. 'Cause if me see him, me gwan chop him raas!"

The family huddled together and made their way down to the cool river, praying that no one was near to witness their disgrace.

Mary never saw Orville again. A few days later a young boy with a mule and cart said that he had come for Orville's things. The boys packed the cart, but Mary kept his large Bible and the planter's chair. The boy said that Orville was living with a woman not far from Ewarton. Satisfied, Mary made no more enquiries and gave the boy two oranges for his trouble. When she saw the cart disappear in the distance, she took an oath that she would never marry again.

The poor folk continued to work the land, while Massa Henry had trouble sleeping at nights, as still more of the workers left the estate to look for their place in the sun. To Mary it was wrong that those who had worked hard on the estate to build it up, should watch it decline into nothing. After all, their mothers and fathers lost blood and dignity on this plantation.

"So while the *mus-mus* ah run 'round with sugar in him mouth, time come fe chat with puss," she decided and headed for the big house on the hill.

It was the first time she had any reason to go and see Massa Henry. There was a time when Negro people couldn't even look at Bucky Massa. However, times were changing. Mary arrived early evening. It was Saturday and she knew that this was his evening of rest. Massa Henry lived in the Great House which overlooked the sugarmill from a hillock. It was surrounded by a large stone wall. The house was run down. The garden was overgrown for no gardener worked longer than a month. They were all dismissed for stealing, sleeping with the maids or lack of effort.

"Good night. Is anyone at home!" Mary called out when she arrived at the gate of the stone wall, fifty yards from the house, and was greeted by two bad dogs that came rushing towards her.

"Please, hol' yuh dog dem!" she cried.

Soon Cynthia, the mulatto housekeeper, drifted towards her at a leisurely pace. Her head was tied and she moved like a queen. To Mary, Cynthia was the prettiest woman in Eden Park. Her only fault was that she knew it. Her lips and nose were African, but her light skin and blue eyes belonged to the white man.

"Is what you want?" she asked rudely.

"Good night, madam, isn't it a blessing from above to be endowed with good manners?" Mary replied.

"Look nuh, me no have no time fe waste, so tell me your business."

"I come to see Massa Henry."

"Fe wha'?"

"None of your damn business."

"Make me tell you somet'ing. Fe a negga gal, you really raas feisty."

"Is who you ah call negga? Look at the likes of you. Jus' 'cause you have a little drop of white inside you, you think you special, well kiss me batty!"

"Me nah stand here fe listen to the like of you, now if you don't leave these grounds I'll leggo the dogs on you."

Mary was so vexed by this fresh 'brownskin bitch' that she took off her leather belt and grabbed her waist through the gate: then she tied her hands backwards. She screamed for Mary to untie her. Mary simply tucked her dress between her legs and sat down quietly, chewing a piece of cane. Her loud bellows soon brought a group of people rushing from the house towards the gate. Amongst them was Massa Henry, a tall bearded white man who was so well tanned he looked like roast pork. He had come to Jamaica when he was 14, after being a failure at school. He took over his father's plantation but by the time he was ready to make big money, sugar went from being king to pauper.

"What the hell is happening here? Cynthia what are you doing tied up?"

"Arrest her, sir, she attacked me and nearly tear off me arm, sir?"

"Massa Henry," Mary said ignoring Cynthia. "I've come here to talk to you in private, sir, if you would be so gracious. Sir, I have a plan to make Eden Park prosperous again. I can make the workers come back to the estate, but we must talk. After all you can't leave a lady outside in this heat."

Massa Henry was taken aback at this woman's courage and, to Cynthia's surprise, he asked her in. Cynthia looked at Mary with fear and horror as if she were a large green lizard. She was confused, for though she hated black and wore elegant wide skirts, bodice and fine head wraps, she and Mary were one. At the time of Christmas 'John Canoe' and the emancipation dance, Cynthia would become excited, taking charge and showing the children how the dances were done in slavery day. Her big show came at the Kumina dance — bwoy, she could whine up and move like any salt-water African. And a friend had told Mary at market that when sickness takes her, Cynthia is the first in line to see the obeah man. Yet she would still go on with her *puppy-show*, boasting how she had been working in the Great House all her life and that her Daddy was Busha Bruns, a 'hurry-come-up' bookkeeper who was sent to jail for horse stealing. Anyway, as Mary passed through the gate she said, "Sir, could you tell your domestic to give me back me belt?"

Cynthia threw the belt at her and rushed back to the house cussing everything in the world — especially those people with a darker skin.

Eden Park Great House had five main rooms on the ground floor with a hall and a closet, and many bedrooms on a second storey. Out back were a kitchen, wash house, buttery, and modest coach-house, and in the stone basement was a hurricane house which was normally used to store linen. Mary knew all of this without ever seeing the inside — "everyone ah laba-laba 'bout the Great House already". The people and the place were an inspiration for gossip.

Mary sat down in the corner of the ballroom. Massa Henry looked uneasy like he was unsure what was going to happen next.

"Massa Henry," Mary began, "we are clearly living in sad times. Now I know you're a man with a good heart. You badly need workers and if the men continue to leave you, well, judgement will come sooner than you think. I can persuade them to come back, but under new conditions."

"What conditions?"

"Well, first is an increase in pay. At the moment a good cane cutter earns 12 shillings a week. This must go up to 16, plus a share in the profits. It is clear that slavery days left some bad habits. More than half a century after it was abolished, the top jobs on the estate are still given to coloured, well that must change — negro workers must be given the same chance."

"You're asking a lot, Mary. I never thought you were a trouble-maker. You are such a hard worker — unlike many of the women around here, whose only use is to breed and carry malice. But you, Mary, when did you start to deal with trouble?"

"These are troubled times, Massa Henry."

Massa Henry couldn't stomach back-chat, especially from a negro woman.

"Now you just wait a moment gal. You know your place!" he exploded.

"I beg you a pardon," Mary said quietly.

"How dare you come in here and make demands. If it wasn't for my family, all the likes of you would be hungry today. My father made this estate into one of the most successful and up to date plantations in the West Indies. He brought machinery from London that was never seen in these parts. As for the workers, they now enjoy rent-free houses and gardens. Anyway, if I paid them any more they would be able to buy an acre of land each and leave me high and dry. But this is a small village which cannot keep all the farmers going. There will soon be a depression and then every one of you will come running back to me. Especially when you're hungry."

"That may be so, but what condition will you be in by the time we come back?"

He rested back in his chair. This man of 60 looked young for his age, unlike many other planters who would eat, drink and fornicate themselves into an early grave. He never drank and was unafraid of coming into the canefield and cussing and joking with the workers.

"You've backed me up against a wall," he said.

"No Massa Henry, things have changed. The old days have gone. We've all got to live together here or we die."

"My father was no lover of slavery and fought hard to have it abolished. So I don't need uppity remarks from you. In any case, I'm sure you couldn't persuade them to come back and work hard. You negroes prefer squatting on the estate to working for wages. The negro is not satisfied with his condition unless he has a horse, a blue-tail coat and land. But the problem is that he wants all these without wanting to work. These men stay at home and come down twice a week and work a couple of days, and return with a bottle of rum and a bag of oranges — both stolen from the estate."

"Please, don't let blood rush to your head. You know that a couple of days work would never provide a horse and blue-tail coat and you are right 'bout land. But if you don't want to pay wages, why not be a middle-man. You could lease them the land and they would work it and sell you the cane, which you then mill and sell at a higher price to England."

"I like it," he admitted. "It's a good idea but let me sleep on it and I'll talk to you soon."

Church was never the same since Orville left. His preaching was missed, but Daphne did a good job as replacement. She was the natural choice to take his place since she was the only one left who could read. The role of preacher gave her a new spark in life. She had just given birth to her seventh child and producing children was wearing her down. She was a tall woman, large, with mighty, bulging breasts — indeed a fearsome figure of a preacher.

It took two weeks for Massa Henry to agree to the plan, and Mary arranged with Daphne to make an announcement in church, after the altar call.

"Well praise the Lord, that he has kept us," Mary addressed the church. "Even through the days of tribulation he has laid a table in front of me. And he shall keep me even through the valley of death. Amen."

"Amen!" replied the congregation.

"Now some of you may have heard that I've been talking with Massa Henry. Well that is so. Now we all know that hard times have licked the planters and you know why, 'cause it is we who is king now. Since freedom come, Bucky Massa ah beg we work fe dem. Jamaica deh like the Bible days when God send a flood fe wash the world 'cause it was evil. We are the remnant of the flood, my brethren and sistren, it is we who God leave in the Ark and we now praise God, that slavery days done."

"Amen!" said the congregation.

"Now the Ark come fe rest and we must come out and do wha'? Eden Park belong to we as much as Massa Henry. It is negro blood that help make it what it is today. Now we can't jus' lef' it so. This land holds bad memories for all of us — the white man worked out our soul case to put sugar 'pon him table — but the answer is not to run. Like Bogle, we must fight and claim what belong to we. Anyway we can't stay out in the hills and common. What happen when hunger lick we? All them that sit here boasy will be the first fe run back to Massa Henry with them little batter pan fe beg him wuk."

Suddenly a young deacon stood up, his eyes glared as he objected. "If you have come to tell us that we must go back to Bucky Massa and cut cane fe 12 shillings a week, then you can keep your words."

"No sir, God forbid. What we want is land and he has the best. So he has agreed to lease some of the land. We sell the cane to him at a good price and then let him deal with the Englishman."

The deacon rose again. "But wouldn't it be better to starve him out and when he can't take the pressure, capture the land?"

"Is what wrong with you, man? Is Bucky Massa have the mill and machinery, you think him just goin' leave it there as Christmas present!"

The congregation roared with laughter.

"No Man," Mary continued. "One hand wash de other, you see that's what's different about the new world. When we come off that Ark, it's partnership we ah deal with, cause slavery business long done, it done!"

The same deacon got up again — 'Bwoy, him 'nuff eenh,' Mary thought. "Will you, sister Mary, be giving up your land to work for Massa Henry? It seems in your case the one hand wash one hand."

People began to whisper as though they thought that Mary was a hypocrite. The women looked at her shaking their heads, ready to pour scorn on her name.

"I will be the first to lease land from Massa Henry," Mary said boldly. She never expected to be the first. She thought she could at least join them later. Now she had to lead by example, all because of that fresh little Deacon.

Daphne then rose and said, "It looks like the Lord has blessed us again, come let us sing that freedom song, God Almighty Thank ye!"

There was a loud cheer and everyone burst into song.

'Oh me good friend Mr Wilberforce make me free God Almighty thank ye! God Almighty thank ye! God Almighty, make we free! Buckra in this country no make we free! What Negro for to do! What Negro for to do! Take force by force! Take force by force!'

As the large figure of Daphne sashayed down the aisle, the men smiled with one eye on her backside and the other on the Lord.

Mary's predictions proved to be right. In surrounding estates poor people began to run back to Bucky Massa as drought licked them, and at Eden Park there was no market for food, more people were selling than buying. But at least people weren't running back into slavery". Mary was seen with greater respect since the deal with Massa Henry, and for that people gave me her the title 'Miss Mary'.

One Saturday, on their usual journey to Ewarton market, as Mary and the children approached the ridge, they saw a white sack lying in the middle of the road in the distance. When they got closer, they discovered it was the body of a white man.

"Come Mama, look, I think him dead!" Richard shouted.

The man was still breathing. He wore a white shirt and black riding breeches. He looked like a pirate. On turning him over, Mary found he was far from dead, but drunk, with the overpowering smell of strong rum clinging to him. They dragged him up to the cart and after several heaves, lifted him in.

"What will we do with him, Mama?" asked Stella.

"Take him back home of course. He's only drunk."

"Him look good, eenh," Stella said smiling. "What if he's a pirate?"

"Well if he's a pirate him far away from his ship."

Their pirate slept all morning under the watchful eye of Stella, who was under his spell. To tell the truth Mary also thought he looked good, especially for a white man. He was tall with straight brown hair to his shoulders. He wore a large gold ring and one earring but he had a gentle boyish look which made her warm to him.

"Where is this place?" he asked in a deep English voice when he at last woke.

"You're at Eden Park in Lluidas Vale, sir," said Stella.

"We found you drunk on top of the hill," Mary added quickly.

"Well I am sorry if I caused you trouble."

"It was no trouble. I'm late for market, but Stella will go instead."

"But Mama..."

"Don't bother argue. Just mek haste and go ah market."

Stella walked slowly to the door, with a smile for the stranger and with vexed eyes for her mother.

"You look so young to have such a big daughter," the white man said.

"I know, I had her when I was a young girl," Mary explained in her best English. "But tell me about yourself who are you? How did we come to find you on the mountain side?"

"Well my name's Cooper, Lionel Cooper, and I am from London originally. I live in Kingston and I'm a commercial traveller. I was riding towards this estate with some rum in my belly, when three men jumped out of the bush, robbed me of my horse and wares and left me for dead. Luckily they didn't find my wallet. And it looks like you've been the good Samaritan."

"Well my name's Mary and that was Stella and the boys," she said nervously. He was so charming, addressing her as if she were a lady. He must have assumed she was without a man, as he never asked her about the children's father. It seemed that as quickly as she had warmed to him, he was only passing through, for he soon told her that he intended to buy a horse in the morning to ride back to Kingston.

"When did you come to Jamaica?"

"Four years ago. I landed here on my thirtieth birthday."

22

"Tell me about London," Mary said eagerly.

"Well it's very dirty, full of thieves and a gentleman is likely to die of syphilis. Apart from that, it's a fine place to live." He said smiling.

"What of Kingston though?"

"I find it a strange place. Everyone there wanting to be English. Even the streets are copied from us. Kingston is more English than England. I do love Kingston at night. Midnight echoes with the rattle of carriage wheels as travellers in silks and satins go home to their beds. But come midday the place is like hell. Those same streets are running with foul smelling sea-bound streams of sewage — it stinks to high heaven. But the air is so fresh here, you must like it in this valley."

"Well the best time of year is now. You'll see oranges, soursops, rose-apples, cocoas and breadfruit — the yellow heart is the best. The children like this time 'cause they roast sweet potatoes and yam in the wood fire. You would love Christmas and August holidays. Everybody comes together to perform quadrille and the band plays drums and flutes. Sometime Massa Henry will send down a pig to be roasted."

Mary tired herself trying to sound impressive but the things of the land were so everyday to someone from London and living in Kingston. She longed to know more about him, but above all she wanted him to be interested in her.

"What do you think London is like?" he eventually asked.

"Well everyone in the village says that the streets are paved with gold, but I don't believe it. I hear that London is bigger than the whole ah Jamaica. The gentlemen all wear top hats and tails and drive in the finest carriages, maybe even made of gold. The ladies go to balls in their fine dresses and wear the best jewels that money can buy."

Mr Cooper laughed and said, "You have a great imagination, Mary."

She didn't know if he was trying to be kind or maybe he was laughing at her, but she continued.

"I think London is full of proud and boasy people, after all they are kings of the world. But me think the best thing about London is that it's firm, it have foundation — the people can look back in the past and know themselves. Whereas in this island we are marooned maroons. All we dealing wid is *puppy-show*. What we need is a real country." She grabbed his arm when she said real, as if he was the word made flesh. He looked up and smiled.

"Has anyone told you that you're a most beautiful woman?", said Cooper, his eyes fixed on Mary's, while hers were turned to the ground.

"No, you are. Don't you ever look at yourself?"

"I don't have a mirror," Mary answered.

"But you must be the cause of many fights round here."

"Not really, some men just want to bed me. I am not really

interested."

He got up and poured himself a drink of sugar and lime, and inspected the small board house as if he was the owner. He was so sure of himself, so sure of his world, knowing he came from somewhere special. His head was stiff, just like the Eden Park men, but he would look Mary straight in the eyes when talking. Eden Park men would look away when she spoke to them as if her eyes were the sun burning their faces.

"I'm sure there's a fine English lady who can't wait for your return. You must have many lady friends."

"No and I'm not going back. I've come to Jamaica to make my fortune. I sell the best English cutlery, made in Sheffield of course, as well as fine Wedgewood pottery that would make any planter's wife the happiest woman in the world."

His dream of prosperity seemed to inspire Cooper like a vision and he began to pace the small patch of earth floor, weaving his way around the three crocus-sack beds. He admired Mary's musket hanging on the wall. She was proud of it because she knew of no one in Eden Park who had one.

"Is this for your protection?" he asked, running his finger along its barrel.

"It's my uncle's. He gave it to me last year, before he died. He got the musket from his father who fought alongside Doctor Paul Bogle at the Morant Bay rebellion. When I was small he would tell me stories of the rebellion. I know those stories as well as I know the Bible."

"Tell me about it," said Cooper excitedly, "I remember reading about the row it caused in the House of Commons."

He took the musket from the wall and pretended to take aim. They went outside and sat on the veranda steps and Mary tried to tell the story the way her uncle would. He would jump up to show you how a man was shot — and her uncle certainly knew how to tell a stirring story so that your belly twisted up with excitement.

"There was a man name Mr Bogle who come from the East, a place called St Thomas. He was a preacher and him stand up fe poor people. Now let me tell you something. The planter think our toil and sweat is the blessing from above, but we know nothing nuh go so. What we treasure is land. You can work us till we drop but tek away our land and judgement will come. Now Mr Bogle he know this too. So when the Custos lick the poor people with high tax, Mr Bogle gather his men and march to the courthouse. What a tribulation! Gun shot bruk out and innocent man a drop like stone. When Mr Bogle see this, the Devil rush to him head and him tek up a cutlass and jook the Custos, kill him dead. Fe dis they hang Mr Bogle, 'til him neck bruk. My uncle say that this musket was Mr Bogle's and he has kept it safe ever since."

"It's an interesting story," said Mr Cooper.

"Uncle said that one day we will rule Jamaica and it won't be buckra making the laws but instead, the poor people will be sitting in Kingston. Then we will know that St Thomas people never died in vain. I don't know... Uncle Jolly love fight and chat foolishness."

Mr Cooper put the musket back in its place on the wall.

"Do you want it?" Mary asked finally, handing it back to him.

"It's beautiful, but I couldn't take it. This must be the most expensive item you have in your house."

"I want you to have it. I said to myself that if I ever met the right man then I would give him my only treasure. My uncle said to me only give up the musket when you think you reach Zion. Well the right time come, the Lord sent you to take me away from Eden Park so you must have the musket."

"Now let's not jump too far. I'm grateful for your help on the hill. But I'm not taking you anywhere. I hope to buy a fresh horse and be off in the morning, alone. Is that clear?" He returned the musket and smiled at Mary as she lowered her head vexed at his rebuke. He then moved towards the planter's chair and noticed Orville's Bible beside it.

"Fine Bible this, leather bound well."

Mary told him it had been her husband's. She told him also that her husband had died of cholera last year. But worse, she told him that she read Psalms to the children every night.

"Why don't you read to me?" He asked.

Mary's words had taken her to the edge of a mountain but she was now likely to be tossed over. She could tell a story but never read. She began to sweat and smiled nervously. She had gone too far with her efforts to impress. He would think that she was a fool. Everything in her home looked *chaka-chaka* and she felt so shamed when she looked at the clay pot catching the rainwater from her leaky roof. She stroked her tightly plaited hair which would never blow in the wind like a white woman's, yet Cooper was saying she was beautiful. She opened the Bible at the first page and read aloud.

"The Lord is my Shepherd I shall not want. He maketh me to lie down in green pastures. He leadeth me in the paths of righteousness for his name's sake. Yea though I walk through the valley of the shadow of death I fear no evil, for Thou art with me. Thy rod and Thy staff they comfort me. Though..."

"Mary, can I ask you why you're reading Psalm 23 from the beginning of the Bible?"

She felt so ashamed. What a fool she had made herself look. She searched for some more lies to spill to him but the thread was done. She felt like an unruly child before her schoolmaster.

"So you find me out. I'm sorry but me can't read nor write not even

25

me deggah name."

"Look I didn't mean to upset you. It doesn't make you less of a person because you can't read or write."

He came towards her, her head still bowed in shame. Then he lifted her chin and his lips dried a tear from her cheek. He looked at her with intense blue eyes and said "Look, I need a few days holiday. Why don't I go to Kingston, get my things and stay with you a few days. If I get a good horse I'll be back in four days. When I come back, I'll teach you how to read and write."

"You mean this?"

"Yes every word, and you can teach me about farming."

The Jamaican sun poured through Mary's window that Saturday afternoon as she and her Englishman held each other close. And yet, this was still a stranger that held her in his strong arms. She felt a tinge of danger as if he had come like a thief in the night and stolen something which she had hidden ever since she chased Orville away. And yet still, it was exciting, different and the man clearly liked her. Mary felt like a child crossing a deep, angry river and Lionel was her bridge to that new world on the other side. She held onto him tight that Saturday, not wanting to ever let him go.

They slept together that same night. Stella, who normally shared Mary's bed, went to sleep with Richard without her mother asking. In silence Stella put up a linen cloth to give her mother and her new love a grudgeful privacy.

For Mary, Lionel brought back memories of Horsemouth. He had gentleness, unlike Orville who was on and off like a tired old billy goat. He stretched his slim arm over her as she lay there, and he treated her the whole time like a proper lady. Mary felt giddy with this gentleman in her bed. It was strange, but she felt a power come over her like a demon. She wrapped her legs around his and they were locked together. She needed him like a man falling from the sky needs wings. She needed his chest, his neck, his seed and his legs. The Devil had taken charge of her soul. 'Lawd God!' she thought as she felt herself floating — it was beyond belief. In the air, the wind blew strongly in her face but she was steady as Lionel held her. She looked down on Eden Park. It was a small basin on the ground. She saw people the size of little ants making their way through long blades of grass and then returning to their holes in the dirt, some looking a woman and others Jesus Christ. Mary was soon in England floating above the gold pavements. She wore an embroidered dress of pure silk which sparkled with jewels of gold and sapphire. She arrived at Queen Victoria's palace and Lionel wore his big top hat and tail. Two little white boys held onto her long dress as she entered the ball to be greeted by Her Majesty. Everyone wanted to meet her. She was the wife of Lionel Cooper, the

26

richest man in the Empire. Mary curtsied to the aged Queen who told her how beautiful she was and that Jamaica was her prize colony. Mary said, "Thank you Ma'am, I am so honoured". There was so much food at the ball — chicken, yam, breadfruit, sweet potatoes, ackee and a wide selection of fruits.

Lost in fantasy, Mary hardly realised that Lionel had come to his peak and was lying on top of her trying to catch his breath. They were both soaked in sweat, both breathing hard. Lionel turned over and rested while she continued to dream of meeting the Queen.

The next morning, Lionel and the boys got along fine and they even started to call him Mr Dada. But well before midday, he was restless to leave as the journey to Kingston would be long. He gave Dudley his gold ring which from then on Mary's son wore proudly on his thumb. Stella hugged him tight and then quickly let go when she felt her mother's eyes scalding her rude backside. Lionel said there was just time for Mary to give him a tour of the estate. He wanted to see a humming-bird so she took him to the calabash trees by the river, where as a child she would dive in naked with the other children and swim like a fish. At the river Lionel turned red with surprise as Mary tucked the bottom of her frock between her legs and quickly climbed up into a tree and sat on a branch. She laughed as he tried four times to pull himself up. In the end she had to grab his pants-waist and drag him up beside her.

"Now you have to be quiet and soon a humming-bird will rest on the branch above," she whispered.

Lionel was still breathing hard after trying to climb the tree. He looked at the woman beside him, unable to work out where she got the strength to haul herself up. After all, he was stronger than her! They waited in silence. Lionel became nervous about the strength of the branch they were sitting on but Mary assured him that when they were children five of them would sit on the branch together without it even bending. Then from nowhere, a beautiful long-tailed hummingbird came shooting by with its long velvet-black feathers, fluttering like John Canoe streamers behind it. It began to suck at the blossoms of the tree in which they were sitting. Mary told Lionel to put his arms out and pretend that he was a branch so that the humming-bird would surely come and perch on him. She couldn't stop herself laughing as he sat there with his arms spread like a duppy.

"So you're playing games with me," said Lionel, trying to push his companion off the branch.

"Stop it nuh man... Look the bird a come closer."

The lovely little gem hovered around the trunk, and threaded the branches, now here, now there, its cloudy wings on each side humming with a noise like that of a spinning top. Its emerald breast flashed

27

brilliantly for a moment in the sun's rays, then it would appear black as the light vanished, then, in an instant, blazed emerald again. Several times he came close to them. They held their breath and sat motionless for fear of alarming it and driving it away. As they hugged each other tight, the bird seemed to look at them curiously.

"Go 'way bird, you too feisty!" Mary cried aloud.

It was as if the bird understood the command. It had another quick look and then vanished into the blue sky. They tried to follow its path but were blinded by the bright sunshine. Lionel carefully balanced himself, and held Mary tighter, kissing her. She slowly pulled him off balance and they both went crashing into the river. Two women were busy washing their clothes by the river bank and turned around when they heard the splash. They must have thought the couple were mad — two big people playing in the river. Mary lay with Lionel on the river bank, dead-tired and allowed the hot sun to dry her. Soon after she watched her stranger ride off to the ridge and as he disappeared into the mountains, she already began to doubt his promised return.

It had been five months since Lionel left and there was no sign of him. Every morning Mary would look up to the steep mountain hoping in vain that she could see him coming. She felt betrayed. Stella would watch her mother's face change from a quiet longing to a deep fretful frown as yet another morning stretched through midday without his return. Worse still, Mary was pregnant for him and the baby would be due in the late summer.

One Sunday, leaving Stella to cook, Mary walked the steep hill towards the ridge. To her surprise she saw Cynthia sitting under the mango tree, crying. Mary felt wary of making a move towards her since she might still be vexed after the fight at Massa Henry's, but she bravely went ahead.

"Cynthia, wha' do you child?"

"Leave me nuh, I just want to die."

"No man, tell me."

Mary got a shock as Cynthia stood up, to reveal that she was as big with child as she.

"Yuh see how me stay. Me expecting fe a white man who mek promise to carry me to Kingston and him no come back. Massa Henry say that too many maids ah breed and him goin' throw me out if me have any more pickney. Lawd, gal you see the trials and crosses."

"Which white man is this?"

"You nuh know him. Him only chat to pretty girls."

"Me expecting too you know for a commercial traveller, a white man named Cooper, Lionel Cooper. A gentleman from London, England. Him promised he would come back after his trip to Kingston, but me nuh see him and five months pass, but deep down me sure is some good reason why him nuh come back."

"You keep dreaming me girl. You mad to think that this sweetboy Lionel will come back to you. He must have women all over St Catherine not to mention Kingston. You're just another that him nyam and lef'."

Cynthia's words hit Mary like a hand slapping her out of a deep sleep. She went on "You think because 'im a white man and drop nice accent 'pon you, that it mean him will come back? Count yourself lucky me dear at least you can say to your brownskin pickney that him daddy was a white man from London, England."

"So Cynthia, wha' yuh sweetheart name?"

"William Frye," she said proudly. By now she had recovered and looked like her old cantankerous self.

"What him look like?"

"Well him tall, has long brown hair and him look young for him age. Yeah and him wear an earring, I think him was a sailor."

"Earring!" Mary exclaimed, her mouth wide open in shock. "So what will you do now?"

"Well me dear, him did leave me some money, so me ah go leave tomorrow fe Spanish Town to stay by my sister and brother-in-law. My sister get me a work. She know 'nuff big people. You must bring your gentleman friend fe a visit — if he comes back," she said with spite.

Mary's heart nearly dropped — it must be Lionel.

"And where did you meet your sweetheart?" she asked eventually.

"Oh Spanish Town of course. He wouldn't frequent these parts."

Mary was seething with anger for Lionel Cooper and told herself, 'If him ever put him backside back in dis yah estate, fire and tribulation ah go bruk out. Jus' mek him set foot back inna me yard and I'll set him a brew that when him done drink it, him have run belly fe a year. That raas, I hope Judgement Seat fall 'pon him backside.'

Cynthia left. She had work to do at the Great House. Mary felt like telling her who her sweetheart really was, but decided to be alone to let the tears burn her face and to cuss bad word to the sun and hills and all creation. She wanted the sun to stop shining and cast a shadow of death over this valley. She turned and followed Cynthia down into the vale. Both carrying burdens much bigger than their babies, for these two women had tasted the bitter fruit of knowledge and now had to survive.

Eden Park's negro church was a Baptist church, but once a month after service was done Mama used to take the young Mary to the revival meeting at a place called Seal Ground. It was on this disused waste ground, surrounded by cane trash, that revivalist or 'Poco' people had their meeting. Mama would dress in white, tie her head and

29

begin to dance with the other women as they made contact with the Spirit. It used to frighten Mary when the women got possessed and they rocked backwards and then forwards. Then they started speaking in a strange language and then rolled on the ground as if they were dead. Mama used to say that anytime Mary found herself in trouble she must go and see the Shepherd, the leader of the band of twenty-five women, who each had a duty to perform. She told her daughter that if she ever had any bad sickness, or if she couldn't breed or if she needed to gain a man's affections, the Shepherd would make it right for her.

That evening Mary went to the mission house where the Shepherd lived alone in a room at the back. It used to vex her that he never worked while the women in his hand would cook and clean for him, and some of the younger ones would even sleep with him. But now Mary had come on business. She would try anything to see Lionel again. She needed to see him, to cuss him and maybe to love him but, most of all, she hadn't given up the dream of going to Kingston with the children.

She saw the mission house from a distance. The white flag drooped in the still air. It was the flag was of Pocomania and it was also meant to attract passing spirits. Inside, the mission house was like a Church. There were benches and at one end, a table on a platform. Near the table was an altar, spread with a white cloth on which candles, flowers, mangoes and other fruits lay. Around the walls of the mission were holy pictures and signs with Biblical verses. The altar was always taken outside into the revival yard ready for a meeting to begin.

Sitting under a wooden cross in the corner was the Shepherd, eating rice and salt fish. He always wore a white gown and turban. He was dark-skinned and his wrinkled forehead and eyes met together at the top of his nose. The mission house had a strange smell of perfumes, oils and herbs, and it was pleasant and heady taking in breaths of this sweet aroma. He talked about Mama and how he knew Mary as a small baby. How he would pick her up and how she would kiss him on his cheek. She took an instant liking to the kindly elderly man. Who knows? Maybe he was the father that she never knew. She told him about Lionel and explained that she wanted him to come back. He was so certain that his magic could work. All he needed was something that Lionel owned and was proud of. Mary told him about the ring that he gave Dudley, and he said she was to return later that night with the ring and they would contact the spirits to bring Lionel back.

At first Mary never really believed that Pocomania could work — she was just trying a thing. But the longer she spoke to the Shepherd the more frightened she became. What was she getting involved with? The fear that one of the spirits might possess her and turn her mad haunted her on the journey home.

30

Mary had kept Mama's revival frock in a box under the bed. As she measured herself against it, she remembered how Mama would talk to herself as she stirred the pepper-pot soup in the yard, cooking for everyone but herself. It was as if she were talking to another person. She would cuss this woman who owed her money, the woman would beg her for more time and Mama would cuss her again. Sometimes Mary would close her eyes and listen to her act out her stories. Some of the sad ones would make you cry living eye water.

Mary took the ring from Dudley, who was fast asleep, and went out into the night. As soon as she crossed the limestone path towards the mission house, she heard the tambourines echoing in the valley. When she arrived at Seal Ground, she was surprised to see women not only wearing white, but reds and blues also. The women walked around in a procession. They stamped the ground with a hard drop that seemed to shake the earth. Mary recognised Aunt Sarah — and what was Miss Johnson doing here? She who would run down negro people day and night. They all looked so different, so serious.

In front of the mission door stood the upliftment table covered with drinks and fruits of all description, and breads of all shapes and sizes. Mary joined the band, following the Shepherd to the table. Then he directed the lighting of the candles. He opened his arms wide, a candle in each hand and said, "Light de light oh." Each person came up and dropped a coin in a box and the Shepherd gave each a lighted candle. The table was then broken, which meant that they could now partake of the fruits and the bread. The procession continued until two boys came in dragging a goat, which they held down on the altar. The Shepherd blessed his knife and quickly cut the throat of the screaming animal. This sacrifice, called the 'sundial', was the second part of the meeting. The Shepherd called Mary over and placed Lionel's ring on the head of the goat. He then smeared her head with goat's blood. What she felt next was the top half of her body swinging while her legs remained fixed to the ground. It was a joyful feeling. She wasn't even trying to move. Her body moved on its own and soon everyone was moving in the same way. It was the beginning of what they call 'labour' — the journey into the spirit world. It was strange how her body suddenly become tense, like she was diving in cold water, and then the tension eased out of her and instead she felt a deep peace as if she were fast asleep. Mary was careful to notice the Shepherd's feet were flat on the ground, as if the 'ground spirits' controlled his destiny. The old man looked powerful and strong, as he spun round. The earthly powers whipping him faster and faster, until all you could see was a white tornado.

Mary felt something warm inside, like the feeling you get when you drink white rum. She found that she was no longer breathing on her

31

own and this warmth would come up to her mouth which then opened to let out a loud groan and the warmth would flow down inside her and come up again and the groan would escape once more. She was joined by the rest of the women and together they uttered a single synchronised groan — the voice of Pocomania journeying to the Spirit Land.

The two boys appeared again, this time carrying a large pan full of water. A tall woman broke from the circle and walked around the pan. She began to swing back and forth, so fast her body might leave her legs. She was the Bellringer and she swung like a bell to call the spirits to make contact with the faithful servants on the other side. An older, dignified woman, walked slowly towards the pan. The rhythm picked up pace sounding faster as all eyes were fixed on her. She was the Rivermaid, who saw to it that the spirits crossed safely. Mary found herself going towards her and holding her hands as they both shuffled around the pan of water. Together they sang, 'One more river to cross,' their bodies rocking, heads bowed and groaning in a constant rhythm. The Rivermaid spun around on her axis. She was possessed, her body no longer her own. She cried, "Pass through me now Poco children, deliverance is thine. Deliverance is thine." She moved over to the water and confronted the hostile Water Spirit who wanted to halt the spiritual journey of those possessed through her river. The chanting and singing grew louder. The Rivermaid then threw water on Mary's head and she felt the warmth turn to a burning inside her — so hot. Mary rolled on the ground, groaning and kicking the air. Three women come across to calm her as the Rivermaid threw more water in her face and said "The waters are now calm. The Spirit has sailed into your soul."

Mary lay there, all the strength gone from her body. She could barely raise her hand, yet she felt an inner peace and a new fulfilment.

The Shepherd told her to go home and rest. He assured her that Lionel would be back in a matter of days.

"Don't forget, the spirit inside you tallawah, it tallawah," he repeated.

The waiting for something to happen was a new burden. After two days Mary gave up and decided that these Poco people were really mad and the Shepherd was reaping his reward on Earth out of all of them. She looked outside at a chopped-down log. It should have made the journey to Kingston to be turned into a mahogany desk or chair for a big man in London or a dining table at the Governor's residence. But this log had been left behind, cast aside for no good reason. It had fallen off the cart and no-one could be bothered to replace it. It was as good as all the other logs, perfect mahogany, but because of an accident, it was left to lie there and rot. So it had lain for the last six months. People sat on it, children played on it and dogs watered it. Time had worked on this log, slowly rotting it — this log which had been chopped down to settle in one place and now had no more purpose than to be left to rot. So time had worked on Mary also. She hated her life. She hated that log.

"Is he Mama, him come back!" cried Stella, with sweat on her forehead and panting with excitement.

"Who?" Mary asked.

"Missa Cooper — he's riding towards our place with 'nuff provisions."

Mary sat in the chair and heard the noise of the children outside as they greeted him, grateful for the gifts he had brought. Meanwhile she thought about how she would cuss him and promised herself she wouldn't listen to any of his lies. When he entered the house, she pretended not to look at him, but then again she was curious, so she slowly opened the small shutter of her eye and peeped out. She looked away quickly, proudly. Part of her wanting him to beg for her attention, but part of her desperate to glimpse him fully again. He started to talk to her about how though they had only met once, it was enough to know that he needed her, that he needed her friendship and love. He said that from their short meeting he had known that she had the ability to make, from something little, something that is great. He'd heard how she was brave and defiant and how she had taken on Mr Henry as nearly "caused a revolution in the place." Best of all Lionel told her that he loved her spirit — that she was a rebel and that he wanted to share some of her wealth. Mary didn't know whether she understood what he meant by that. The rest she understand well enough but it sounded anyway like lots of words to her. Nothing he said really made her know why he came back but with one eye on the future, she knew she would hold onto her chance this time.

Mary finally turned around and faced him. He was as she had remembered, but his boots were new and stiff and his white shirt was dirty from his long journey. As she turned he realised she was pregnant. If he had any doubts about whether he was the father, what he saw in Mary's face must have quelled them. He came closer and kissed her and then gently rubbed her belly as if he were comforting his baby inside her. He kissed her again. But she knew she would never let herself go again, never lose herself in the waters of his soul. This time round she knew what she wanted from him. It would be a fair exchange — he could have her body and emotion but she would have his knowledge and she would keep her soul.

Lionel said that he had enough money to stay until the baby was born and that they would then go to Kingston to live in his house. Mary knew that this could never happen but allowed him to think that she shared his dream. He was full of promises of them going to London and getting married and such like. The more he stood there promising her heaven and earth, the more the fear that he would soon be leaving again began to grow within her.

Mary's reading and writing went well. Lionel was a patient teacher but her will to learn was so strong that he would often have to beg her to take a rest. He lay in the hammock, tired after the long lesson, looking like an empty well that she had drunk dry. She wondered if her power to drain Lionel was the reason he began to drink. Mary warned him about the rum but he never listened. Mama used to say that a man turns to rum when he has no true loving — in Lionel's case he certainly wasn't a drunkard through idleness.

They now worked the three adjoining lots having bought the lease at the estate for little or nothing and settled on the idea of raising cows. Lionel and Dudley worked long hours fixing the fence, milking and slaughtering for market.

At nightfall when work was over the family would all gather in the yard to hear Mary tell stories. Some she made up, but most were the old Annancy tales which her grandmother used to tell her. Before she began she used to say, "There are times when the Lord allows us to peep into the future and it is through tongues, prophecy and parables that He speaks to us."

One night Mary surprised her assembled family with an announcement"

"This is a story specially dedicated to Lionel."

Everybody clapped, Lionel bowed gracefully. The children looked eager as usual, especially Richard, who sat cross-legged at his mother's feet, like a puppy hungry for food.

"Alright, I will begin. One day when hunger ah lick every jack, man and animal, there was a blackbird who had a feedin' tree in the sea. And every day Blackbird go and feed. Annancy say to Blackbird, 'Please, Bro'er Blackbird, please carry me over to your feedin tree.' Blackbird say to Annancy, 'Bro'er Annancy, you so craven, I know you will eat every bit from me.' He said 'No, Blackbird I won't do it.' Brother Blackbird say to Annancy, 'How you ah go fly an' yuh nuh have no wing?' Well Blackbird take out two of him tail feather and stick upon Annancy, he take two feather out of him back again, stick upon Annancy, two feather out of him belly feather and stick upon Annancy. Well! Blackbird and Annancy fly to the feedin tree in the middle of the sea. But every time Blackbird go fe pick, Annancy say that one ah fe him.

Blackbird go upon the next limb, Annancy say ah fe him. Blackbird

34

go upon the third limb, Annancy say ah fe him. 'Til Annancy eat a good tummy-full. Annancy drop asleep upon the tree. Well! Blackbird tek time, pick out all the feather back and Blackbird fly away. When Annancy wake out of sleep, him say, 'Mek me fly.' But he can't fly. He broke the branch of a tree, t'row in the sea. The branch swim. Annancy say if the branch will swim him will swim, and he jump off a tree, drop in the sea and sink.

An when he go down a sea bottom he meet Sea-mahmy. He said to Sea-mahmy, 'Sea-mahmy, tell me if me have a cousin down ah sea bottom yah!' Sea-mahmy put a pan of sand in the fire fe well hot. When it get hot she take it off ah the fire, give to Brother Annancy to drink it off. An' Sea-mahmy say, 'Well, since you drink it me know you and me is cousin.' Annancy say, 'Cousin Sea-mahmy, send fe one of your son fe carry me to the land.' Sea-mahmy give him one of her son, name Arnold. Well Arnold and Annancy travel, then make it to the middle of the sea, when Sea-mahmy call. An Arnold say: 'Stop, Brother Annancy, I think I hear my mother calling me back.' Annancy say, 'No man, it's the sea, it ah get rough, come nuh man!' An' Arnold sail with Annancy on him back till they reach shore. When they go to shore he say, 'Bro'er Arnold take this bag weigh me, see how much me weigh.' Arnold lift him up and say, 'Yes Brother Annancy yuh heavy.' So Annancy come back out of the bag. He say, 'Brother Arnold, you come in mek I weigh you see.' Arnold went into the bag. He tie Arnold, tight-tight. Arnold say, 'Brother Annancy you ah tie me too 'trong.'

Annancy say, 'Me ah tie you fe see if you heavy. You heavy-oh! You heavy enough fe me wife pot.' An' fe all the bawl Arnold bawl, Annancy take him back to him house an' eat him."

After some loud applause, Lionel looked at Mary confused, "What's the meaning behind the story?" he asked.

"Well I suppose it has different meanings to different people. To me, I love Annancy. My Granny said to me that really he is a spider, a trickster. When hard times lick you, you have to be Annancy to stay alive. That's how Granny say she manage through slavery times."

"So who's Blackbird in the story?"

"Blackbird can be anybody who can help you. Blackbird have wings but poor Annancy nuh have none and him hungry. But Annancy is also greedy and him care 'bout no one else but himself. In the end he loses his power. This nuh worry Annancy cause, though he was cast in the middle of the sea with nothing, he can still use him brain. Like we in Jamaica. We come here with nothing but God leave us with brain so Annancy use it fe work a next trick and him gone home with him belly full."

The baby was born in the Summer and they called him Gladstone after one of Britain's Prime Ministers. Nana Ethel the midwife held up the new born baby as if he were a prize. Nana had delivered all Mary's children and most of the babies in Eden Park. She was a woman of mystery — nobody knew her age but she never seemed to change. Her hair was always white as long as Mary had known her and she would shuffle on her thin legs, calmly drifting from house to house — heaving, pulling and smacking new life into the world. She always carried a crocus bag round her shoulders where she said she kept her tools for work. Mary watched her as she rubbed the baby with different oils and herbs and then carefully cut his navel string which she silently buried under the breadfruit tree in the yard.

Most of the village women came to see Mary's brown baby. They were proud of him and adored his colour. Dudley played with his tiny fingers as Mary looked on — they were both her children and she loved them equally but Gladstone — if he kept away from rum — would have a better chance in life. He would not have to work the land. He could get an office job in Kingston. He would be able to go to big schools like Wolmers and learn mathematics, Latin and Greek and all those big subjects. While his brother Dudley knew his place. He would go nowhere but the canepiece.

Lionel missed the birth of his son as he was fast asleep after being carried home too drunk to walk. Still, Mary had reason to be grateful to him; when he was sober. He would still give her lessons in reading and writing. She could walk around Eden Park with her head lifted high — soon she would be asked to read the lesson in church. Some women began to chat against her though and spread rumours that she was a witch and that she turned Lionel into a house slave — for them no white man is going to love an 'ole negga' woman, the only thing he would want is her sex. The others held Mary up high and were proud of her. For them, "negro man nuh have no use," to have a white man was to have "everything."

They say that a woman is vain but Mary had learned that men are worse. The secret is that when you have an idea and you want him to agree, let it appear that it was his idea in the first place. This was the only way she could calm her restless Englishman. One early morning, before the sun had gathered its strength and the ground was still cool and dewy outside, she was there doing her spelling at the same time as trying to stop Richard and Dudley from fighting. Lionel sat half-asleep in the planter's chair.

"Lionel, how do you spell ladies, with 'ys' or 'ies'?" Mary asked.

"It's 'ies'. Have you nearly finished?"

"No, this is really hard; it's no use Lionel, I'll never become a lady, it's impossible. As they say in these parts — you can dress up a pig but it will always go back to its pen."

36

"Look, don't cry, I'm sure with patience and hard work you'll at least be able to read and do some basic writing."

"And be a lady like those in Kingston and Spanish Town who grace the balls and speak with an English voice? I want fe talk more genteel, and you promised me that you would make me a Duchess."

"Did I?"

"Well I suppose not in so many words. Anyway, nobody in Eden Park thinks you could do it. They all say that only the living God could change negga gal from darkness to light. Them say negga people too ignorant for learning and too backward to be a lady. But, you know Lionel, I jus' cuss them yuh see. Me tell them that you can do anything. That you is a learned Englishman an' nothing is impossible for you. You can turn water into wine if necessary."

"And what do they say?"

"Them just laugh and call you a waste of time. Them say the only 'ting you good for, is to ride 'ooman."

"They do, do they!"

"But me bet them all my donkeys that you is not a waster and that you are an intelligent and great teacher. So I told them about your idea of making me a lady within five months."

"And what do they say to that?"

"They say it impossible, 'nuff of them even bet them horse that you couldn't do it. But I just say to them that once you think of an idea you never waver; you are like Christ walking on the water. All them do is laugh and cuss bad word and say all you want is fe breed an' lef' me."

Lionel was now standing, his face red with anger. He wanted to know who these people were.

"Just you go to them and take up as many bets as you can. Tell them that when I am finished with you they won't be worthy to walk in your footsteps."

"You mean you will change me into a lady?"

"Yes, I will. It will take some time but I reckon that I'll have you transformed in six months — and if you're good, in three."

"Like a caterpillar changes into a butterfly?!" Mary screamed.

Lionel looked her up and down as if she were a block of wood that he had just hewn and would now carve into shape.

"I'll have to work out a full timetable." Lionel's face was eager and he was as excited as a young child. "This will include elocution lessons. That means lessons to make you sound like a duchess. Also lessons in good manners and decorum."

If anybody had changed, it was Lionel. He was a man inspired, a man with a purpose and a challenge. Mary had caught her butterfly and kept her hands tightly cupped knowing that he would fly away through the slightest opening.

37

The lessons were long and they had more time when the children were asleep. Lionel showed her how to style the morning cap that he had brought from Kingston. This had to be worn on the back of the head. Mary learned that dresses, like people, were placed in classes. There was undress, half-dress and full-dress. As well as costumes for morning, walking, promenading, carriage, afternoon, evening, concert, opera and balls. Shoulders should always be straight and one sits with buttocks caressing the edge of the chair — this gives extra poise. When it came to reading, she should have a book only slightly open and held out in front of her. She had to keep remembering to keep her back straight. A lady never slouches. For morning wear, a lady is allowed a diversity (she loved that word) of attire, especially caps — silk lace is the best. For outdoor wear, there are a variety of bonnets. Straw bonnets for walking, silk ones for promenading and, of course, a carriage bonnet. A lady never goes out without her fan, which she gently waves at arm's length from her face. Mary really did want to be a lady because she never knew a lady who had to suffer hard like a negro woman. Lionel said that a lady in Kingston does not go out between breakfast and dinner except on special occasions — that's to stop her fair skin from being darkened by the hot sun. In the evening a young lady looks forward to being taken to a ball. Lionel tried to teach the waltz, but Mary found it too stiff and in the end it always turned into the quadrille at which she was much better. The hardest thing was speaking like an English lady. Lionel's accent was so deep and at times hard to follow. They found that it was easy if she practiced nursery rhymes. "Mary had a little lamb, her fleece was white as snow." Apart from the Bible, she read Lionel's collection of the Waverley Novels by Scott. In two months she had mastered so much, it was like she had been blind all her life but could see clearly now. She read about other places and her English accent was coming on well. In fact she was doing so well that sometimes the children couldn't understand her. They complained at her new attempts at English, but when the rest of Eden Park people began to comment on how they liked Mary's new accent, their embarrassment turned to pride. As for Lionel he was amazed at how quickly she picked up his instruction. She was like Miss Henry's poodle which she trained to do anything — the only thing left for that dog to do was to speak.

Three months had passed and Mary was ready to read the lesson in church although Lionel had his doubts. There seemed to be more people than usual for the Sunday service and as she went forward to read Psalm 23, she remembered Orville and how she hated him for not teaching her. Mary read the passage with ease and the congregation looked up at her with pride, awakened by the sweetness of her English pronunciation. At the end of the service Dexter and Titus, two cane-

38

cutters, bowed as Mary walked past them out of the church.

"Your Royal Highness, may we rise in your presence?" Dexter said laughing.

"The two of you are so silly this morning," she said smiling.

"Wha' you mean by 'you are'— is 'you is'. That is negga chat an' that is what you is," a vexed Titus said pointing his finger at Mary. "You t'ink you can come wid yuh pretty accent and impress me. Gal yuh mad! Me did know yuh when yuh batty did outdoors, so stop try fe mek we look small."

"Tell her, Titus," said the shorter and darker Dexter. "Yuh come from the same canepiece as me an' no pretty talk will change that."

"You two are just ignorant. You are like crabs. You see one person ah climb out of this cess-pit and all you want to do is drag them back down. It wouldn't bother me if I didn't speak to the likes of you ever again."

Mary left the church vexed. Titus and Dexter had been her friends from childhood — in a matter of minutes they had become enemies. She had said nothing bad to them, yet their eyes were bitter, it was the look they gave Massa Henry after he had cussed one of them in the field. Mary wondered what the rest of her friends really thought. For the first time, she realised how important they were to her. All her life she had wanted to run from them but they were part of her. However, she had changed and now needed Lionel and his world more.

Meanwhile Lionel was more and more restless and at times Mary wouldn't see him for a whole week. She feared that one day he might never return. She knew he had other women but as long as she didn't see them, she didn't mind. She had never felt so clear in her head about what she wanted and didn't want. She did not need a man for love, but for help. Mama had an unusual way of looking at the story of Creation. She used to say that God made woman out of the ribs of man so that woman could take care of herself. Mary hoped that she could take enough from Lionel to be able to fulfil her dream of raising her children in Kingston. This was her dream as she watched the Eden Park men walk slowly towards the estate; they were driftwood coming from nowhere and going nowhere. But she had to act quickly because she was certain Lionel would soon leave her.

One evening, Mary made her way to the hospital. It had once been the old slave sick-house, near to where the overseer had lived on a hill where the healthiest spot on the estate was supposed to be. The hospital was managed by Massa Bremner, a big fat Scotsman who Massa Henry had helped by giving him the job of estate doctor. People say that he ran from the Army after killing another soldier who had eaten his salt-fish ration. He was so dirty that most of the estate workers would rather suffer or took their business to the Obeahman rather than be treated by him. Bremner loved three things in life: woman, food and drink. Most of the time he was content with any old *streggah* woman who would have him; that was when he wasn't too drunk to do anything. Mary would look away from him every time she saw him — he simply disgusted her. She breathed deeply to fight down the bile as she knocked on his door.

"Come in, come in Mary; can I be of assistance to you?"

"I don't know sir, but if you can help me, I'll help you," she said smiling, although she certainly wasn't feeling happy.

The treatment room was surprisingly tidy; everything seemed to have its place. There was a large bed in the corner and paintings on every wall of great Scottish soldiers. On top of the medicine cabinet was the tiger's head belonging to the tiger which Massa Bremner always said killed his father in India.

"So, I hear you're living with an Englishman. I hope you're taking care of him; make sure you bathe him when he's sick."

"Yes, of course, sir."

She hated every part of him. He was fat, but yet strong; he smiled as he sat in his large armchair, his face was red, his eyes red with last night's drinking and his hair red like fire. His belly and chest were like a stone wall and his head peeped over the top. He stared at the woman who had paid him a visit.

"You like me, Massa Bremner?" Mary asked.

"Well of course me dear, I love every part of you."

She pulled up the top of her frock and her breasts fell in front of Bremner's glaring eyes. He reached for them but she stepped back.

"If you love me, will you promise to help me?"

"That depends on what you want, but I'm sure we can arrive at an amicable arrangement."

Mary moved closer to him and allowed him to suck at her bosom. He became excited and started to grab at her. She felt sick to her belly; he sat there big, bloated and red, with his pride rising. She pulled away and he became vexed.

"Don't you toy with me as if I'm some young stag. Now come here, or God in heaven help you."

Mary was afraid; she had woken up this ugly bull and if he was not fed, he would eat her like a gravilicious beast. She had never before given herself to a man that she hated, but nevertheless she moved back towards him.

Bremner eyed her as if she were a roast pig, waiting to fill his empty belly. Mary dared not look at him, but looked through him searching for that rib inside so that she could tear it out and build something of her own on his bones. She moved closer to him and slowly undressed, watching his smiling face buried in his many chins. Then he asked her

40

to strip him like the mistresses had to do during slavery days; Mary obeyed meekly.

It was over so quickly and he sat back and groaned like one of Massa Henry's new steam engines. Mary had made sure that it was the right time of the month; she would rather die than breed for Massa Bremner. He must have had at least 15 children around the estate, all freckled, with dark red hair and damn feisty as well.

"Can I beg a small fava, Massa Bremner?"

"I can't do anything more, I am tired; come back later," he said, using a filthy cloth to wipe the sweat from his neck.

"Is jus' something I would ah like you tell Missa Cooper. Tell him me have a blood sickness and that him have to take me to Kingston to see one of your doctor friends who can treat me," Mary pleaded.

Massa Bremner pushed her off and jumped up from the chair, looking like he had seen a duppy.

"What! You come jump on me and you have the clap!" he cried.

"No, is not true, I just want you tell him that I have a blood disease."

"Oh, I see," said Massa Bremner, smiling with relief. "Why do you want me to tell him that?"

"It's a private reason, will you do it?"

"That's a tall order. I don't like lying to a gentleman, it's un-Christian and I'm ashamed that you even thought of the matter young lady. Clearly, young Cooper has not got you under discipline." All the same, Mary felt that he wouldn't need much persuading. He soon changed his mind when she promised to come every night. Once dressed she hurried to the door. Bremner let her out.

"Remember, this belongs to me," he said slapping her backside. His evil smile brought bitter gall to her throat. "But, do you really think Lionel is going to stay with you in Kingston and look after all your children? His friends will give him hell."

Without Mary telling him, he had already guessed at the reason for the lie.

"What are you going to do when you arrive in Kingston and he finds out you're not sick?"

"I'll worry about that when we get there. Well, will you help?"

"You have the word of a gentleman," said Bremner, glowing red with laughter. Mary stepped out into the rain, wanting it to wash away the sins of the night and cleanse the memory.

The chains of slavery were gone but the untold stories welled up inside her. She sighted Nana the midwife through the rain. No-one knew where she stayed; the children said that she was a duppy living in another body which she "teef". That was it: a duppy living in a borrowed body. All she ever knew was the world of massa and slave;

41

now she has been washed away with only stories that are too bitter to tell and memories too shameful to remember. She had been set adrift with nothing but a 'free paper' in her hand, cramp-up like an old crocus bag. Mary lost sight of her in the distant mist and rain.

The next evening she saw her again. She had just put Gladstone to bed when there was a loud bang on the door.

"Mary, open the door, it's Sammy."

She opened the door to see Sammy Henry, a boiler worker at the mill, with Nana Ethel in his arms. She looked like an old wet sack.

"I think she might be dead. I saw her lying near the factory entrance; she must have been there nearly a day and what with this bad rain."

They laid her on Mary's bed: Stella went to get Nurse. By the time Nurse came, Mary's little house was packed with most of the women in the valley. Those who couldn't get in were singing *Sankey* hymns outside. Mary looked at Nana. She never really knew her granny though since Mama dead, she would always tell Nana her problems. When she had finished talking she would realise that Nana hardly ever said a word, but somehow she always found an answer.

Now as she lay dying, it seemed to Mary that a link with the past was about to be cut. Nana used to tell stories of the old slavery days: great tales of runaways, of rolling caves and of terrible duppies. She knew everyone in Eden Park and she knew to which slave owner their parents belonged. Now, as she lay on Mary's bed, she was nodding in a short, jerky fashion. Her lips were open and Mary heard her mumbling in a sort of sleepy sing-song. Her voice was weak; it sounded like the rustle of slight breezes through sun-parched leaves in the bush. As the rain gathered force outside, Nana's voice strained to muster strength. Mary thought she heard the creak of ox-carts, the curses of bookkeepers, the grunts of the negro people bawling, 'Lawd have mercy', in a chorus of pain. She knelt down and began to cry.

Nana rested her trembling hand on her granddaughter's bowed head and began to talk in a voice more like the voice Mary was used to, her toothless mouth moving slowly as she spoke.

"Save your tears my dear, let the dead bury the dead, but before me pass over I have a story fe tell you. It happened before we negro people get we free paper. It happen right in this plantation of Eden Park. The overseer, a big Irish man name O'Malley, him was real vex that we get we freedom. Him never want it fe come. Him is a man that like fe breed young fresh gal all 12 and 13. Me 'member the night it happened, when him come to the house-slave quarters a look fe a young fresh thing. His eye catch a young girl who ah pretend that she wasn't looking. This girl was about 19, but she was married to a tall spanking young man. The girl cry, 'Let me go, Busha. Let me go,' and when her husband hear her scream him come running in and tek up a spade and lick down Busha. When dat red-face man pick himself up, him redder than poinsettia rose in June. Him cuss 'nuff bad wud, an' de more him cuss, de more him get vex. Him decide fe punish de gal and him shout to her husband, 'No nigger mustn't lick white man!' An' him order de young gal fe strip naked an' four men tie her to a wagon wheel. Then him order the husband to give him wife forty lashes. Why him do that Mary? Why?"

The little old woman began to cry. It took so much strength to cry those tears that Mary thought she was about to die. She calmed herself and went on.

"While de red-face Irishman counted slowly up to forty de young gal's husband, with guns point at him, beat his naked wife, while she cry an' she twist. While the slaves looked on like black duppies, each crack of the whip snap a vessel in them soul. When de beatin' all done, an' de gal look as if she dead, de white people left him with what was left of his wife. She didn't know what happened next, but later people tell her. They tell her seh, she husband, the handsome strong black bwoy, begin to cry and him turn mad. So him tek up a cutlass and burst into Busha house and with one swing him cut off the Busha head. Then him run like jack rabbit for the woods. Them send out a big party but them couldn't find him. The next day them find him near the Great House a hang by him own rope, tie by him own han', from a cotton-wood tree."

Nana Ethel lay back on the bed and began to breathe heavy, her strength spent. But only for a while. She stared out of the dark window, drew back her eyes inside the room, looked around at those who were standing by her dying bed, and quite suddenly turned herself over on her face, lifted up her clothes and revealed her bare back and buttocks.

"See dem, these are the marks of that night of beating. See dem!"

Mary stared shocked at Nana's disfigured back, those marks of her beating lay stiff and criss-crossed on her skinny back.

"It was me who cried that night, just a day before we get we freedom. It was my husband Thomas who hang himself in the Great House yard. All my life I wanted to tell Thomas that it wasn't his fault, that's why me never marry again. Now, me chile, me is happy, for now I can go and put his spirit to rest when I see him in glory. We can catch up on the times we missed and I can tell him that he must now sleep easy for we are together forever."

Nana turned to Mary and smiled. The singing outside got louder as if they sensed the coming of the Lord to take away his servant. "Listen, I know everything in this valley," she told her granddaughter. "And I know you want to marry the white man, Lionel, and go to Kingston. I know your plans me chile, even before you mek dem. Look in me crocus bag, you see a jar with a drink that look like milk, tek it, me dear, you might need it. Only drink it if yuh desperate, for it strong like any lion."

Mary waited for more words but they didn't come. She knew Nana had gone to Thomas. One woman cried out and tied a large band around her waist and fell to her knees. They sang *Jesus Will carry Me Home* and all night people came to the house to pay their respects to this old spirit.

By early the next morning more people from Ewarton had heard about her death and came to pay their respects to this woman who had brought so many lives into the world. Indeed many of them were delivered by poor Nana. They asked about the manner of her going. The story was told to each group who wanted to hear every detail. The body was washed and laid out to be anointed. One woman insisted that the death bed be put outside so as to "fool the duppy." A hog was quickly slaughtered by the men and everyone ate roast pork and sang sorrowful choruses that echoed like a spirit through the mountains and valleys.

It was time for the speeches, and the white rum had made the men's tongues loose. An old man raised his voice the loudest.

"Dearly beloved," he began, "is a sad 'ting to see our sweet sister has now left us on the Lord's chariot. She was dear to me soul though she was apart from us even as she was amongst us. Now me is a man which hear de Spirit, an' when de Spirit tek me all raas bruk out. I beg your pardon - all hell break loose. Now the Spirit say to me that there is a brother who has two box of white rum lock-up inna him house... Bring it forward for the sustenance of the congregation!"

Everybody looked at Mr Davis who had come to the funeral with his wife and baby. He was a brown man who was a manager in Massa Henry's distillery. He went home and soon came back with two boxes of the best rum.

After the funeral Mary slowly went inside, everything seemed empty and her body was chilled as she heard the women singing.

Sleep on sleep on
sleep on an' take thy rest.
We love thee true
But Jesus love thee best
Good-bye—good-bye—good-bye.

Everyone knew that the spirit of the dead was still active for nine days after the death. They had to keep 'watch' during this time, so for the next nine days people took turns to sing and look out for the wandering spirit. Everyone loved Nana and none of them wanted her spirit to get vexed.

The evening following the 'nine-night' Lionel was unusually sober. He lay in the hammock whistling, while the children were at the front making a mess with the ink and quill. Mary sat near him breast-feeding Gladstone, wanting to ask him a question but not knowing how. She struggled for a long while and then took a deep breath.

"Lionel, why don't we get married?"

"Married for what?"

"Well I feel that we should, to make things right."

"I don't understand, we're together, you're not going anywhere. Don't be foolish, woman, marriage is out of the question."

"Well, I will be going somewhere soon, if I don't reach Kingston first."

"Where?"

"To heaven or hell. I went to see Doctor Bremner and him say I must go to Kingston because I have a blood sickness."

"I don't believe you. I know you too well. I know you want to go to Kingston — me, you and the children — but let's not rush things. We'll be there within a month."

"Look Lionel this is no joke. Me sick. Me sick bad and when death tek me I hope you know is you response."

"Well you look fine to me. You've never complained you were unwell up to now."

Mary went to bed early, thinking about her uncertain future. Lionel didn't believe her. She thought of the white liquid that Nana Ethel had given her. She took it from under the bed and drank the bitter waters; it left a bad taste in her mouth. After an hour she was completely wet, every pore was sweating and the room began to spin out of control in front of her. She tried to get up but fell to the ground.

A long while later Mary awoke to see two blood-shot eyes peering down on her; it was Doctor Bremner, his raw tobacco breath was strong enough to wake the dead. He smiled at his patient and then winked his eye — they were partners in crime. He left after shaking Lionel's hand.

"Mary, how are you feeling?" asked Lionel. He look worried as he sat beside her on the bed.

"Much better now. It was like a man just give me one lick in my head. I felt so weak."

"Dr Bremner says it's your blood." Lionel's eyes look filled with pity. "I'm sorry I didn't believe you. Dr Bremner says there's a physician on Duke Street. We shall move to Kingston very soon."

"You mean we'll all be moving — me, you and the children," Mary said, rising up to kiss him for his generosity.

"Well yes, but only for a while until we find out what's wrong with you. Then it's back here until we can work things out for the future."

45

"When do we leave?"

"In the next few days. I've already told Stella to get things packed; you'll have to find someone to live in the house while we're away or squatters will take the place over."

As he got up from the bed he noticed that Dr Bremner had left his stethoscope.

"That drunken fool," said Lionel picking, up the instrument. "I'll just go after him."

"No, Lionel, take it to him in the morning; stay with me, nuh. Tell me about your wife in England." It was only now that Mary found the courage to talk about Cooper's life before he met her.

"Why do you ask?"

"I love you Lionel, but me don't know you. You never tell me hardly anything about where you come from. Yet I know there is something eating inside you."

He was silent awhile and then began to talk slowly. He seemed to be far away but yet was telling Mary more about himself than he ever had before. He spoke of his wife who was called Clarissa. He said he hadn't seen her for four years.

"When we married," he said, "I thought of her as truly beautiful. She was everything I wanted. I worshipped her — she was my goddess. But I found out that she couldn't fulfil her wifely duties. So at nights I began to go out drinking and took my pleasures elsewhere. She never complained, and of course we were still married."

"Did you and she have any children?" Mary asked, surprised.

He told her that they hadn't and said his wife had blamed herself. Her desire for a child became so strong that she pretended she had a son. Lionel said she would get up in the morning and rush out of the door, returning with a pillow which she put to her breast. She had gone mad. And then Lionel had sailed for Jamaica.

He looked hard at Mary. He had stopped talking and she knew he wasn't going to say any more. He gave his usual excuse about having to see one of his friends, yet she knew he was off to see his mistress — perhaps to tell her he was going. As soon as he left the house, Stella entered her mother's room. She had become a woman and now when she walked to church, the young men would look eagerly. She would tease them by holding down her chin shyly and wriggling her backside as she passed.

"Mama, tell me de truth, you sick bad?"

"No me dear, to tell you the truth, a lie me ah tell, my body is in good health."

"But Mama, we all ah fret that you soon dead."

"Stella, I'm sorry me chile — I was going to tell you. I want us to go to Kingston. I want the family to settle in Lionel's home in Town. Now that you can read, you might be able to get a job in a shop or maybe even a hospital. I want us to leave this place. Beyond Eden Park everyone ah move with the times and we just ah stand up and mark time. Look at you, so pretty, like the rose of Sharon, and yet you ah bend yuh back ah plant yam an' milk cow; you should be a schoolteacher, postmistress or even a nurse."

"Mama, I don't mind it here. I don't want to leave."

"Don't bother with that, young lady; when your grandfather ah feel the whip 'pon him back, or when him leg bruk in the man-trap as him a try fe runway, him never say him nuh mind it here. Stop that kind ah chat gal, the only thing that ever kept a black man alive in Eden Park is the dream that his children will one day leave."

"But Mama you think Lionel will want us to stay with him?"

"I don't know me chile, but I know it is what we need."

"So where him deh?" asked Stella.

"Him gone look fe him woman."

"If you never have pickney fe him, him gone long time. Why yuh nuh jus' run him?"

"Gal, have manners — jus' go ah sleep, yuh too fast, yuh love dip yuh mout' into big people's business."

"Mama, it can't work, stop dreaming. Please — I beg you."

Vexed, Stella turned her back and shut her eyes. She was right about Gladstone, thought Mary. In Eden Park there was a high crop of brown pickney, most of them would leave and go to Kingston, or London. Their white fathers loved their brown offspring with a passion — they could see their own image and so they had to treat them good. Gladstone was Lionel's pride and joy; he was now a year old. Lionel used to be a father to all her children, but now he had only time for his little 'prime minister', Missa Gladstone.

The day of the journey came and Mary rose early; the morning was misty and cool and the smell of dawn was of green leaves and fresh cow dung. She felt like an excited little girl, skipping in the yard as she swept. She collected the eggs from the layers and then got Dudley to go to the river for water. All her morning chores were completed quickly and — she hoped — for the last time. They were to travel by horse and trap along the Rio Cobre gorge until they reached Spanish Town, and then rest the night, to start early the next day for Kingston. Mama and Stella were busy packing when Dudley called from the door.

"Mama, Mama, Massa Bremner say him want fe see you at the hospital. Him say is urgent."

Mary's heart sank, a dark cloud loomed over her new dawn. She decided to take a basket of fruits to him hoping to make sure he kept his promise.

The hospital door was open, but no one was in. Mary would have left the basket on Bremner's desk, but as she turned to leave, an arm snaked around her waist.

"Missa Bremner, why yuh do that? My heart nearly drop out of me mouth."

"At last you've come back," he said, feeling her bosom.

"Well, I can't stay," she said slipping out of his arm. "I jus' come fe thank you for your hospitality and help, and me lef' some fruits on your desk, sir."

Dr Bremner smiled. He went across to the front door, turned the key and put it in his shirt pocket.

"Missa Bremner, open the door, nuh man — me have plenty things fe do. Stop the joke business and let me go man."

"You think you can just brush me aside?"

"Look Missa Bremner, me nah stay with you. Me have a lot a business fe do an' me children need feedin', jus' open the door."

"You think you can come here and buy me with fruits. I lied for you, broke one of the ten commandments. Who knows, I may spend longer in purgatory because of you. Now take off your clothes or else I'll do it for you."

He rushed towards her, his arms wide open, his yellow teeth grinning. Mary ran towards the door banging and screaming, but Dr Bremner scooped her off the ground and threw her down on his bed. She then felt his massive weight pressing down on her, crushing her chest. He ripped up her best dress, slapping her across the face every time she scratched him. As he leaned over her she caught sight of his red ear, and bit it as if she were tearing into a tough piece of cane. Mary gripped the ear so long that blood filled her mouth. Dr Bremner jumped up like a man shot; he fell over and rolled on the ground. Mary struggled to his desk and picked up a razor holding it firmly in both hands.

"Open the door and let me out or I'll kill yuh!"

"You filthy whore. You animal. You tried to bite off my ear!" Bremner yelled as blood ran down the side of his face. He slowly got up holding his left ear. Not satisfied, he stretched across to her again but she cut him with the razor. One arm of his shirt quickly became red as blood dripped down onto the floor.

"So you want to fight me, you slut. I'm going to give you a good whipping. And when I'm finished, you're going to lay down."

Massa Bremner stood still; he took off his leather belt. He suddenly pulled back his arm and lashed Mary across the face. Her cheek was on fire and she could see nothing. She fell to the ground hitting her head on the desk, her body seized with pain. She tried to get up but her head was heavy and began spinning in circles. Dr Bremner turned her over and in the same movement ripped away what was left of her

48

undclothes. The blood from his ear dripped slowly onto her breasts. Mary had no strength left so made it easy for him, spreading her arms and legs like a crucifixion. Just as he bent over her there was a knock at the door.

"Bremner, are you in there man? I've got your stethoscope. Open up; I'm in a hurry."

"Lionel," Mary screamed. "Help, him want fe kill me. Lord God, help me!"

Lionel broke through the door only to find Dr Bremner waiting for him, waving the razor, half-dressed.

"So you've come for your whore, the slut who gave herself to me so that she could go to Kingston."

Dr Bremner stabbed at Lionel with the razor but he forgot that his breeches were still around his ankles and fell crashing onto the table. Lionel jumped on top of him and began to hit him in his head and back, but Dr Bremner just soaked up the blows. He then hugged Lionel's slim waist, lifting him off the ground and like a bull smashing him against one of the Scottish generals hanging on the wall. He simply rained blows into Lionel. When Lionel's eyes got big and blood dribbled from his mouth, Mary tried to stand up to help her man, but it was no use. Dr Bremner then picked Cooper up and began to squeeze the life out of him; Mary was frightened that he might break Lionel's back. Thankfully, in one last effort, Lionel managed to grab Dr Bremner's bloodied ear and pulled at the wound. Dr Bremner looked possessed as he screamed out, shaking his head, and dropped Lionel like a hot Dutch-pot. He held his ear and stumbled out of the room, no better than a drunken man vexed for rum. He soon came back holding a large army revolver. There was a loud crack as he fired a shot.

"So you want to fight a soldier, well no one comes here and makes a fool of me! You've drawn your last breath — you and your whore."

But Bremner was having difficulty aiming the gun as more blood ran from his ear and down his arm — he seemed maddened by the pain. Lionel dragged his woman quickly out of Dr Bremner's hospital and the next thing she remembered was waking up in her own bed, heavy with the pain of knowing that Kingston was far far away.

Mary felt pain also for the children. Stella helped undress her mother, while the boys looked on, little Richard kneeling by her bed praying to Jesus to let Mama live. All Mary needed was a rest and she told Stella to stop fussing and to send the boys outside. Still weak, she drank some bush tea and looked across to Lionel who was at the window, his back to her.

"How are you feeling?" he asked coldly, too angry to turn around.

"Not too bad - but Lionel, mek me tell you what happened."

"Don't bother trying"

49

"You vex with me, yes?"

Lionel's veins stretched out of his neck as he shouted his anger at Mary, calling her a whore, a slut and that he was ashamed to think he could have lain with her.

"You can call me what you like, Missa Cooper. But look 'pon me and tell me if you ever intended fe tek us to Kingston to live in your fine house."

"Listen to me, you filthy whore, Kingston has nothing to do with this; you not only lay with that fat old dog but you and him plotted and lied, to try and make me look a fool. I've lived with you and helped you with this place but when I turned my back, you were gone with other men."

"So what's going to happen now? No, don't answer, let me tell you; you're going to do what you always planned and that is to tek off to Kingston."

By now Gladstone was awake and needed feeding. As Mary reached for him, Lionel dived across the room and snatched him from her.

"You think I'm going to let my son drink milk from you? Don't you dare feed my boy. You joke about having a blood disease, but after you've been with that stinking Bremner, I'm sure you've got something. I will take my son before allowing him to feed off your milk."

Gladstone began to cry, he was hungry and upset. Lionel tried to comfort him but Gladstone only cried harder.

"Lionel, please give me my baby, he needs his mother," Mary pleaded, her arms stretched out. But Lionel held him closer and Gladstone screamed even harder.

"He won't stop crying. Lionel, give me my baby, nuh man."

As the cries got wilder, Lionel finally gave in and pushed Gladstone towards his mother. She snatched him to her breast and he slowly quietened. Lionel looked at Mary as if her milk were poison, but he said nothing. The silence was interrupted by a soft tap on the door; Mary thought it was Richard playing, wanting to come back inside so she shouted at him to keep away. The door slowly opened. Mary looked over to where Cynthia stood holding a baby closely to her breast.

"Is what bring you here!" It was many months since Mary had seen Cynthia — Spanish Town must have been good to her, for she looked well rounded and pretty. Beyond the open door Mary saw Cynthia's sister and brother-in-law in a fine looking buggy. Lionel sat down, a pained expression across his face, as he tried to make sense of what this new morning had brought. Mary almost felt sorry for him. She looked across to the other baby mother holding her child before her like evidence in a court. Cynthia looked like a lady of substance, with her elegant frock gathered at her full hips — her brown skin, her city perfume — Mary hated her for having all the things she wanted.

Lionel walked over to Cynthia. He had shaken off the confusion that came over him when she first walked in. He was confident now — the English gentleman. He looked into the bundle in her arms, searching the baby's face like a doctor, only he knew what he was looking for — maybe a special Cooper mark.

"This is not my child!" he deduced.

"Cynthia, mek me see de baby," Mary demanded. "Is it a boy or girl?"

"A boy — a young gentleman, like his father."

"What's his name?"

"Oliver."

The first thing Mary noticed was how similar he was to Gladstone. His complexion was a lot lighter but he had Cooper eyes and, as he clasped his tiny hand around her finger, he gave Mary a Cooper smile; the smile which left you unable to feel anything bad towards them, no matter what they had done. Lionel and Gladstone used it on Mary every day.

"You lie, Lionel — you is the baby father. We may be poor and simple but we nuh fool."

Cynthia turned to Lionel in anguish, "Why did you say you were coming back when you knew it was untrue? You said you loved me and that you would tek me to Kingston, but I find you living here with this negga woman."

"What? Is who you ah call negga woman? You think 'cause yuh brown, yuh special? Lionel, how you mek this woman come inside my house and cuss me; you were taking me to Kingston, not her."

Then, in a great chorus, as if prompted by their mothers, both babies began screaming loudly. This was too much for Lionel who stormed out to find some rum. As the door slammed shut Mary knew it had closed on her.

Cynthia looked at her with pity. For the first time she frightened Mary — the light-skinned mother's new power towered over her.

"You really need Lionel fe true," she said, looking Mary up and down with scorn as if trying to see how she had managed to keep Lionel for so long.

"Yes I do, and I know I love him more than you."

"I suppose you're right. I loved him once too, but I don't need him any more. I won't take away your English gentleman."

"You mean you'll go away?"

"No better still, I will help you make certain that you keep Lionel and go to Kingston. Now what have you got that Lionel really loves?" Said Cynthia looking down at Gladstone, smiling, her eyes concealing a plan Mary couldn't read.

51

"Is what you want with Gladstone?"

"Listen, me have a perfect scheme. I'm on my way to Kingston now, let me take Gladstone with me. Tell Lionel that if he wants to see his son then he must take you and the children to Kingston, and when you get there you'll give him the address of my uncle where I'll be staying."

Mary stared hard at Cynthia. She seemed out of place in the simpleness of the country, she was now a city girl. Her painted face and the gems on her fingers came from a world far from this bush and stinking sugar cane. She sat only half on the bed as if she might catch something; she was now only a visitor to Eden Park — she could tell her fine friends how she came from the country and how she would visit but couldn't live there. Mary felt like the girl Cinderella in Lionel's story, who couldn't go to the ball. But could Cynthia really be the fairy godmother? And yet Lionel would surely follow his child to Kingston. Mary's head was confused after all that had happened to her since morning, but the plan seemed good.

Still, she wanted to know why Cynthia was so ready to help her.

"You and I are in the same boat," she said. "Even if Lionel leaves you, when you get to Kingston he'll at least help you to get a start. He has cheated both of us and it's about time we both got our revenge. Don't look so worried me chile. You're Kingston bound; jus' trust me."

Up until then Mary always felt that the harder she tried to leave this place the more chains were wrapped around her. Why hadn't she just given up and accepted her lot? God must have put something inside her because she had a permanent burning desire to smash down walls, run up hills and fly to the other side of the moon. Mama lay dead in her Eden Park grave, yet she was so intelligent; she knew how to make five loaves feed fifty — no one could turn her fool. Mama would work her piece of land till she tired and then sit down in the night to watch the stars. She had so much 'brain' but like a soldier without a war, she had no choice but to sit looking at the moon waiting for it to change into the sun. It was worse for Mary because she would look to the moon and need to know where else it was shining, to what city did it give light and was there another Mary on the other side so that she could shake hands and say, "How de do?"

Mary felt guilty as she looked down on her helpless baby, who would be the bargain for her freedom.

By early afternoon, the hottest time of the day, Cynthia sat in the buggy with Oliver in her lap. Her sister was holding Gladstone, fanning herself rhythmically — she was now part of the plot, but she stared her charge's mother with eyes that judged. What kind of mother could give away her beautiful baby? When Cynthia had torn Gladstone away from his mother, placing him in her sister's lap, it was like she was tearing away Mary's own flesh and leaving a bony shell. The sister waved slowly to Mary as the buggy moved towards the edge of the valley. It was a wave that you give the dead before the coffin is lowered into the ground. Later as the sun changed places with the moon, Gladstone's mother knelt down in the field and wept for her baby.

Mary returned home just before dawn and fell asleep on the dining table but awoke shortly after when she felt a hand on her shoulder.

"Mary, what's happened to Gladstone? He's not in his crib."

She was surrounded by the whole family waiting to hear the story of why Gladstone was missing — Lionel stood in front of them.

"Don't fret, I've given him to Cynthia — as a guarantee."

"For what!" screamed Lionel.

Mary explained, but things didn't seem as clear to her now as they had before.

"Mama, you mean you sell Gladdy!" cried Stella.

"No, I haven't sold him. It's just that if you want to see your son Lionel, you must take us to Kingston."

"And what if I refuse. What will you do then — have him killed?"

Lionel paced up and down the room punching his open hand — he was red with anger and Mary was worried she had awakened an evil spirit.

"So Mama, are we going to Kingston fe look fe Gladstone. Should I go and put on my best shirt Mama?"

"Dudley, stop yuh noise!" Mary said quickly and sent Stella and the two boys to fetch water. Stella pushed her brothers out of the house, slapping Dudley who didn't want to leave. She looked back at her mother confused as she went out.

Lionel burst out, "No white man in the world would suffer all this from a negro peasant. You don't deserve to be free — they should have kept you in chains. This house stinks with your lies!"

"Well get out if you don't like it!" Mary cried.

"It's I who built this house and my money which bought those cows. I decide when I leave and what I will take with me."

He came forward and grabbed her arms. Mary struggled to get free but Lionel's grip was too tight. He began to puff heavily as he dragged her towards the door while she clung to the table. He smashed her fingers with a spoon until she had to let go and then he dragged her along the floor, throwing her on the dirt outside. She heard the bolt violently thrust in place. Then to make matters worse, of all the people who decided to pay Mary an early visit, Mary looked up to see Horsemouth. She smiled nervously and tried to wipe sweat and dirt from her body in an effort to look presentable.

"How de do Horsemouth, lovely mornin'".

"Yes and me come fffff...fe some breakfast," stuttered Horsemouth.

"Not this mornin' me dear, come tomorrow."

"You look like yuh have fffffee...ver, Mary."

"A lickle chest cold that's why I'm out here to get some fresh air."

Horsemouth walked away slowly. He had got broader since Mary last saw him, but he still looked as fit as he was at eighteen. He had not married, but many a girl had babies for him. Mary turned and banged on the door but there was no answer.

"Lionel open the door!"

She banged again — the door flew open. Mary walked in quickly but she couldn't see Lionel. He was laying in the hammock. The quiet tingled her spine. His boots were on the dining table — something he knew she hated. Mary picked them up and polished them till they shone, washed her hands and gathered the Dutch-pots to go and prepare breakfast. All this time he watched her as if she were a walking razor that would tear out his heart if he lowered his guard. That night he lay in silence, believing that Mary had despised him while he thought she worshipped him.

It took Lionel until the next morning to announce that they were leaving for Kingston the following day. Mary tried unsuccesfully to feel the joy of victory in battle. She needed to feel whole again. Part of her was laying in Kingston in another woman's arms. Her breasts itched to feed her baby son. She wanted to put her finger in his tiny hands and watch him smile as he gripped it tight. Mary finally lifted herself out of these thoughts, as there was much to do before she would be ready the next day, to take her first steps away from Eden Park.

The house was noisy with excitement as Mary and the children packed their things and argued about what was rubbish, what was too heavy and who was the real owner of certain items. During this confusion, Lionel lay in the hammock still silent, bitter. He was in the house but somehow no longer part of the household and spent his time brooding about being cheated of revenge on Bremner. The doctor had disappeared from Eden Park like a thief in the night. The first people knew was when they found the surgery shut up the next morning.

By nightfall the housework and packing were done. They were ready to leave at last, but Mary was uneasy.

Before dawn the next day, she set off with the boys one last time for Ewarton market, wearing her best dress again, hastily mended after what took place at the hospital. She also wore her pretty shoes which Lionel had brought back for her from Kingston. These weren't market clothes, but today she wanted to look special.

As the sun began to dry the wet grass, the donkeys found it heavy underfoot. The rainwater rested on the mahoe leaves high above them; the shadow of the tree formed a tall woman tenderly holding a child. Mary's shame would never end until she saw her baby. It must have been the same way Mama felt when she was told that her womb was barren. Only in her Mary's case she had given her child away. Although she would soon see him, she was fearful that something would go wrong; she hoped that the Spirit which the Rivermaid said had sailed into her, would be strong enough to take her back to Gladstone. Soon she would be free from this bush knowledge — a new voice was calling her to come out of the bamboo, the palm tree, the sugar cane — to reach a new horizon.

Many people were on their way to Ewarton driving donkeys hidden beneath heavy loads of mint, onions, nutmeg, papaw and pumpkin. Mary was going to market so she would have some money in her pocket — that way she wouldn't have to rely totally on Lionel when they got to Kingston. As she drifted with the crowd Mary felt confident that things would work out right. She felt sorry for these poor wretches she would soon leave behind. They were travellers with no fire at night and no cloud to guide them during the day. Mary now felt she was not of them but that she belonged to a new country; they were now foreign to her.

"Mornin', Miss Mary me hear you turn big time and ah go ah Kingston."

Mary didn't recognise the voice behind her, but when she turned around it was Miss Lottie, riding a donkey that was suffering under her big frame. Mary only intended to tell a few people that she was leaving, but trying to keep a secret in Eden Park is like trying to keep the rain from your head with a plantain leaf. She told Miss Lottie she expected to be gone by noon. Miss Lottie was so proud of her that she began crying with joy. They went to sit together near the water fountain. Mary looked around at all that she knew and for the first time felt that she would miss it. She would miss Obediah, the madman, who came up to her to wish her well. His matted hair hanging from his slim face, his grimy rags barely covering his *maaga* body. Then there was Miss Iris and her drunken husband, Skipper. They ran the small rum bar just before the market square. They would argue every market day. Their tortured marriage provided the market people with fun and excitement. Miss Iris was a real joke. When she was done with Skipper she would start on the rowdy crowd, who would laugh even louder, especially when she turned her back and lifted her frock. Then she would go back inside the bar, but always returned later to give the next show.

The market was a real piece of excitement. Every week some incident happened that would either make you want to run with fear or cry with laughter. Only last Wednesday a madman from Mary's area of Eden Park came rushing through, swinging a machete. He chopped four women before the militia shot him. He said he was the Angel of Death and had come down to destroy the earth of all its wickedness.

Jamaica must have more prophets than words in the Bible, all telling the people that they should repent because judgement is at hand. The best prophet in St Catherine was Brother Joel. He had the sweetest words and yet a thunderous voice which made Mary shiver when she was younger. He thought he was Christ who had died and had risen and was here to judge the world. Mary, usually never paid him any mind but on that last day she listened carefully as this old prophet preached the morning message.

"Look at me hands — the nails were driven in by those wicked Roman soldiers, and my feet — them did ram one big rusty nail inna me foot."

He then tore his white garment to reveal his skinny side.

"And my side where the Roman soldier rammed his spear and forthwith came there out blood and water. Oh my followers, I have once again come amongst you. I, who dying on the cross, cried out on the ninth hour, 'E-li la ma Sa bach tha-ni'. My God, my God, why has thou forsaken me? But now I am risen and let me tell you all, there will be blood and fire 'pon all those who do not call on my name. For my Father will destroy them with thunder and lighting — selah. Look! There is Mary Magdalene."

Mary looked around and realised with shame that Brother Joel was pointing at her.

"Mary, Mary, the mother of James and Joseph and the mother of Zebedee's children. You who kept me safe from the wickedness of Herod when I was a suckling. Mary who wept at the cross and sat by the sepulchre."

The crowd was now laughing and Mary became vexed as she realised she was part of this show. Brother Joel then threw himself down at her feet and began kissing them. Mary put her foot on his head and forced it on the ground.

"Move yuhself nuh, man, before I tek up a stick and bruk it 'cross yuh back." She walked away quickly as Brother Joel's blessings turned to vicious curses. She was no longer the gracious Mary Magdalene, but the evil Jezebel.

In a way Mary felt a strange freedom buzzing in that market air — a freedom that meant you could be whoever or whatever you wanted and people would take you seriously. Even though they may laugh at you, they would never ignore you. Obediah the madman was king, Queen Victoria, a goat or a mango tree — whichever took his fancy. But what kind of place was this? A place where mad people were taken seriously. Where you could be who you want for the day. Surely this was a place where people were lost, not knowing who they really were. Mary had formed new lands in her mind, with big people — a place with gentry and ladies, where people were serious, not *puppy-show* people. She was glad she was going to her unknown place, towards real freedom.

As she turned the last bend before the valley of Eden Park opened before her on her journey home, a flock of crows settled on the road and Mary felt cold for a moment wondering what evil luck lay ahead. Before she reached the church, she saw Stella running toward them. Her clothes were dirty and ruffled, and, as she got closer, Mary saw tears streaming from her daughter's eyes. Breathless, she fell to the ground.

"Stella, what's wrong?"

"Mama, the one Cynthia, she did trick we. When I come back from the river me catch Lionel leaving the house, him seh to tell you him gone with Cynthia. Mama, where is Gladstone, when will he be back with us?!"

Lionel had left as soon as the carts had disappeared over the hill on the way to Ewarton. Mary screamed for her baby and asked God to curse him and Cynthia. She ran chasing nothing but the hot breeze; then she collapsed not able to catch breath. Dudley and Stella helped her back to the house. She hated herself for being so foolish as to risk her baby for everything and now she was left with nothing. There was a letter on the table from Lionel. As she opened it she thought how nearly a year earlier she could just about write her name; this man had dressed her for the world and he had now stripped her of her hope and future. Mary's tears smudged the ink of his handwriting as she read his cruel judgement.

Dear Mary

A messenger brought a letter from Cynthia early this morning. She told me where I could find her and my child. She said she had to take the child from you because you were behaving so oddly, she thought my son was in danger. When I think back to the way you have been behaving over the past while, how you have deceived me, how you tried to trick me, how you fornicated with that filthy, lecherous Scotsman, I know that Cynthia is indeed telling me the truth and I am grateful to her for protecting my child. What kind of mother could you be to my son?

Maybe it would have been better if I had never taught you a thing. Perhaps you were happier, and a better person in your ignorance. Knowledge can be dangerous, that's why God knows best. You must accept fate and know your place, we each have our work to do, no matter how small, as the hymn writer says:

'The rich man in his castle,
The poor man at his gate,
God made them high and lowly,
Each to his own estate'.

I intend to marry Cynthia and Gladstone will be brought up with his half-brother, Oliver. As soon as he is old enough, he will be sent to England to receive an education befitting a gentleman.

I took the liberty of taking the musket and I shall pass it on to Gladstone when the right time comes.

I have left some money as I would not like to think of you and the children meeting hardship, despite the way you have behaved towards me. I hope you will remember me as a fair man.

Yours with God,
Mr. Lionel Cooper

Mary knew that she would never see Gladstone again. She was sure that Lionel would make up a story when in the future her baby asked about his mother. Lionel would say that she died while she was giving birth or that she was licked down by cholera. Even if Gladstone knew about her he would certainly feel shame that she was poor and a negro, he would never bring his friends to see her. She would be a negro *duppy* that he would be happy to forget. She went across to the empty crib; it had been used for all her children as they screamed into life. But now it was a grave. She had sacrificed her son for nothing. The world was unfair to allow a white man to take his son and the mother to have no say because she was poor and negro. Mary looked into the crib and saw Gladstone, crying out at feedin' time, his tiny arms and legs kicking. She picked him up and gave him her breast — would he suck and feel content? Then she rocked him gently. She felt glad that he had now come back.

"Stella come, look who has come back to us, it's your brother, Gladdy."

Stella rushed inside and looked confused.

"Stella, come and hold Gladstone fe me, look, him come back. He never really did like it in Kingston. Him prefer country wid him people."

Stella took Gladstone from her mother, silently looking at her with those wide eyes and then dropped her arms.

"Stella, watch out, you ah drop Gladstone!"

Mary quickly dived to Stella's feet and saved her baby just in time; she could have cussed Stella for her carelessness. Instead, Stella rushed over to the old planter's chair, sat down and began crying. She must have been ashamed for caring so little for her brother as to drop him. By this time Gladstone had started to cry. Mary rocked him in her arms, smiling as his tears turned to a smile as he looked up at his mama. Mary began to sing to Gladdy, he loved when Mama sang.

58

Me carry me ackee a Linstead market
Not a quatty worth sell. Oh what a losses!
Not a quatty worth sell.
Me carry me ackee a Linstead market.
Not a quatty worth sell. Oh not a light, not a bite!
Not a quatty worth sell.

Mary's singing was interrupted by the boys rushing into the room hearing her singing to Gladdy. Dudley looked at his mother as if she were a witch.

"Now boys, we are not going to Kingston anymore; Lionel has left, he had to go back to England but come and give Gladdy a kiss, 'cause him back and I know you two did miss him."

Stella quickly grabbed Dudley and Richard, marching them outside. Mary didn't hear what she said but after a short while the boys returned, nervous but smiling and Dudley carefully took Gladstone from his mother's arms and showed him to Richard. It was like the return of the prodigal son — if Mary had had a spare goat she would have cooked it to celebrate. Gladstone could just about walk, he must have learned that in Kingston. Mary told Dudley to set him down on the ground and her little boy managed to cross the whole room without falling.

Gladstone stuck with her everywhere. He went with her to church, where she showed him off proudly to the members and she asked everyone to thank the Lord for his safe return. Gladdy was with her when she went to the field to plant; Mary would strap him to her back while she planted or let him practice his walking by wondering among the yam heads. He was a little devil at home. He would steal honey and bring dirt from outside which his mother had to stop him from eating.

Stella and Mary never really saw eye to eye after Gladstone's return. She no longer helped her mother with the cooking although, as the girl child, she should. Mary hoped Stella didn't expect Dudley or Richard to wash, cook and clean.

'The gal worthless, all that interest her is man. When Gladdy is crying at nights I can't remember once she getting up and taking care of him. I don't know how she goin' manage when she have pickney,' she said to herself.

One night after Gladstone's crying had kept her from sleep, Mary sat next to his crib singing quietly to calm his spirits. Although his eyes were closed his little hand clasped her finger pulling her down as if he wanted to tell her a secret. He told her not to worry about Kingston, as long as they were together that's all that mattered. He never felt bitter about Mary giving him to Cynthia, she was a cheat and a liar and her day of reckoning would be a judgement according to her deeds.

'He tells me he loves me. I tell him that I will never lose him again. I don't know how he came back to me but I'll never let him go. Perhaps it was the Rivermaid who brought him to me. I tell him he must never forget his Mama. I am in the soil in which he was kept warm and strong, I showed him the sunlight and the rain. I know all his little secrets. I know his past because I am his past,' she would tell herself. "Not to know me is not to know yourself," she told him, "and if you deny yourself you will be nothing but a shadow for someone else. Never leave me Gladstone or I lose a part of myself and you lose all."

As Mary turned away a loud scream tore into her spine. She turned back, there was no scream, just silence. No tiny baby asking to be fed, no Gladstone — just an empty crib...

BOOK TWO

...There was another break in the shooting but no one wanted to leave, David Cooper once again became the focus of attention. This time the orange sellers led the cry for people to buy their goods. Cooper began to cough blood, yet there was still no sign of a helicopter. He turned his head enough to see the crowd all jostling to get a good view of his dying body. These spectators were not going to be denied the taste of death and refused to leave until the last drop of blood had oozed out of their Prime Minister's veins.

Growing weaker, Cooper remembered when he was fit and strong, standing on this same platform, the people's messiah. Why should God take his life now, he deserved to be rescued. If only he could stand up strongly on the stage and tell the people to rest all their troubles and fears with the Independent Party of Jamaica. And they would listen to him as they always did, because he was a modern day prophet to whom the people had given their hearts and souls.

"Marva, it's so damn unfair," he whispered in his wife's ear. "What have I done to deserve this?"

Tears streamed down Marva's face. Cooper turned and glared at Ken Williams, the so-called loyal Brigadier-General who was screwing his wife. Marva thought he didn't know about it, but in Jamaica nothing is a secret. Williams had youth and good looks on his side. Even as he lay bleeding to death, David Cooper wondered whether Williams' cock was bigger than his own, and whether he kept it going for longer. Cooper hated Williams for succeeding in seducing Marva. The vision haunted him as he lay dying, of the both of them lying on his cold grave, with Marva, her legs apart, screaming with joy as she felt Williams' long cock.

Cooper had become hysterical, all he could see around him were traitors. Breaking into a cold sweat, he began to scream.

"Jesus Christ help me! Lawd Jesus help me!"

"David, easy now, drink some water," Marva reassured him, her dress soaked in his blood.

"Marva," Cooper said regaining his composure. "What was it like fucking Ken?"

"What do you mean? Please David, don't talk. You're saying things you don't understand?"

"Don't tek me for a fool!" he spluttered in her ear, feeling a sharp pain in his side as he did. "Was he as good as me Marva, tell me."

"Please David, you're hurting yourself even more."

"I want to know!"

"David," she said, "you're going to be alright. They'll fix you up. You'll be alright. Wait and see."

"Cut the bullshit Marva, tell me was it good?"

"Yes it was, will that make you happy?"

"Was it better?"

"No, it was the same." Marva began to cry. Her face was covered with blood and tears. Cooper motioned to Ken, who lowered his head tentatively to his boss' parched lips.

"When I die, if you ever lay your raas hands on my wife, I will haunt your backside forever. Do you hear me?"

"Yes sir!"

Cooper felt detached from Marva, she suddenly became ugly, pathetic, covered in her tears and his blood. He could feel her trembling against him as she looked away racked with guilt. He felt a sense of satisfaction that he made her confess, he knew she would live with that for the rest of her life.

A sudden burst of energy revived David Cooper. "Bring me the microphone, I want to talk to the people!" he commanded.

His head soaked in blood, he was helped up by two soldiers and stood in front of the mic, flopping like a puppet on a string. It was a sad sight. The entire auditorium fell silent with hushed anticipation.

"People... you have come to see your leader die! Well see me deh!"

Cooper collapsed in a heap as if someone had cut the puppet's string. He was still alive though, and winked at his brother Rodrigues.

"They can't keep a good Cooper down," he said.

"Yes David, you're as stubborn as mother," said Rodrigues.

David loved his mother, who although in her eighties, was as active as a woman half her age. She was from England and would often tell him stories of how she first met his father Gladstone...

...There were no early roses to be found in any college in Cambridge. It was May and the last of the daffodils and tulips struggled to make one more dramatic appearance as their fellow players bowed out until next spring. But what of the early roses? Those early buds that saw nature breaking her waters before the birth of summer. It was the signal for picnics on the lawns and reading Keats by the Cam. The end of heavy coats and huddling in tea shops and the coming of cider, lemonade and butterflies. The head gardener searched every corner of this ancient academy but not one early rose was to be found. What a calamity! In his thirty years of service this had never happened not even in his father's day, who was head gardener during Queen Victoria's reign. Then as he stood in the quadrangle of King's College he nodded to himself with a satisfaction that perhaps only Galileo would know. It was the women of course. It was the arrival in recent years of those bloody damsels. They must have caused some imbalance in the earth. It was nature's way of heaving scorn on the Vice-Chancellor's folly for letting them study here in the first place. He marched away, his head buzzing with his new theory. Who knows perhaps they would allow him to give a lecture? He was sure he could show those dons a thing or two.

Virginia first met Gladstone Cooper several years after the Great War, on a night when Cambridge was alive with the May ball. She sat in the corner of the ballroom with her two girlfriends Felicity and Angela. She could feel a suspender clip pinching the inside of her leg and she shifted around uneasily to work the skin free.

So there she sat like a mechanical doll half in heaven and half in hell, smiling at the gentlemen as they walked past. If it were not for Virginia's ginger hair, people might think the three women were triplets as they sat with their white, frilly ball gowns and Japanese fans. Felicity and Angela were brunettes but they all wore silk ribbons and their cheeks became red puffs if a young man came too close.

This was a strange ball. The band played some of Scott Joplin's ragtime numbers, but no one was dancing. The undergraduates and dons drank wine, talked politics and joked about their schooldays. While Virginia sat dreaming of suddenly getting up on the podium and doing the can-can, something to give the old dons an early retirement.

"Virginia, you haven't said a word all evening and you've been staring at that piano for the longest while," said Angela.

"It's not the piano," said Felicity, "she's been staring at that tall chap near the piano."

"Oh, you mean the coloured fellow," said Angela smiling at

Virginia and winking mischievously.

"Don't be silly, I was just thinking about the piano — what a clear tone it has."

Virginia looked over at the man in question. He looked lonely, as if he were looking for a friend who hadn't turned up. He was definitely ex-army, you could tell by the way he never slouched but stood upright almost to attention. He slowly leaned back on the piano and their eyes made contact.

"Look Ginny he's smiling at you," said Angela. "He's from the West Indies you know, I think he's a medic."

He was still smiling at her. She tried to pretend not to notice and then in a sudden fit of madness poked her tongue out at him.

"Virginia, my God, what did you do that for?" Angela examined her quizzically.

"I don't know, I just did it. He reminded me of when I was a girl and the little boys in the park tried to kiss me. I don't know, it was stupid."

"Now look what you've done. He's turned away. You've embarrassed the poor fellow." Felicity said half-seriously.

"Do you think I hurt him?"

"For someone who wasn't even looking at him you seem awfully worried."

Suddenly feeling unaccountably rash, Virginia announced, "I bet you two cigarettes that I'll go up to our West Indian friend and ask him for a dance."

"You wouldn't dare. You'd really ask a man to dance? Ginny I know you've done some mad things here but this takes some beating. Alright you're on, but if you lose you have to do watch for a week. Felicity has a week's supply of cigarettes and I know matron is suspicious."

Virginia made her way slowly through the sea of gentlemen who looked at her with undisguised wonder. She felt like saying, 'Yes it walks you know and smiles, and it bloody well would like to bash some of your stupid heads together.' She felt a touch of sympathy for her West Indian who looked distinctly uneasy at the realisation that she was advancing in his direction. What if he decided to run from this mad woman? She might end up chasing him around the ballroom like an evil vampire. His apprehension quickly mastered, he greeted her with a warm, charming half-smile.

"Good evening, sir," Virginia said nervously.

This was followed by a silence, she could say no more.

"Good evening, it's good of you to come over to me. Forgive me for staring at you earlier, but I couldn't help myself. I was, as they say, enchanted."

"Do you like dancing?" she asked.

"There's nothing I like better," he replied.

Without another word spoken, they were holding each other in the middle of the hall, the band playing a slow romantic number. Virginia felt ashamed and wonderful at the same time. Soon there was a large space around them, everyone watching this outrage. Professors looked down at her through their thin-rimmed spectacles and cursed again the day the University allowed women to enter its hallowed chambers.

"What's your name?" he asked softly.

"Virginia, Virginia Langbridge. And I'm reading art history."

"You're not by any chance the Virginia Langbridge who..."

"Yes," she interrupted, "I'm the ballet dancer who fell from a horse and will never dance professionally again."

"I'm sorry, I read about it in the papers."

"Never mind, what about you?"

"Well my name's Gladstone Cooper, I graduate this year in medicine."

"So you hope to be a doctor?"

"Yes, I want to start my own practice, but back home in Jamaica. I've been away since I left school, but I've always intended to go back."

They became aware at the same moment that they were still the centre of attention. Gladstone suggested that they go outside for a walk and the two students headed for the door. On the way out, Virginia smiled triumphantly at Angela who returned a pretend cigarette puff.

The two walked through the college arches and then towards the river. They cut across the perfectly manicured lawn, the river was opposite, glistening in the moonlight. Then, like an awful looming shadow, a college officer appeared in the distance. Waving his arms and jumping up and down, he came steaming towards them. He was about fifty, an old military type, with a bald head and a medal that never left his lapel.

"What on earth do you think you're doing, madam?"

"I beg your pardon, sir," Virginia said surprised.

"You are walking on the grass. Ladies are forbidden to walk on the turf - only gentlemen are allowed. The college rules were explained to you. Ladies must use the gravel path, not the grass!"

"If you ask me, that's a damn stupid rule," said Gladstone.

"Come on, Gladstone, I better stick to the path. Who knows, I might turn into a frog otherwise."

It seemed that Cambridge reluctantly suffered the presence of female students, and they were given 'grace' status rather than full admission. The women's colleges were glorified slums with few books and no leisure facilities, while the men's colleges had tennis courts, cricket pitches, grand libraries and, men could walk on the grass.

Unless women students were invited to a special lunch, they had to suffer the rigours of almost unpalatable food. The usual starter was a bowl of plain gravy soup, so watery that the women mistook it for a finger-bowl. The main course was typically under-cooked chicken, two over-cooked sprouts and an abundance of floury potatoes, all washed down with the regulation glass of water. Dessert was a miserable rhubarb submerged in luke-warm custard. It felt like the female students were being punished for being women. Meanwhile, the men dined in real style with wine flowing freely. Soup and shrimps were given as starters, followed by duck, served with parsley and stuffing. Waitresses served a variety of sauces as Britain's young elite gentlemen filled their stomachs. They lived the lives of the rich upper-class while their female counterparts were the paupers, grateful to be allowed into the king's palace, but not permitted to share at the king's table.

Virginia tolerated the social segregation but she refused to accept academic inferiority. The previous week she had needed to look at one of Milton's manuscripts at the King's College Library. She was told that the library facilities were not available to her unless accompanied by a Fellow of the College or failing that, with a letter of introduction. She felt humiliated at being locked out and not taken seriously.

Gladstone explained that he would soon return to Jamaica after his finals, while Virginia was to complete her first year. Cambridge had been a big disappointment for her and meeting Gladstone seemed to promise something more exciting. They arranged to meet the day after the ball in one of the many quaint tea-houses that were scattered through town.

They sat silently over the hot-tea, searching for interesting stories, then, in a burst of excitement, Gladstone asked his companion to paint his portrait. She hadn't told him that she painted, but he said he guessed from the way she dressed. She became conscious of her baggy corduroy breeches and floppy hat. They were so unalike in that tea-shop. He, of course, came in his fine two piece suit and silk tie. His shoes were immaculately polished and tied so that each bow was in symmetry with the others. His shirt was starched and his collar stiff.

They decided that Gladstone would sit for her in the small field behind his college — a remote spot where local girls would meet with their beaux. Certainly, Gladstone could not come to Virginia's college dormitory since the rules forbade such visitors.

He was a great model, tall with black curly hair, that waved slightly. He would stand legs apart, almost to attention and would give her a half-smile from the corner of his mouth. He was so charming, like a Greek god looking down on the mortals of the Earth. He looked irresistible. Already something inside Virginia was leaping up in response to him, and watching his face, she saw some quality which

66

separated him from any other man that she had met.

Although Gladstone appeared supremely confident, Virginia sensed there was something else under that persona, that was hurt and vulnerable. It crashed forth at the Varsity cricket match. Gladstone was forced to open the batting because the opener was injured; a position he hated, preferring to bat at number four or five. In fact he was one of Cambridge's star players, a brilliant all-rounder and player of the year of the last two seasons. Unhappily, on this occasion, he was clean bowled after only the second ball of the day. He looked furious as he strode back to the pavilion. Then a spectator shouted, "These darkies can't play an Englishman's game. Bloody cheek having one at the crease in the first place."

Almost before the man had finished his statement, Gladstone had veered from his route to the pavilion and was heading into the crowd. He grabbed the offender and beat him about the head. In the end it took four men to restrain him. It was so strange, so out of character. Normally he was so measured that you might think he was really rather a prig, but the beast that roared under that mild mannered chest, made Virginia feel that they had one similarity — a bloody bad temper.

Later, after he had changed, Gladstone and Virginia walked along the Cam together. She teased him about his show of temper but he was clearly not in the mood for idle banter.

"I don't know why you find the incident so amusing, but then you would, wouldn't you? You're a white woman, what would you know? When I was in London last summer, seeking lodgings, I ended up having to stay with one of the lecturers because no one would rent me a room."

"But why do you let it get to you? You managed to get somewhere to stay."

"But that's not the point. It's people's attitude towards me. I never experienced anything like it in Jamaica and yet over here everyone thinks they're better than the ignorant fools in the colonies. It bloody well annoys me. There are chaps in my island many times better than they are. As for cricket, I'm sure a team from Jamaica would give a bloody good hiding to any team here."

Virginia was unable to reply to Gladstone's hurt and realised how insensitive she had been. They walked on in silence for a while and then, without warning, he took her hand, leading her down some stone steps to the bank where they sat comfortably in each other's company beneath the bridge.

"So at least in your years at Cambridge you have discovered the secret hideaways," Virginia said smiling.

"Well it's better than carving up dead bodies."

He opened up his arms as if he were about to catch her and held her close to his chest. They kissed, at first gently and then in a passionate grip. Virginia wanted to make love to him and somehow she knew that she soon would.

Virginia had a skip in her stride the next morning and her head was filled with Gladstone. She daydreamed of things they would do together in the future. Her Jamaican man moved her imagination and yet allowed her to to be herself, in all her wildness. He was no trend-setter or life of any party, but was like a wide, bare canvas she could paint across.

Virginia had no lectures until the afternoon, so she turned into King's, hoping that she might accidently meet Gladstone. Several young men lay on the grass reading and making small conversation. There she was on the edge of the lawn. Their stupid rule told her that she had to know her place and keep to the gravel. What the hell, she would show them... She walked onto the grass, right up to a group of men with their backs to her dimunitive figure.

"Excuse me, gentlemen, but you're blocking my path."

"What the bloody hell are you doing on the grass!" bawled a red-headed young scholar who could have passed for her brother. Then she recognised him as the Cambridge cricket captain and an overrated batsman at that.

"You're blocking my path."

"You bloody well get off the grass right now!"

She walked around them but they moved across to block her. Then she ran to one corner but they came at her like a rugby pack. Soon, what was a peaceful, lazy morning turned into a grand show as about a hundred men in black gowns came onto the grass and formed a semi-circle around her. Then they began to clap slowly with a frightening beat. Virginia took off her shoe which had a sharp heel.

"Touch me and I'll let you have it!" she shouted, trying to sound threatening. Then she heard the voice of the cricket captain.

"Porter, bring us a pair of scissors."

Her red-headed adversary then stepped forward, scissors in hand, smiling smugly.

"So you want to walk on the grass like a gentleman do you? Well in that case, you can't be a lady. Can she gentlemen?"

"No!" went the loud reply.

"But a gentleman doesn't have long flowing hair. So we are going to let you walk on the grass, but not before we give you a haircut."

They rushed Virginia, lifting her off her feet and placing her on the ground. Her arms and legs were pinned to the grass by four men, while the one with the scissors cut her hair like he was shearing sheep. Her screams were choked by bits of chopped hair falling into her mouth. It was no use struggling as every joint seemed to be held down. The shearing completed, the men scattered back. Virginia was left on the grass sobbing, red hair in little piles about her. She raised her hand slowly to feel her head and touched scalp. She was almost bald. She took her hand away quickly as if her head carried a disease. She could not move but looked up into the sky and asked God to let it fall on her miserable soul. She grabbed a lump of grass lying beside her and squeezed it, only to find it was more hair. She cried until the tear-maker inside her died of dehydration.

On the last day of the Summer term, the final cricket match of the season took place. Virginia had not seen Gladstone since the incident on King's lawn. He must have heard about it, yet he had not been in touch with her. She knew he would be playing in his favourite place in the batting order and hoped he would see her if she waited outside the changing room just after the start of the match. As Virginia expected he soon emerged, looking as if he had been expecting her.

"Virginia, how are you? Look, I've tried to see you, but you know how it is, unless I'm invited and you can supply a chaperon, then there's no way into your college."

"You don't have to explain."

"To tell you the truth, that was only half the story. I couldn't bear to look at you with no hair, plus..."

"Go on say it you didn't want to be associated with a mad rebel, who could even be one of those awful feminists."

"Alright, I wanted to get away from you. You were embarrassing me."

He reached for her hat and removed it from her head, and with a mischievous grin said, "But now I realise I'm in love with you — even though you're bald!"

They both laughed and Virginia wished him good luck as he went to the crease. She noticed someone else in the dressing room. It was the ring leader at the King's lawn, with his back towards her as he tried to get his box into his trousers. Virginia reached into the changing room without thinking and grabbed hold of the nearest bag. As she had hoped, she found a white pullover inside and slacks as well as pads and a bat. Then, slamming the door shut, she locked the cricket captain in the dressing room. She could hear him banging and swearing, but the crowd was large and noisy and his cries were drowned by the excitement. She ran behind the ladies' toilets and changed with her floppy white hat covering her shorn head, she was ready. As soon as she was padded up a wicket fell, so she marched smartly to the crease.

Virginia knew the game of cricket well. When she was younger, Nanny used to take her to the park in the summer. There, Virginia would sneak away when Nanny was sleeping to join in the makeshift game which the poor boys played in the square. They were really frightened of her, this strange high-born, playing with the raggamuffins. And if they wouldn't allow her first bat, she threatened that her daddy would arrest them and throw away the key.

Virginia found her line at the crease and settled herself to receive the first delivery. Gladstone at the other end of the wicket, stood nonchalantly looking about him, one hand at his waist. She did not know whether he realised at that point who his batting partner was. The first ball came and she hit it with pace down the pitch, straight for four. The crowd stood up and applauded, Gladstone shook his head in amazement. The next ball, as she expected, was a bouncer. She stood back, gave herself some room and hooked it past third man for another four. When Gladstone came to bat at the next over, he continued the onslaught, hitting the ball for four straight boundaries. Their partnership brought victory to the team and the crowd rushed onto the pitch, lifting Virginia up high. Some of the stronger men patted her on the back nearly dislodging teeth from her mouth. Then an unsuspecting young scholar suddenly embraced her.

"Wait a minute, it's a woman!" he shouted. "He's a bloody woman!!"

They removed her floppy hat and pulled off her jumper. Yes, her shirt had two bulges. Clearly, she was of that alien species called 'woman.' The celebrations ceased and the inquest began. The opposing team were awarded the match because Cambridge had broken the rules by fielding a woman. Virginia was ordered to report to the Vice-Chancellor's office the first day of the new term, where disciplinary action would be taken. She sat down in the middle of the pitch and Gladstone came to sit beside her.

"Look, don't worry. They'll probably suspend you for two weeks, nothing worse."

"My father will kill me when he hears about this."

"Anyway, we beat them together, that's all that matters."

"What do you mean 'we' beat them?" Virginia asked smiling.

"Now wait on, you did great support work, but when I came to form we were unstoppable."

"Rubbish, it was only when I arrived that your innings got going."

"What do you mean? Clearly your job was to take the shine off the ball, while I cracked home the fours and sixes. Anyway, baldy locks..."

"Who are you calling baldy?"

Virginia chased Gladstone round the wicket wielding her bat. They both collapsed finally, laughing and tired.

They returned to the courtyard, careful to stay on the gravel path, but this time they turned left into King's chapel. It was a grand building which smelt of history and deep religion.

"I really love this chapel," said Gladstone as he looked up to the roof which seemed to rise to heaven itself, "let me show you my favourite stained glass window."

There it was high above the altar, it was truly magnificent.

"Do you know who that is sitting on the throne?" Gladstone asked excited.

"No, I haven't a clue."

"It's Caiaphas, the Jewish high priest and that's Christ being dragged before him, just before they turn him over to the Romans. I often look at that window and ask myself why the Jews and Romans get so heated about a man claiming to be the son of God? Why didn't they just ignore him? Save themselves a lot of trouble. Why not let him go and form his own kingdom and let the better man prosper? It's pride and vanity. I believe there's room in the world for other countries as good as England, the British are simply too vain to give us a chance. They would rather crucify us, than see us rule ourselves."

"Gladstone, can I be frank with you? I think you're the best looking, most charming man in Cambridge, but you seem to carry around a bitterness. Why?"

"What do you mean?!" Gladstone snapped.

"It's just that you seem to carry round a hurt."

He was silent for a moment and then came to sit close beside Virginia in one of the choir pews. He started to talk and as he did so she felt the force of his pent-up emotion and sadness.

"I first came to Cambridge 11 years ago during the war, but decided to join the army after my first year," he began. "It was a natural decision — I am part of the British Empire and we were under threat from an aggressor. Although I was born in Jamaica, I always felt British. At school I proudly raised the Union Jack every morning and amongst my friends there was no question that Government and loyalty lay in England. So when the time came to defend my country, I did not hesitate to fight for King and Empire. I remember feeling a child-like excitement when I entered the crowded recruitment station in East London. I was fired up with the fervour of embarking on a just cause.

"Once in the army, the cockneys welcomed me although they found me to be rather strange — a 'darkie' and yet a 'gent'. After the men had unpacked in the Canterbury hospital, now converted to a barracks, a trooper from India walked past, looking totally lost. I was pleased that at least another dark face was in my Company.

'I think your bunk is on top of mine,' I said holding out a hand in friendship.

'Thank you sir. My name is Dilip Patel,' said the well-spoken Indian. He looked a frail specimen but he was stronger than he appeared, for I found it hard work helping him to pick up his pack which he nevertheless took from me with ease. His hair was greased

71

back like an American, to reveal innocent good looks.

'Are you a student?' I asked.

'Yes, I'm an Oxford man, I'm reading law. Rhodes scholar.'

'Oh! I'm from Jamaica, doing medicine at Cambridge.'

"Well, that's how the Gladstone-Dilip partnership began. We quickly became friends, sharing experiences of university and looking out for each other.

"One dinner-time I was squashed between two East Enders, while Dilip sat opposite.

'So what's your name, darkie?' said a small, freckle-faced fellow who couldn't have been more than nineteen.

'Gladstone,' I answered proudly. There was a loud cheer around the table.

'When yer standing for Prime Minister?' cried a fat little man at the other end of the table. I hated that word 'darkie', but I thought the best form of defence was to ignore them. This was fine until the trooper to my left, decided that it was time for fun.

'What makes you think you should be fighting alongside us Brits. I bet you can't even use a gun,' said the dark-haired trooper. He wasn't as raw as the others, possibly grammar school educated.

'Why not, I fight for King and country.'

'When did you darkies learn to fight? You should be pickin' cotton or singin' the blues. This is a man's war.'

'Well, what are you doing here? Seems to me you'd be better off picking daffodils,' I retorted. There was a roar of laughter. The trooper stood up, aiming a right hook at my head but his arm was caught mid-swing by the Sergeant Major. Everyone flew to attention.

'I thought we'd signed up to fight the Hun, not each other. Now look here, Green, you're not in the ring now. Your boxing days can resume when you get to France, there'll be plenty of fighting to do, don't you worry.'

'Permission to speak, sir,' I said, looking up at the six foot-four sergeant, who was once a Covent Garden market porter, 'this man is bloody rude and has something against foreigners. I'd like to teach him a lesson over ten rounds.'

"The Sergeant turned red. 'Are you sure about this son? I mean Billy Green is London's light-heavyweight champion.'

'I was school boy champion of Jamaica for three years running.'

'Where's Jamaica?' someone shouted.

'It's a town near Scarborough!' cried another. The canteen erupted in laughter.

'Alright everyone, calm down. Tomorrow evening at six, ten rounds of three minutes and I'll be the ref. In the meantime you two shake hands.'

'I'll never shake hands with a nigger!' said Green spitting on the ground, his eyes full of hatred. The Sergeant didn't pursue the issue but walked away, perhaps happy that he had organised exciting entertainment for the following evening.

"Lights out was at ten. I lay on my bunk, brooding over whether I'd made the right decision enlisting as a private or enlisting at all. The so-called six weeks training had been little more than a three week scout's camping trip. I still didn't recognise the sound of a machine-gun much less have any knowledge of how to work one. The officers, who seemed to live the life of Riley, had servants, young boys who served eggs and bacon in the morning and gave them sex at night. These same officers would call us out for drill and start telling us lies about how well the push on the Western Front was going. We were informed that the war would end by Christmas but I never believed that. To be patriotic began to be a pale shadow of what I expected. There was no integrity in lying to young men about fighting for your country, when at night they grunted and groaned lying with their young servant boys.

"Hypocrisy existed throughout the army. Each time a unit was about to leave for France, the chaplain would come to give his usual blessing. He wore his black and white clerical robes, his eyes set back in his plump, complacent face. He told them that God was with them and against our great foe. The vicar would then send them on their way, safe in the knowledge that he was only going as far as the train station. I wondered if Dilip was asleep in the bunk above me.

'Are you awake, Dilip?'

'Yes, but I think you'd better get some rest. You have a big fight tomorrow.'

'Dilip, why did you join up?'

'Why do you ask?'

'I don't know, why does anyone want to die for their country?'

'I thought I knew when I joined, but I'm not so sure now.'

'No, nor am I. Suffering colour persecution and seeing the way people who are supposed to lead us behave, I don't really feel I'm fighting for King and country. There doesn't seem to be any point to it.'

'Suffering my dear fellow, is the price of peace,' said Dilip speaking like a wise old guru, 'and we have no rights to enjoy any of its fruits unless we have fought for it.'

'I agree, so that means you and I will soon be able to claim our piece of Empire, it'll no longer be something we've been given, but something we've really fought for.'

"I heard no reply from the top bunk, Dilip was asleep. This war had changed my whole view of the world. I began to see myself as more than equal to those who lived closer to the seat of empire. I wasn't taken seriously as a member of this club, yet I felt I was better than

73

most, and those considered better seemed pretty mediocre to me anyway. All my young life in Jamaica, I was told that the world spun around Great Britain, so it was a revelation that the best was not here, just like they discovered that the Earth was not the centre of the Universe. I now knew that God scatters perfection like a farmer scatters seed. It was clear for any man to grasp, to believe otherwise was to believe a lie.

"The next day's military training consisted of picking apples in the local orchard and towards evening, we were given our introduction to first aid. This was the first time that the realities of the war were betrayed to us. We were given graphic details of the kind of injuries that could occur at the Front. As the doctor talked of wounds and blood, I thought of my other fight, the one scheduled for that evening. What had I taken on? Yes, I was a good boxer but that was at schoolboy level, clearly Green had more experience. I wasn't even angry with the daft fellow but it was a question of honour. The gauntlet had been thrown down and a duty was to be fulfilled, even if it meant having my head bashed in.

"The entire barracks was full of talk about the big fight and betting was brisk. Green was evens favourite so there were side bets on which round I would fall. By six o'clock, the dining-room was cleared and the chairs were evenly spaced so that a large square was left in the centre and there was much jostling for ringside seats. The large figure of the Sergeant Major walked around inspecting and making sure that spectators were well back. He took his job seriously, strutting about in his white vest, proudly displaying two tattooed nude ladies on his powerful forearms. There was a large cheer as Billy Green's entourage entered the dining-hall and made its way to the 'ring'. Green was bobbing and weaving — he looked a sharp and seasoned professional. The cheer became a mighty roar as the hero stepped into the square. He bowed to his supporters and began dancing, occasionally boxing the air with a flurry of punches that whipped up the crowd's excitement.

"I entered slightly after, Dilip walking proudly in front carrying neatly ironed towels under one arm and a bucket in the other. We were received with universal loud booing and abuse. I realised afresh the deep hostility they had for those of us with dark skins. I was a dangerous bull that the crowd wanted Green to kill. It was awful, I knew that despite my white father, in this world I was a negro.

"The first round had me struggling to fend off blows that were coming from all directions. My only hope was to cling and cleave to Green, soaking up the body punches and praying for the bell to ring. I didn't manage to land one punch and when the bell finally came, I dragged myself to my corner. Dilip looked worried.

'Gladstone, do you want me to throw in the towel? You're taking far

74

too much punishment.'

'No, there's going to be no giving up tonight.'

"Dilip wiped the blood from my nose and I entered a second round, to continue my punishment. Then from nowhere, came an upper-cut that nearly sent my chin into my brain. My legs became like solid blocks of iron and I keeled over. I could clearly hear Dilip's cry of 'Stay down, stay down!' But I managed to get up by the count of eight to the thunderous approval of the crowd. Green delivered two more blows to my body and sent me stumbling around like a baby in a playpen, crashing finally into my corner.

"The Sergeant Major was standing over me, unconcerned with my injuries, just making the count. By the time he had got to nine, the bell rang inciting the crowd to fury. The referee was condemned for counting too slowly, but a growl from him soon silenced his critics. Dilip pulled me onto my chair, saying nothing this time, resigned to scraping me off the floor in the next round. The bell rang and I was facing Green again. I changed my tactics and tried to frustrate him using the last of my strength to run from his punches. It was working. Soon he began to swing wildly and he left himself open on two occasions. On the third I got him with two mighty left hooks that sent him tumbling to the ground. But over-confidence would prove to be my downfall. He got up quickly and I came rushing towards him spurred on by my knockdown. I walked straight into another upper-cut and the next thing I knew it was morning.

"I had never imagined that before I saw action I would be travelling to the Front with an eye half-closed and my nose nearly broken. But I had gained respect after the fight, even though I had lost.

"We sailed the Channel in a small passenger boat which the army had commandeered, landing at Calais which looked bland, its sober-coloured countryside nothing compared to the beauty of Jamaica. The troopers tried to fool themselves that they would be back by Christmas opening presents with their families and eating plum pudding.

"Preparation was hard work. Around thirty of us would leave our camp at about five every evening, to walk ten miles to where the shells had been dumped by lorry. Then, arriving at nine, we kept on working, sometimes until as late as four in the morning, carrying boxes of shells about two miles to where gun pits had been prepared. Then we would have to walk the ten miles back to camp. One night, on the return journey, I heard a vehicle coming round the corner from behind me. Thinking it was our chaps, I slowed down but when I glanced back I realised it was a German convoy. I dived into the bushes but two soldiers behind were sighted and instantly shot.

"Not long after, we were sent to the Somme. The battles were bloody and four months of fighting brought a limited advance. The cost to life was enormous — maybe half a million men were lost. I was desperate to get away from the water-logged trenches, from the pathetic soldiers looking out into the foggy wasteland dreaming of Christmas turkey, while gunfire, mortars and rockets exploded around our ears. It will take me years to rid my brain of the haunting laughter of machine-guns rattling in the distance.

"Out of all that awful time, I remember one day in particular. We were pinned down in our trenches by a torrent of machine-gun fire from a German unit on a small hill about 200 yards away. Myself, Dilip, Green and a man named O'Brien were ordered to scout ahead and take out the offending gun. A decoy would be offered by the rest of the troops, keeping the Germans busy with continuous fire. Green looked at me and smiled.

'What's the matter nigger, you scared?'

'My name is Cooper to you and of course I'm scared. I'm bloody scared.'

"The covering gunfire came and we set off, knowing that if we were sighted it was certain death. A strange sensation came over me. I felt all-powerful, above mortality and immune to the danger about me. I could see the two Germans who manned the machine-gun. I could almost see the whites of their eyes. Then O'Brien was hit in the chest and fell crying down the hill, knocking Green over as he went. I threw a grenade at the gun post but it missed its target. Suddenly I heard the cry, 'Gas! Gas!' A mustard gas bomb had been hurled at us and the stench began to burn my nose and grip my throat. I noticed that Green was pinned to the ground, struggling to push off O'Brien's dead body lying on top of him. Green couldn't reach his gas mask and was coughing up blood. The German soldier was taking aim at him. Not thinking of the danger, I dived across and dragged O'Brien's body from on top of Green. It seemed that the machine-gun had jammed and Green, although winded, was able to crawl to safety. Dilip and I threw grenades and a loud explosion silenced the gun post for ever. The lads in the trench pushed forward to praise their new heroes.

"Later that night, I sat down and dreamt of Jamaica. I could never get used to the cold of Europe. I dreamt of strolling in the sunshine with a lovely dip in the sea and horse riding on my father's ranch in Hanover. I missed the hot wind that caressed your skin like a warm fire and the people, their dark faces holding so many stories and who loved me as one of theirs. Back home there were greens, oranges, reds and yellows, here it was all grey and pale and colourless. My daydreaming was interrupted by Green, who came towards me, his hands in his pockets and his head bowed.

'Hey Cooper, I just want to thank you, mate, for saving my life. I was on my last breath out there.'

'It's OK.'

"Green sat down next to me and offered me a cigarette.

'Why did you do it? You were in the line of the Hun's fire.'

'Wouldn't you do the same for me?'

'Not bloody likely. I would have gone for the German.'

'And left me to die? I don't believe you, you would have helped me alright.'

'You're really sure of yourself aren't you? And how come a nigger like you speaks like a gentleman?'

'Where I come from we're taught to speak the King's English. But since I've been here, only a few people seem to speak like the King. I suppose in many ways we're more English than the English.'

'You're from the West Indies aren't you?' Green said, sucking the end of his cigarette. 'What are the damsels like over there? I'd quite fancy one of them negresses.'

'They say that the women in Jamaica are the most beautiful in the world.'

'Is that so? Yer reckon, that after Christmas, like, when the war is over, me and you could take a trip back to Jamaica. You reckon you could find me a lovely dark beauty?'

"I laughed and looked back at Green. In a strange sort of way I liked him. He was raw and didn't give a damn but he gave out a sense of red and yellow colours in all this dark grey.

'Where are you from Green?'

'The East End of course. They used to call me Bethnal Green when I was a boxer. Me ole man was a tram driver. I was the second of eight children and we all slept in the same bed, boys and girls. Each mornin' you'd get up and 'ope that someone 'asn't wet themselves on yer shorts. It was a bit like the army; you had a bath once a week if you're lucky and we all suffered from lice in our 'air. In the end it was too much for the ole lady and she died of consumption. It broke the ole man's 'art and his pocket as well, 'cause he would booze away his wages. In the end they put 'im in the Poor 'Ouse. So at fourteen I was on the street fending for meself. That's 'ow I learned to box. A coach spotted me fighting this copper, so it was either I stayed with 'im or go to prison.'

"Before I could find out anymore there was an order to move forward to fresh trenches thirty yards ahead. When we arrived we realised that we had really made no progress. We were now occupying the same trenches we had dug a week earlier. All that effort and thousands of lives, for thirty yards of French mud.

"We had seen many of our unit die. It was a thought that pressed down on our minds as I crouched close to Dilip in the cold trench. I smoked a cigarette that had been passed down from about fifteen men,

77

each one taking a puff. Dilip looked anything but a soldier. He was too elegant, better suited as a politician or a lawyer. He told me that his family were so proud that he had managed to win the scholarship to Oxford, especially when his whole village had held a week of festivities in his honour. Dilip had been paraded shoulder-high around the streets, while little boys looked up to him with bare feet and a hungry belly knowing the impossible could be achieved and the old men rested all their unfulfilled aspirations on his young head. Now he sat in a rat infested trench.

"He was about to tell me something and perhaps give me a token from his pocket, when there was a loud manic cry to evacuate the trench and retreat. The Germans had broken through and we had come under heavy fire. I got up and ran as the loud shrill notes of the shells sang out before crashing to the ground. I turned around to see Dilip go down, his eyes stared aimlessly at the sun as if he had seen a monster in the sky. I knew he was dead. I had become an expert on death. My old rival Billy Green was slightly behind me. He stopped suddenly, and to my amazement went back for Dilip, maybe he thought he was still alive. He carried him on his shoulders and began running towards me, jumping over dead bodies and ducking shrapnel. I shouted, 'Come on, Billy, come on!'

"Then he too saw horror in the sky, killed by a shell that burst a little distance off and sent a small fragment of its casing straight into his heart.

"Long after the onslaught had ceased, we went back to bury Dilip and Billy. It was only in the cruelty and chaos of war that Billy could overcome his bigotry. I believed then that it was possible to mould a world where men could live together, no matter what their colour, but today it seems like that was wishful thinking."

Gladstone looked up at Caiaphas and then turned to Virginia. Recalling his war experiences had left him exhausted, but a calm had replaced the anger and bitterness. He took her hand and they sat together for a time. Then, unexpectedly, he said that he couldn't leave England without her. Virginia assured him that she would at least visit him in his little island. They still had some time left and Virginia was determined to enjoy it, right up to the last second.

Gladstone's finals came and went. To celebrate, the couple decided to spend a weekend together at a lodging house, something which was forbidden and certainly immoral. Virginia suggested the small village of Girton. Gladstone was surprisingly reluctant, objecting to staying together in the same room as they were not married. In the end, it was as if Virginia were seducing him, assuring him that they would have separate beds and that nothing untoward would happen.

Although she had never been conventional and hated those passive women who enjoyed playing foolish to please their men, Virginia nevertheless felt she may have gone too far with Gladstone.

They cycled to Girton, soaked to the skin as the rain lashed down. All the time Virginia was worried that Gladstone might think she was a loose woman. At the lodging house they were welcomed by a sour-faced landlady with spectacles resting on the end of her nose.

"Good afternoon, madam," Virginia said. "My husband and I would like a room for the weekend."

They were both nervous. There would be no chance of sharing a room if the landlady suspected they were not married. The woman turned to Gladstone. He was wearing one of his many suits and genuinely did look like he had just got married.

"You're a student here, aren't you? From foreign climes, I'm sure I've seen you in town."

"Yes, you have and this is my wife."

"And you, madam, you're a student as well?"

"Oh no, I'm from London. I'm a nurse and we got married yesterday."

The landlady glanced sceptically at the cheap metal ring on Virginia's wedding finger.

Gladstone was getting impatient with this cross-examination.

"Look, madam, we can take our business elsewhere. Now are you going to let my wife and I have a room or not?"

She nervously handed him the book, frightened by this quick-tempered foreigner.

The room was basic. Two single beds, a wardrobe and a small desk and chair in the corner. A pathetic porcelain dog rested on the table, while an awful picture of a black cat with its paw raised, hung over the beds. They bought a bottle of wine and Virginia drank until she was tipsy. Gladstone modestly limited himself to one and a half glasses. Virginia's shoes, rain mack and stockings lay strewn on the floor where she had thrown them. She watched Gladstone, as he neatly pulled off his coat, hung up his jacket and then picked up her things and carefully put them away in the wardrobe. This annoyed her. She loved to be a little untidy, in fact, she enjoyed the comfort of disorder. Anyway, who did he think he was, her wet nurse or nanny?

It was too grey and miserable to go out, so they played checkers until evening. Gladstone had brought some rum punch to the lodging house. It was a bottle he had been saving, he said. His brother had sent it out from Jamaica.

"This rum punch is delicious," Virginia said, wiping her mouth. "Tell me about your family, you've never really talked about them."

"Well, my father is still alive. He's in his sixties now. He owns a chain of stores in Kingston. I was raised by my step-mother. I never knew my real mother. My father claims that she died of cholera just after I was born, but somehow I doubt it. I always felt there was something he was hiding about her."

"So didn't you ask him about her?"

"Yes, but he wouldn't say. He hated it when the subject of my mother came up."

"And your brother who sent the rum, what's he like?"

"Oh Oliver, well, we have different mothers you know. That might explain why we're so different. He's a rascal, a womaniser. I wouldn't trust him as far as I could throw him, but he is my brother so we are close nevertheless. I was always my father's favourite. I don't know why. Even when we were younger, father always found time for me, but gave Oliver short shrift. When father travelled on business, he would always bring back a wonderful present for me, while forgetting altogether about his other son. Father refused to allow my step-mother Cynthia to discipline me, however. It caused so much friction that he finally threw her out of the house to raise his two ten-year-old sons by himself. Oliver's never said anything about it, but I remember how as a child, father would sit me on his knee and talk about how I would someday become the first Prime Minister of Jamaica as if he didn't care what Oliver did. Anyway, I went on to college, while Oliver left school early and now runs my father's business. You can't dislike him, I would say he's a lovable rogue."

Gladstone lay on the bed reading a book on human anatomy, while Virginia set out her pencils and pad to sketch her feelings of the day. She liked to do this each evening. Sometimes she would draw just a circle, other times it would be animals, nature or maybe patterns. Today she sketched a daffodil growing between barbed wires. She felt that a new beginning had come but she was uncertain of where the end was. Gladstone came over to her and gently pushed his hands over her shorn hair.

"Well, since this is our 'honeymoon', we might as well make the best of it."

"Now what do you mean?" Virginia said teasing.

"You know what I mean."

Virginia undressed quickly, making sure that this time her clothes were neatly placed in the wardrobe, and then dived under the sheets pulling them up to her neck. Gladstone turned around and smiled, he was in no hurry. He drew the curtains and then slowly undressed. He was soon lying beside her in the bed. Virginia shivered as Gladstone kissed her, reaching out his arms towards her and gently easing her closer to him. As she nuzzled her face into his shoulder, she felt reassured by his familiar scent. Virginia allowed Gladstone's heavy weight to settle on top of her while her fingers moved through his curly hair and along the smooth valley of his back. Virginia turned her head towards the mirror and glimpsed the contrast of her white legs wrapped around his brown torso. This turned her on even more and she was seized by a force that compelled her to kiss and suck every part of Gladstone's body. She loved it most when he pushed his brown seed from behind and she lay stroking the inside of her vagina with his fingers. This was double ecstacy. He was also intoxicated by her white skin against his brownness, as he pushed his seed deeper and deeper inside her. It was her 'difference' that he loved. He came with a loud groan and she followed with a yell that slightly frightened Gladstone as he lay exhausted on her back.

Gladstone pulled from inside his woman and rested. He both looked and felt content. For Virginia, there was no longer an insistent feeling of disquiet or nagging sense of the loss, she had now found joy.

The weekend over, Gladstone and Virginia travelled together to London. Twiddling her first-class ticket in white-gloved hands, Virginia stared through the carriage window, the landscape slowly changing from green fields, scarecrows, rows of cabbages, to the fog of London as the train pulled into Kings Cross. Neither of them spoke a great deal during the journey, but were at ease in each other's silence. Before parting, they agreed that he would come to dinner at her parents' house the same evening.

Virginia decided to take a cab home to the Bayswater Road. The streets were full of beggars. The country had now basked in the sunshine of peace for a decade, enough time for the great divide between rich and poor to return in place. The country had had time to forget how war had helped to bring people together, as everyone had suffered some loss.

The Langbridge house had four storeys with the servants quarters in the basement. Mrs Langbridge came out to help her daughter with the luggage. She was a small woman who dressed simply, usually in greys and blacks and often indistinguishable from the servants. She spent her time reading romances that were serialised in the newspapers and organising charity events for invalid war veterans. She was bigger than this confined world, but in her day a lady from a good family looked for a husband of means and substance, there was no other ambition. With her daughter, Mrs Langbridge was a different woman, displaying intelligence and a great sense of humour — they were like sisters. But when Mr Langbridge came home, she became timid and withdrawn again. His authority within the household was never challenged. Mrs Langbridge knew Virginia could not suffer the humiliation of not being taken seriously. When her father started cursing feminists, Virginia would leave the table as discreetly as possible, biting her tongue in disgust.

Once the suitcases were unpacked, Virginia sat in the drawing room with her mother and told her everything about Gladstone apart from the weekend at the lodging house. Mrs Langbridge was as excited as her daughter and hurried to make preparations for dinner — everything had to be just right for their special guest.

Mr Langbridge arrived from the Club at six. He kissed his daughter, but before he could take off his coat, she began to talk of Gladstone.

"I know you'll like my new friend Gladstone, Father. He's handsome, he'll soon be a doctor."

"Slow down. I'm sure I'll like him darling."

Virginia's father was a tall man who was hardly seen out of uniform. He had grown handsome with age, his silver hair bestowing a dignity and elegance to his demeanour. He was the personification of military efficiency, though personal charm was not his strong point and he made no pretension to it. He was aggressive and blatant. All the same he was good at his job and for that his family respected him and were grateful.

Langbridge stared at his daughter as if she were ill or there was something wrong with her face, then Virginia remembered her hair. She had left home after Christmas with a long red mane, now it was cropped. As far as she was concerned the Cambridge men had done her a favour since short hair was now the fashion of the independent woman. School girls who once looked forward to the day when they could put their hair up, now felt an equal longing for the day when they could cut it off.

"Virginia, your damn hair is too bloody short!" Langbridge blurted and then marched off to the dining-room.

Gladstone arrived early. He looked immaculate in his dark suit and gleaming shoes. Virginia noticed that he had neglected to tie his laces in their usual perfect symmetry. She had not mentioned to her parents that Gladstone was coloured, as she didn't think it was important until she saw her father glaring at him wide-eyed and tight-lipped.

"Father, Mama, this is Gladstone Cooper."

Gladstone approached Virginia's mother and charmingly kissed her hand.

"Welcome Mr Cooper, my daughter has not stopped talking about you all evening."

"Thank you, Mrs Langbridge, and good evening to you, sir." Gladstone shook Langbridge's hand nervously.

Dinner was tense. Langbridge hardly said a word, Gladstone was clearly embarrassed and it was left to Virginia and Mrs Langbridge to make polite conversation. Eventually, Langbridge made the kind of contribution they were all expecting.

"So, you're from the West Indies. It must be damned hot out there and full of mosquitoes. I don't know if I could live in a place that's so backward."

"Well with limited resources we are making slow progress," Gladstone answered wearily.

Langbridge was clearly unimpressed with this reply and continued to make derogatory comments about the colonies. Gladstone appeared to be making a strenuous effort not to enter into an argument. He was keeping his responses as bland as possible, but in the end he could not contain himself and sought to assert his position.

"My view is that it was a bad thing that the Jamaican Assembly was abolished. We could have made it the basis for some sort of home rule," he insisted finally.

"Home rule! You must be out of your mind, man. These countries are much better off in the safe arms of the Empire."

"I beg to differ, sir. I think we're ready to begin to stand on our own two feet."

"You negroes don't know anything about government. It's best left to the white man. You mark my words. Without the white man there to separate all the factions there'd be a bloodbath."

"How can you sit there and talk about bloodbath? We've both fought in the biggest bloodbath perhaps in the history of the world, and for what? A few hundred yards of French beach. All those millions of young lives wasted. No, sir I've seen nothing in England that tells me that my colony couldn't do a better job." Gladstone was by now standing, enraged by Langbridge's comments.

"Now you just be careful of your tone young man. You seem to have forgotten your place."

"Father," Virginia pleaded, "please let's not argue."

Ignoring his daughter, Langbridge stood up so Gladstone would not remain looking down on him.

"And as for my daughter, I hope you haven't any ideas about marriage or love because that's out of the question."

"Father, what are you saying?!" Virginia cried, frightened.

"It's alright Virginia, I'll be off."

Gladstone stormed from the table. Virginia caught up with him in the hall, where he was calling for one of the servants to bring his hat and coat.

"Gladstone, I'm sorry, I don't know what's come over him. He was so awful. He's not normally like that. Please, can we meet and talk tomorrow?"

She stretched on tip-toe to kiss his cheek. He walked out into the cold London wind, which rushed into the house after·him before Virginia could close the heavy front door. She did not return to the dining room, but instead stamped her way upstairs so that the whole house could feel her anger. She lay on her bed, tears scalding her cheeks. There was a firm knock on the door which slowly opened and there stood Langbridge, his hands behind his back.

"Can I come in, Ginny?"

"Yes, you can do what you want, after all it's your house," she snapped.

He sat down at the dresser astride the stool.

"What's the matter, darling?"

"Father, I can't believe you can honestly sit there after insulting Gladstone and not know what you did. The war has changed everything. For the first time, men from all parts of the Empire are meeting each other on an equal footing. Things have changed for women too."

Virginia went across and knelt down, resting her head on her father's lap. Langbridge hated this outpouring of emotion and he began to cough nervously.

"Father I'm in love with Gladstone and I want to marry him. The coloured race is a reality. Gladstone is the result of negro and white coming together. It has happened and will continue. I want to have children who are proud of who they are. They must be proud of their brown skin. I want us to have children who will grow up with a strong character that can withstand any amount of ill-treatment."

"Ginny, even if I said 'no', you're so mule-headed it would make no difference. I don't approve of races mixing but if you love this Gladstone chappie..."

"You mean I've got your blessing!" she said excited.

"Well, I couldn't bear it with you and your mother sulking all day. Do as you wish. But don't come crying to me when things go wrong."

Virginia jumped up and hugged him. Langbridge became red with embarrassment and struggled to leave the room as his daughter peppered his face with kisses.

West London could never hold Virginia Langbridge's interest. It was littered with young, rich bohemians calling themselves artists. These people pretended to paint but had little or nothing to show for their effort. They just talked about creating, but their studios were only used for dressing-up for parties and dances. They thought that a painter should have a touch of disorder in life and cheerful bad manners, no fixed hours and no sexual standards. Their claim to revolution was the fact that they spread butter with a cut-throat razor and drank tea out of a brandy glass. Virginia was interested in thinkers and artists who really wanted to change the world and had some political awareness. Instead, she suffered those who loved to speak

French loudly in a crowded tea-room in order to impress rather than to be understood. The thought of going back to Cambridge was no solace but she knew she couldn't give up. So few women had been admitted — it would boost those bigoted dons to see a woman fail.

Exactly four weeks after the disaster at dinner, Virginia set out for Shoreditch, where Gladstone had informed her by letter, he was living at the house of his old Professor from Cambridge. He greeted Virginia, an excited and determined look on his face. She had hardly entered the house before he informed her of his plans.

"I'm sorry Ginny, I've had enough of life in England. I've made up my mind to go back home. There's a ship leaving to Jamaica tomorrow and not even the forces of hell will stop me from being on it."

Though she had been expecting such a decision for some time, it nevertheless struck Virginia like a bolt of lightning.

"And what about us?" she appealed. "I thought we were getting married."

"Lectures start in October. You go back to Cambridge and finish off your degree and then you can join me in Jamaica. And there's the summer holiday, you could come and visit me next year."

Virginia realised it was pointless arguing. Gladstone would only be happy at home in his island. So she mustered an understanding smile and helped pack his suitcases. She told him that he could stay the night in the spare room at her parent's place. Gladstone agreed.

Langbridge behaved surprisingly civilly to Gladstone, especially when he heard that the Jamaican was leaving the next day. He hoped that distance would help his daughter end her silly infatuation and find a true English gentleman instead.

Virginia was too upset to travel with Gladstone to Southampton. As he loaded the cab for the station, he turned and walked back to the front door.

"Take care of yourself, Gladstone. I love you. I want you to write to me every week. It's going to be hard not seeing you," she said, tears making her vision hazy. Gladstone held his love for a brief kiss and then rushed into the cab. Virginia was sure that if he had stayed any longer he would have started crying also. She looked out at the streets of London and she too began to feel like a foreigner, displaced and hungry for a land with adventure and surprise. She felt empty as she closed the door on the familiar streets of West London.

Virginia had only been at Cambridge two days when she was sick all over her sheets. Grace and Felicity, her room-mates, thought she was dying and rushed out to get Matron. Matron marched in dressed in black, and her head covered like a nun. With her icy face, she resembled a jailer rather than a caring substitute mother. To complete the image, a large bunch of keys rattled at her side.

"Now, what has happened to you Miss Langbridge?"

"I don't know Matron. I felt a little faint and then I was sick."

She looked at Virginia suspiciously, as if the young woman had committed some grave sin. Grace and Felicity for their trouble, were ordered to clean up the mess and the patient was led out wearing her dressing gown, to see the University doctor. Virginia was confused. Surely if she were ill, she should be treated with care and sympathy. Instead, Matron bundled her into the office and, to make things worse, locked the terrified patient in like a prisoner while she went to get the doctor. The little office was neat and mean with a large plaque on the wall carrying the inscription, 'And it shall come to pass, that whosoever shall call on the name of the Lord shall be saved.' Virginia cast an eye over Matron's small desk and saw a copy of the popular magazine *Lucky Star*. On the cover was a picture of a young girl crying on her shocked boyfriend's shoulder. The caption read, 'This week's story is of the young girl at No 20 who was trying to keep her secret from the neighbours — but the gossips were determined to make Joy Binns hide her head in shame.' She didn't have time to read further, before the doctor burst in, holding what looked like an oversized test-tube. The Matron followed swiftly in his wake.

"Right, clothes off, completely naked and please could you urinate in this!" said the little man, shirt sleeves rolled up and smelling of disinfectant. He examined Virginia's stomach and shook his head in disgust.

"What is it, what's wrong with me?" she asked frightened.

The doctor ignored her pleadings and turned to Matron.

"Yes Matron, you're right. I would guess she's pregnant."

"Pregnant! You mean I'm going to have a baby!?" Virginia shouted with disbelief.

"Come and see me in my surgery tomorrow and I'll give you something for the morning sickness. May God help you!" said the doctor gravely. He picked up his equipment along with Virginia's urine and left, still shaking his head.

"I'll have to report you to the Vice-Chancellor, this will be trouble. I suggest you go to bed and remain in your room until you are called for. You think you're clever, young lady, but you have soiled the name of your family, the University and you have sinned against God with your lustful act of fornication. Get out of my sight!"

Virginia rushed from Matron's castigation back to her room where she expected to find sympathy from her two friends. Instead, they looked at her with disgust. They too had guessed the secret of Virginia's illness.

"You're pregnant aren't you?"

"How could you do that? You've ruined yourself. If your father didn't have money, they'd send you to the workhouse. You know they'll send you down and you'll never get a degree," said Grace.

The force of her hostility was surprising, but she was not alone among Virginia's friends in condemning her. With hardly anyone expressing understanding, much less support, Virginia was given a foretaste of the isolation to come.

As expected, she was sent a message to go to the Vice-Chancellor's office later that day. Solemnly, she put on her gown, combed her hair and sprayed on some French perfume, as if preparing herself to meet her executioner. A relentless rain beat down as she stepped outside, still feeling queasy. By the time she reached the Vice-Chancellor's office, her red hair was matted to her forehead and her gown soaked with rainwater. His office smelt of oak, history and cigars.

"Please come, Miss Langbridge," said Dr Walker, the Vice-Chancellor. Virginia was surprised to see the college doctor and Matron already positioned, flanking Dr Walker on either side, as she sank in a low chair opposite, to face her judge and jury. Walker was an old man of nearly seventy, his bald head buried in a mass of papers which probably contained the incontrovertible evidence of Virginia's guilt.

"Miss Langbridge, not so long ago, when prostitutes were caught with students, they were tried and sentenced by what were called 'Vice-Chancellor's Courts'. This University even had its own cells where these lewd women were imprisoned." He got up, clasped his wrists behind his back and began to slowly pace up and down. "Now, some say we are more enlightened today since we've abandoned that practice and furthermore we have actually permitted women to study at Cambridge. In both cases, I went against the tide of the times and the reforms got my support, but, Miss Langbridge, I will never compromise on the question of fornication. You are a disgrace to your class and may I say to your sex. The institution is a place of learning where young men become gentlemen with great intellects and wonderful manners. We allowed the fairer sex to join us but what have you done, young lady? Let me tell you, you were given a yard and you took a mile. Now I cannot afford to allow this cancer to spread. It must be cut out at the root."

"Here, here, Vice-Chancellor! Cut out indeed!" sang Matron.

"In this regard," he continued, "I have no choice but to have you sent down. We cannot be seen to condone immorality and, indeed, will not do so. Who knows, this may well spread into the male colleges. Now before you are dismissed, do you have anything to say?"

Virginia stood up and looked this old man straight into his self-righteous eyes.

"Nobody here has asked me how I feel about the situation. I'm going to have a baby and I'm proud of it. I didn't plan it this way, but a new life is growing inside me. It doesn't, however, make me any less competent to be a student. This has got nothing to do with my morality, but it's your own fear and guilt. And as for polluting the morals of your sacred young men, you don't ever comment when they go to London every week and indulge themselves at brothels. Why aren't they in front of this high moral court? I suppose you will tell me that those women tempted the young men all the way from Cambridge to London. To be frank, Dr Walker, I'm glad I'm leaving. You're not shocked by my morality, who knows, you've probably got a litter of children for poor domestics all over London, and if you haven't, several of your precious young gentlemen undergraduates certainly have."

Virginia flew out of the office leaving three red faces, whose owners were convinced that she was only fit for the workhouse.

Before she left Cambridge, word had already reached her parents that their daughter was pregnant and that she had sworn and blasphemed in front of the Vice-Chancellor. Virginia was not prepared for the second inquisition. Her mother had drilled into her from when she was small, that a good marriage was the main and only proper aim in life for a girl of good breeding, but she had now caused the family shame and failed as a daughter. Virginia kept thinking about Gladstone. She wanted to tell him about his baby, but worried that he, like all the rest, might turn against her.

The inquisition at home was surprisingly short-lived. Mrs Langbridge cried a great deal but her husband saw the situation in terms of a military manoeuvre which needed precise planning. His daughter sat in the drawing room while he paced back and forth in front of her, firing a number of options in her direction. The usual one for a girl in Virginia's position was to be sent away to the country, London was too public a domain to raise a 'bastard.'

Virginia was told that a lengthy visit to an aunt in Bournemouth would be appropriate and, as she was not earning any money to keep herself let alone a child, she had no choice but to comply with her father's orders. It was made perfectly clear to her that the child would be put up for adoption. At the conclusion of the 'discussion', Langbridge retired to his study with a stiff whiskey, cursing that she hadn't been born a boy.

Virginia was not prepared to accept her fate without some resistance however, and decided on a course of rebellion. She declared that she would not eat until her wish to be sent to Jamaica was granted. If she had anything in common with her father, it was the fact that they were both stubborn — a tough battle lay ahead.

By the fifth day of her 'hunger strike', Langbridge was driven to breaking point at the possibility of his daughter dying upstairs. Poor Mrs Langbridge was too upset to eat anything either. The mental pressure drove Langbridge finally to Virginia's bedroom. She hadn't expected a visit from him so early in the morning. Unbeknown to her parents, the baker's son had been blackmailed into throwing cakes and bread up to Virginia's window first thing each day. She had warned him that, if he failed with the supplies, she'd tell the police where he and his mates held their dog fights. There was not a chance that Virginia would starve herself or her baby on account of her stubborn father and his bigoted ways.

At the knock on the door, Virginia quickly swallowed a Chelsea bun in one bite and frantically dusted the bedclothes, then lay back pretending to be poorly.

"Come in," she whimpered.

"How are you feeling, Virginia?"

"Is that you, Father, I can barely see you. I feel so weak, I think I'll be gone by the end of the month and then your troubles will be over."

"Well, I've been thinking. It's no use my fighting you — you're not a Langbridge for nothing. I can't prevent you from going to your Gladstone. I've fought many battles in my day, but I always knew I'd lose against my own flesh and blood."

"You mean I can go to Jamaica?!" Virginia screamed.

"Yes, you can go, but I'm doing this mainly for your mother's sake and you remember that."

Forgetting her 'illness', Virginia jumped out of bed and leapt at her father's neck. He quickly retracted out of the bedroom, but not before saying, "Oh, yes Virginia, I nearly forgot, you could tell the baker's boy to leave two french sticks for your mother..."

Later, after a hearty meal, Virginia ran upstairs to write to Gladstone giving him the good tidings.

Dear Gladstone,

How are you keeping in your sunny island? I hope you think of me every day just as I do you.

I have some wonderful news although I'm not too sure how you're going to feel when I tell you. You're going to be a father in March. As you can imagine Father did not receive the news very well. We had quite a tussle about what should happen to me and the baby, but in the end I persuaded him that my plan was the right one. For me to come and live with you in Jamaica (just as we talked about in the summer). I know it wasn't really our plan for me to come so soon and I know you wanted me to have the opportunity to finish my studies. Well things didn't work out that way — pregnant ladies are not thought to be capable of writing essays or sitting exams (apart from the fact that we might contaminate others with our immorality). Anyway I wasn't left with any choice in the matter and was summarily sent down at the beginning of term. So much for that. Well, we'll be together soon. Of course we'll get

89

married. *Remember how we planned for the ceremony to take place while we waded in the sea?*

I really miss you Gladstone and wish you had been with me to face all the disapproval and hypocrisy — I really learned who my friends were over this.

It's a natural consequence of an incompletely lived life to fall into the habit of always looking into the future. For me England has always been a place where my personality has felt confined — I can now understand so clearly what you meant about the hypocrisy you saw every day in the army. I remember every word you said to me while we sat below Caiaphas in the chapel. You and the baby and your little island will be my permanent future from now on.

I shall be setting sail within the next few weeks and will send a telegram with the exact date of my arrival.

Until I see you, lots of love and many kisses from me and our baby.

Virginia

The day before she was meant to leave, Mrs Langbridge brought Virginia a letter from Jamaica. Excited, she rushed upstairs, and nervously sat down at the bureau to read the greetings from her new home.

Dear Virginia,

How are you darling? I hope you and the baby are fine. At first I was shocked when I read you were pregnant, but it's fantastic news although totally unexpected. I miss you so much. Everything seems to be happening at once, both joy and pain. Two days ago father died, he was nearly 65 years old. He didn't want us to bury him with my step-mother in Kingston, but said before he died that he wished to be laid to rest in some plantation in the country, where my real mother is buried. Anyway, before his heart failed, I told him about you and about his grandchild. He said that he knew you would be beautiful because he and I both had the same good taste!

Father left some money so I will be able to set myself up with a good practice in Kingston. At times, darling, I wonder if it was foolish to turn down the chance of doing research, but I just couldn't take England anymore. I hated being second-class. In England I realised what it must be like to be a full negro at home. As a child, I never saw myself as black or white. I also understood in England about how the mass of people are trained solely to serve a small master class, with pittance for a reward. We have this disease also but I will make it my future to fight it.

Jamaica must sound like a strange sort of paradise to you, but it's home and it's where I should be.

I am now living with my brother Oliver in a pleasant house, on the Hope Road in Kingston. By the time you come I may have my own place just down

90

the road from here. Oliver has done very well for himself, especially after he took charge of my father's shops. I've told him about you and he says he can't wait to meet you. He's a sly fox, so be warned. When I told him about me becoming a father, he was overjoyed but couldn't understand why I hadn't had many more children in England. Oliver by the way must have about fourteen children all over the island. He's rough and he doesn't give a damn. He recently became union leader for the wharf workers downtown. Such is his influence that in a few weeks he made me second in charge of one of Jamaica's biggest unions, the aptly named Cooper Federation of Workers.

When I came back to Jamaica, for the first three weeks I was shocked at the total barrenness of mind. I had nobody to talk to about anything, because nobody is interested in anything. There is no theatre to go to, no concerts, one can't talk about books because nobody reads any. When I talk about important events in other countries, hardly anyone is interested. Since those early days I have managed to meet a group of people who one could bracket as intellectuals. Otherwise Jamaica is still an empty desert. A lot of work needs to be done, but there's a great swelling inside me to reach out to the poor. Something exciting is going to happen here and I feel we can both be part of it.

I hope this hasn't put you off. I know that Jamaica is the soil in which our relationship can grow and develop. I've missed you so much over these past weeks, life is pretty dull without you, darling. There are so many places I would like to show you. Discovery Bay where Columbus landed, the beautiful fishing town of Port Antonio in the East. The Blue Mountains where I'll show you that even Jamaica has snow. But all of that will have to wait until after our child is born.

Last night I wrote these few lines of poetry which I dedicate to you:

Stretching forth from England's shores
I can't wait for you
To splash my dullness with all your wonderful colours.

My Rainbow girl,
Your exciting mixture intoxicates me
And I become drunk on love.

You who came to me after the shower,
After the floods, after the hurricane.
My Rainbow lover.
Let us intermingle and show them our display of colour.
As a Peacock spreads its feathers.

We are now so close
Our Rainbows dart into each others heart
To kill the gloom

91

And open up
A Springtime.
I hope to hear from you soon.
Love and kisses my darling
Your waiting love

Gladstone.

The day of departure arrived. The Langbridge's drove quickly to Southampton, the English countryside flashing past. It no longer held any interest for Virginia, it was too familiar and the prospect of a new beginning made this landscape dull. Langbridge concentrated on driving and was silent throughout the journey, while Mrs Langbridge sat in the back with her daughter, crying all the way to the busy dock. They kissed and said their good-byes. Virginia wished her mother could accompany her into her new life — maybe she, too, would have found a release from the dowdiness of her existence and marriage. Langbridge stretched out his hand as if to shake his daughter's, but changed his mind and instead, moved a step closer and gently stroked her cheek.

The vessel to Jamaica was called the 'Tornado'. Virginia hoped the name was not a bad omen. It was scheduled to arrive at Kingston harbour by the end of the month by which time she would be six months into her pregnancy. She was already having to be pretty inventive about her attire to conceal the expanding stomach. How was she going to find an appropriate dress for the wedding?

At dinner, on the first evening at sea, Virginia was joined by a middle-aged couple who realised she was alone on this long voyage. Virginia was sitting at the table staring at a picture of a sugar plantation in Jamaica, thinking of how ghastly it must have been for those poor Africans making the journey across the Atlantic, packed together in those terrible slave ships.

"May we join you?" said the man.

"Please do," Virginia replied smiling.

"My name is Hargreaves, John Hargreaves. And this is my wife Linda."

"Virginia Langbridge."

Linda didn't seem as open as her husband and she sat smiling awkwardly.

"So what takes you to Jamaica?" said Hargreaves.

"I am to join my husband, he's a doctor." Virginia glanced at her belly, and congratulated herself on avoiding calling Gladstone 'my fiancé'. "Are you going to Jamaica on business?"

"You could say so. I'm the new Governor of the island. It's our first time to Jamaica but we're looking forward to the job. We were in Kenya before this. I hope we find the locals as friendly to Europeans as those in Africa."

During lunch, Mrs Hargreaves became more relaxed. She confided to Virginia that sometimes it was harder being a Governor's wife than being the Governor himself.

"The greatest quality, my dear, in this job, is to be able to withstand criticism. And that's what I hate," said Mrs Hargreaves, her tongue loosened by the wine.

"What do people say?" Virginia asked.

"You get it from both sides, from the ex-pats and the natives. What you wear, how you walk and there's always a rumour that you're being unfaithful to your husband." She winked mischievously at her husband.

They showed Virginia a picture of their son, who was at Cambridge doing his finals. She didn't tell them that she too had been an undergraduate or that she recognised their son as a young man who was disciplined for urinating on students as he leaned from a window during a lecture.

"He's a bright lad you know, he should get a First if he works hard," said Mr Hargreaves.

"You must be proud of him," Virginia said smiling.

On the morning of the arrival Virginia woke early. The island rose above the choppy water and in the background she could see the range of mountains called the Yallahs Hills. The hot wind blew in her face and like a magnet she was drawn into the warmth of the landscape.

They disembarked at Kingston harbour. There was no time to relish her first footstep on Jamaican soil as Virginia was immediately overwhelmed by a deluge of black men all offering to carry her suitcases. She was frightened as they jostled and pulled her towards the waiting cabs, horse-drawn or motorised, whichever she wanted. As she pleaded with them to let her through, they suddenly scattered and in the clearance stood the figure of Gladstone. For a moment, he didn't move towards her, his face slowly, tentatively melting into a smile. In that instant the hubbub vanished and Virginia was aware only of her fine young man. In three strides they were kissing and hugging each other tight, relieved to be in each other's arms. Gladstone had gained weight — a larger chest than Virginia remembered, squeezed into his short-sleeved shirt. He looked so much at home, hardly bothered by the burning sunshine.

The drive up King Street on their way to Gladstone's house gave Virginia her first taste of Kingston life. She watched in amazement as a barefoot woman balanced three suitcases on her head at an angle of about forty-five degrees. She walked so easily, displaying a total grace — Virginia was mesmerised by her. They drove from the commercial chaos of the harbour, to the lush vegetation of the residential areas. Virginia became self-conscious realising that everyone was negro and she white.

Gladstone's house was only a few blocks away from his brother's. Oliver was already waiting to greet the English woman about whom he'd heard so much. The moment she saw him, Virginia knew he was a Cooper — this tall man, with a self-assured smile walking slowly to the car.

"Virginia, meet my brother Oliver."

"It's my pleasure. I've heard so much about you and I must say you are exquisitely beautiful. My brother is a lucky man."

He kissed her hand and then helped to carry her things to Gladstone's bedroom. Virginia was a bit embarrassed as, although she was pregnant, she was not married, but Oliver seemed to think nothing of it. She was fascinated by Oliver — his bad reputation intrigued her. He was much lighter-skinned than Gladstone — almost white. His hair was cropped short and he gazed through half-closed languid eyes which suggested a man of leisure.

Virginia enjoyed her first Jamaican meal, which Oliver proudly announced he himself had prepared. She noticed the picture of Lionel Cooper which hung imposingly above the planter's chair. His piercing eyes and sensuous half-smile had been handed down to both sons.

"Gladstone tells me that you might eventually want to teach out here, but I think you would be wasted in that profession. You could come and work with me. I've set up a trade union, the biggest in Jamaica. I will need someone to work as an administrator."

"Don't trust him Ginny, Oliver's the first shopkeeper to run his own union," joked Gladstone, but Virginia sensed a serious edge behind the comment.

"Thanks for the offer," she said, "but what I would really like to do, is set up a dance company. Is there much organised dance here?"

"Well, apart from the Kumina jump-up in the country and the white people's can-can, there isn't anything," said Gladstone.

"But why you want to work in dance? There's no money in that. Take my advice, there's money in unions," Oliver said confidently. "A group of workers will pay high dues for me to go and negotiate better conditions for them."

"You don't pay him no mind," said Gladstone, finishing off his wine, "my brother sees unionism as business when it should be seen as politics. You go ahead and start your dance company, you should do it, because it's something you believe in."

"I believe in unions," Oliver interrupted, "but I suppose Gladstone is right, you must have a heart-felt conviction. But let me warn you, Virginia, Jamaica people, them nuh easy — if you give them too much of your heart they'll surely break it."

Entrusting her with that thought, Oliver took his leave of Virginia and Gladstone.

The house was basic and Virginia was already working out changes to make the place look brighter. She laughed when she saw the mosquito nets over the bed.

"You won't laugh when the mosquitoes have your fresh English flesh for dinner," teased Gladstone. He switched on the radiogram and tuned into a Cuban station playing jazz music.

Virginia noticed a somewhat ornate musket hanging on the wall.

"Where did that come from?" she enquired.

"My father gave it to me. He said he got it from my natural mother."

"Have you found out any more about her?"

"Yes. Before my father died he told me the whole story. She was a woman of the people — a poor woman who lived in the countryside. The strange thing is that sometimes I sit down and I feel her presence when I look up at the musket. I don't know anything about her, but I'm sure it's her presence."

"Do you think he was in love with her?"

"I don't know. She must have made some impression on him. He asked to be buried at Eden Park in St Catherine, that was where she lived and where she's buried. She died about ten years ago after a long illness."

"I'd like to see Eden Park. Could we go there tomorrow?"

"Don't you want to rest? I'm sure you must be feeling like you're still at sea."

"Perhaps a little, but I still want to go."

Virginia turned off the lights and went to the open window, where she crouched on the floor with her chin on the sill. Outside, the moon was shining between the trees and nearby, a nightingale sang its broken tune. In the distance, a chain of mountains was lost in drifting white mist. Jamaica at night, Jamaica in moonlight, Jamaica that would take this English woman's heart and mind.

"Gladstone, I'm so looking forward to tomorrow, to us seeing Eden Park together, " Virginia said.

"Haven't you forgotten something that we need to think about first?"

"What, you mean for us to get married? Yes, let's do that in the morning!"

"No, we'll need to make some preparations first. For one thing the church needs about two weeks notice and, anyway, I shall need a new suit."

"That's alright, then. We shall be married in a fortnight and we can still go to Eden Park tomorrow."

Gladstone looked a little pained at Virginia's impetuousness but decided not to oppose her.

She was happy to get out of the heat of Kingston and drive to the cool St Catherine countryside. The couple rattled along the terrible roads in Gladstone's Ford, a car that he loved for its reliability, certainly not for its comfort.

It was amazing how so many people knew Doctor Cooper, waving to them and shouting plenty of 'Good mornings'. Virginia was fascinated by the children as the car rolled through the small towns along the way — often they stared back at her, openly aghast, regarding her as if she was a ghost.

The sunrise ahead was glorious, bringing to life the sleepy market women who sat by the roadside, almost indistinguishable from the bundles of goods that lay before them. They were determined-looking women, with their plaid headcloths, heavy men's shoes and thunderous voices, who defied science every time they balanced those giant baskets on their heads. Virginia was reminded of the poor classes in England, their women were also tough, but these peasant women had a strength and dignity which inspired admiration and also fear.

"I can't stand the way they stare at me," she said wiping the perspiration from her forehead.

"Don't worry, darling. Look at it this way, when I first arrived in London, little children would run up to me and rub my hand. I suppose they thought my colour was painted. You'll soon fit in."

Virginia already sensed a gap in Jamaica between the town and country which was as big as the class gap in England. She heard talk of 'Kingston people' as if they were a breed apart, yet she saw no difference.

The Rio Cobre, an exquisite deep-green river, kept them company for miles, until it became lost in the undergrowth. Soon the car was heading towards Ewarton and from there, Eden Park. Gladstone stopped the car at the top of a ridge and they both got out to appreciate the magnificent view which unfolded before them. It reminded Virginia of the rolling Welsh valleys. She could see why the British loved it there. Falling away to the right, was the most striking feature of all, the quadrilateral pattern of the canefields and beyond, like gods in a Greek amphitheatre, were the huge mountains inspecting the mere mortals below.

"Gladstone, it's beautiful here, like a fairytale and the air is so fresh. I can see why your father wanted to be buried here. I'm sure he must have had some good memories."

96

"Well all I can see is a sugar plantation," said Gladstone coldly.

"I'd like to think he fell in love with a special lady who stole his heart," Virginia said enthusiastically.

"Perhaps, but knowing the old man's reputation he would have had little time to fall in love. If anything, I reckon the old rascal wanted to be buried here because he broke someone's heart and still felt guilty."

"You mean he broke your mother's heart?"

Gladstone looked sullen and offered no reply. Instead, he turned back to the car and pretended to be inspecting the tyres. They drove on, into the Vale, past the plantation house which Virginia learned had recently been bought by an Englishman not long in Jamaica. She watched as workers drifted into the sugar-mill from houses owned by the planter. Children, who seemed as young as ten, were going to work in the field; they strolled behind pairs of oxen that would be used to drag the carts of freshly cut cane. She felt that Eden Park could have changed little since the last century.

Lionel Cooper had bought a small plot of land for himself where he now rested in the shade of a cotton tree beneath a simple stone which bore only the dates of his coming and passing. As Virginia looked down at the grave she longed to piece together the mystery of the Cooper family. Who was Gladstone's mother? And what of the jolly rascal who lay dead at her feet? She was frustrated at Gladstone's apparent indifference to his family history. As they drove away from Eden Park, a breeze blew in the surrounding trees. Virginia's body froze in response to a loud cry rippling through the branches. It was the cry of a woman, and the trees bent towards the car begging its passengers to stay. Virginia looked across at Gladstone. He clearly had heard nothing and did not perceive this eerie shrill voice which had called from the valley.

The wedding was held at St Andrew's Parish Church (more formal than those Cambridge dreams of a wedding service while the couple waded in the sea), with the reception taking place in Oliver's superbly tended garden. There must have been two hundred guests — mostly Gladstone's relatives and then some of his medical friends. In all those people, the bride only knew two — her husband and his brother. How dearly she would have loved to have had her mother by her side or even her stuffy father there, to give her away. Not surprisingly, Oliver was not only best man, but also master of ceremonies — a role he played with gusto.

"Now, come Mr Bridegroom, your time now sir, we all want a sweet speech or you nah go have the bride tonight," said Oliver who was half drunk, "but before you take the stage, my brother, a few humble words of advice from a man who is overjoyed to see his kin married to such a delectable beauty. My brother went to England and plucked nothing but the best. However, there is some men sitting in this very wedding who think that when God say that woman was made from the rib of man, that mean she must know her place in the world and be man's servant. Some men here, who shall remain nameless because I want a favour from them, think women's only use is to carry water, pickney and gossip. Well nothing nuh go so! Me feel seh that God use up at least half the rib cage of man, when him made woman. Therefore, my brethren, a man is only half a man if he doesn't allow woman to make him whole. And it is the same for woman, she must allow the man to make her whole. And that is what happens in marriage. There is a unique oneness. That is why the whole of creation cries out, 'Amen'. It is the nature of things. A man must learn to humble himself, allow the woman to come right inside and sit next to him. So that they can be King and Queen of creation, which is the duty that God laid on them."

"Then how come you're not married, Missa Oliver?" shouted a guest.

"Cause God curse me with a badly shaped rib cage and out of the 60 woman which try, them just can't fit. But fret not my good man, for I'm still trying!"

Everybody roared with laughter as Oliver called for a toast to a happy future with many children.

The guests were entertained by a mento band, called How Sweet It Is. They played quaint Jamaican adaptations of traditional English folk songs and sea chanteys. It reminded the new bride of England and once again she felt homesick. But the pain soon passed in the joyful realisation that Jamaica was her new home, and she was here to share it with Gladstone.

Virginia was to meet the colony's elite at the select 'Jamaica Club'. Gladstone and Oliver, although both members, only reluctantly took her along. She was told firmly to behave herself. Women had only recently been allowed to attend, and then only accompanied by their responsible husbands. Virginia got another taste of home as she walked into the lobby — a distinct smell of cigars and a large Union Jack displayed on the wall above a picture of the King. There were glass cabinets proudly showing the trophies that had been won by club members in activities ranging from chess to tennis. Oliver proudly pointed at himself and Gladstone in the picture of the current Jamaica Club cricket team.

"Why are there no negroes in the team?" Virginia asked.

Gladstone and Oliver looked at each other as if they were hiding some deep secret.

"It's the rules," said Gladstone, "to be in the team, you have to be a member, and in order to be a member you have to pay a membership fee. Most negro people can't afford it."

"Is not 'most'," interrupted Oliver, "is all, and it's a raas shame. I'm sure the team would benefit from a different policy. This country is a pox, Virginia. They keep the poor black man out of everything, even the vote. If you don't own so much land and earn a certain amount of money, then you don't vote. You certainly don't play cricket, ole chap."

"Then why are you a member?" she said annoyed.

"Because I want to play cricket," said Oliver smiling.

Gladstone explained that the wise men who ran Jamaica never made any decisions at their Council, rather they came to the Club, and in the comfort of lunch and a drink, these predominantly white men conducted their business. This ritual would be practiced every day and, like the changing of the guards, Virginia was in time to see them finishing off lunch and retiring to the bar. It was amazing to see the major bankers, lawyers, doctors and the Brigadier-General all under one roof.

One of the women, who was called Martha, bored everybody with a stone by stone description of her house, then a long tirade on the falling standards of domestics and all of this coated by an attempt at the Queen's English; but she kept coughing up her Creole, a just reminder of her real place in the world. Her husband, Stephen, had a somewhat crude sense of humour.

He had progressed from whiskey to neat white rum and in the presence of his wife began to recall his sexual exploits as a school boy in Kingston.

"Virginia, mek me tell you about this prostitute name Shaggy. Well me and me best friend Tomlinson, we were about fifteen, we steal away from school one lunchtime and we go down to Half-way Tree. Right near the clock-tower, we sight Shaggy. Every time me see her, my cock just stand to attention. The gal have a massive batty and her breasts stretch from Parade to Kingston harbour. Anyway my Uncle did go America that week, so him did give me sixpence — so me and Tomlinson went fe ride Shaggy. When we go up to her she just run we — say she nah trouble no pickney and we so small it might bruk off inside her. Me jus' flash her de sixpence and everyt'ing fine; but me say that's fe two ah we. Tomlinson go first. Bad Shaggy strip off and lie down, her legs apart. Tommo climbed in a little jumpy; when she done wid him, Tommo bawl 'Lawd have mercy! Lawd God almighty'. She fling him up and pull him down, the bwoy cry living eye water. When him done, him crawl out weak to rahtid. Then like thunder ah clap, she shout, 'Next!'. Raas, when me look 'pan Tommo a shiver in de corner, me decided fe run. By de time me did reach de fence, Shaggy grab me, tear off my pants and bwoy not a thing coulda save me. She left me on the ground weary. When she ah leave, she turn round and say we must come back when we turn man."

Everybody laughed loudly, even the people on the next table joined in the mirth. It seemed to Virginia that the story only betrayed the man's contempt for the woman. He drunkenly plunged on:

"You know, I'm sure is that bitch give me de clap. Bwoy it nearly kill me. In school me would sneak out and go up to the wall fe piss. I would have to spread-eagle, tearing my hands down the wall as me willy feel like someone set it 'pon fire!"

Oliver suggested playing tennis. Virginia told Gladstone that she preferred to sit alone in the sun. After warning her about heat-stroke, he went off with the others.

Virginia sat enjoying the sun, until a middle-aged man who, instead of looking tanned, seemed rather to have been bleached by the sun, interrupted her repose.

"Afternoon... may I join you?" he asked politely.

"Be my guest."

His breath smelled of rum. This frail old man carried a permanent-look of concern on his face. Through his creased cheeks he smiled, as he carefully sat next to Virginia.

"The name is Wells, Colonel Wells."

"Virginia Cooper."

"I haven't seen you here before... are you new to Jamaica?"

"Yes, I'm a recent arrival."

"Cooper... is that Dr Gladstone Cooper? Didn't he study at Cambridge?"

"Yes, that's where we met."

"Thank God for Cambridge, with standards falling we have at least one institution to be proud of."

"Standards?" Virginia repeated, puzzled.

"Well I damn well had to walk out of the Colonial Club this morning. They've allowed a nigger in as a member."

"Why, shouldn't anyone be allowed to join?'

He turned and smiled and continued, as if to a naive child:

"You've only just arrived in the colonies... you wouldn't understand yet. One couldn't bear to have niggers breathing curry in ones face while playing billiards. Thank God for the Jamaica Club, at least it's holding up standards."

"There you go again, about standards; all I've seen since I've been here, are ex-patriots doing their best to crush black people and a load of arrogant browns who don't want to admit they're black!"

"Poppy-cock! It will be over my dead-body that a nigger gains membership to this club. Things in Jamaica are deteriorating as it is. I've lived here for ten years now and I can remember a time when if a

100

black walked past you, he would bow his head in respect — and if he was insolent, you could beat him there and then or send him to the jailhouse with a letter that said, 'Please give the bearer 20 lashes.' "

"And is that how you'd like to treat brown people also?"

"Do you know what prestige it gives to a coloured to belong to a European Club? One old boy offered me his car, if I'd give him a reference."

"So you think they're inferior?"

"They have white blood in them that's true, and that does give them superior intelligence over the blacks, but at the end of the day, they too are niggers. I would allow only a small number into the Club and they'd better not forget their place."

Virginia decided to get out of there quickly, before she began to smash the furniture or maybe hit this buffoon next to her with a rum bottle. She looked around her, at this so-called 'high society' and all she saw were dull, drunk, witless pot-bellies. How could they go on day after day, repeating the same senseless conversations, laughing at the same stale dirty jokes? Had the English come to this? England was at rock bottom and these expatriates had a nerve to talk about being civilised and cultured. Virginia longed to get out into the fresh air of the ordinary people, who still retained dignity under what, at times, seemed impossible odds. She cast a last dismissive glance at the old fogey in front of her and wondered if he too didn't have a black mistress to warm his bed.

Although Gladstone wouldn't admit it, money was short especially with the baby coming. Virginia got work as a teacher in a mission school, run by the Methodist Church. Her pupils were young girls up to the age of 14, the children of the poor. Of those who completed their allotted time at the school, most would graduate to sell in the market or look for a job as a maid. Half of the girls, however, became pregnant at which point their studies terminated as the Church refused to teach such sinners. The school didn't employ sufficient staff so it operated a system whereby the brighter children ended up teaching the slower ones.

Virginia had only been teaching a month, when she entered the staff room to find her colleague, Grace Samuels, in tears.

"What's wrong, Gracie, are you sick?"

"No Miss Virginia, is George, me can't tek the drinking no more and me find that me pregnant. Last night him come home and wake me out ah me sleep and tek up a broomstick and beat me. I spend the whole ah last night outdoors. Is nearly every day the man tek set 'pon me." Gracie pulled her blouse and showed her colleague the five marks across her back. "Then the little money which him earn on the wharf,

101

the man jus' drink it off. We have fe live on my teacher's salary alone. Miss Virginia, me 'fraid fe go home tonight, cause I know him goin' beat me again."

Virginia held the woman in her arms as she cried with fear. Grace was usually so full of energy. The man she lived with was a Jamaican Indian. They called him Fire-Tongue on account of the way he would drink white rum like water.

"Listen, you come and live with us. There's plenty of room at our house. You don't need to go back to him."

"But what about my things?"

"You don't worry, I'll go round to collect them."

Gladstone was not happy when his wife told him that Grace would be staying, but when the guest cooked him hot pepper soup that evening, his tune soon changed. So much so, that he decided to accompany Virginia to confront Fire-Tongue.

They drove into a dreadful slum area of Kingston where a terrible stench of sewage hung in the air as they walked to the wooden house. Many of the residents watched them with hostility and suspicion, while others cast an aimless curiosity in their direction. Even the scrawny looking pigs and goats seemed to stop in their tracks and look at the two strangers. Virginia remembered the animals in the countryside and how they were fat and healthy compared to their malnourished city cousins who had to root along gutters to find scraps.

"Hey bwoy, is the coolie man inside?" Gladstone enquired of a little boy, who was using a piece of wood to wheel an old tyre down the road.

"Yes sah, him deh inside. Him ah sleep, sah, knock de door hard," said the boy.

Gladstone did as advised. Eventually Fire-Tongue appeared. He was a short man, although stockily built.

"Is what you want?!" he demanded, eyes blood-shot with drink and lack of sleep.

"We've come to collect Grace's things."

"And who you is?"

"Virginia Cooper, I teach with Grace."

Fire-Tongue's reply was to slam the door in Virginia's face. After two minutes of waiting, Gladstone knocked again and the door flew open. This time a large suitcase and two parcels were thrown out, into the street. Then came a wooden box and finally two Crocus bags, which hit Gladstone on the chest causing the crowd, who had gathered to savour the commotion, to erupt with laughter.

"Tell that dirty ole negga, nevah fe put her backside in here again. Next time me go chop her!" Fire-Tongue growled, disappearing back into the darkness of his house.

102

When Gladstone was working late Virginia would sit on the veranda perfecting her newly acquired skills, plaiting Grace's hair and singing favourite folk songs. One evening Grace sang the first verse of 'My Bonny Lies Over The Ocean'.

"Where did you learn to sing that?" Virginia asked surprised.

"Oh my mother taught it to me and she got it from her mother. Why, do you know it?"

"Yes, of course, but you sing it so beautifully."

"Miss Virginia, do you think the devil is a man or a woman? Fire-Tongue say that all women are just like Jezebel," Grace asked picking up the topic on her mind.

"I don't know, Grace, isn't the devil a spirit?"

"I reckon the devil must be a woman because no matter how God try to make man keep his commandments the devil always make man break them. And they say it's woman who is behind men's weakness."

"If that was true, then women would have power and money. The devil is inside all of us, both men and women. I think the devil is an 'it', men use it for violence and oppression, while we women use it as guile and tactics to stay alive and feed our children. We are all devils, only some of us are good devils and some of us bad."

Grace laid her head on Virginia's lap as her hand stroked the English woman's belly.

"I'm certain that my baby is a boy."

"Well, whether it's a boy or girl, I'm sure it will be perfect."

"Just like its mother!' Virginia teased.

"You know, Miss Virginia, you've been so good to me, I really do love you."

Every Saturday morning, Grace and Virginia would make their way downtown to Coronation Market. They, like all the other customers, would have to pick their way around the piles of produce which the market women laid out next to where they sat on the ground. Only a few were lucky enough to have stalls. Virginia loved the taste of jelly coconuts which were always in abundant supply. They usually bought theirs from the same old man, who was an expert with his machete, skillfully slicing off the top to get at the cool water inside. Little boys carrying a tray around their neck, would sell cold sweets, cigarettes, dried shrimp and even guava cheese while singing witty songs exalting the virtues of their wares. Skillful cyclists, who rode as fast as any vehicle with an engine, darted through the market, even though they might be carrying a considerable load. They once saw two men, both on bicycles, balancing a huge wardrobe between them. Mayhem was only just averted by the timely appearance of a member of the constabulary. But sometimes, no such happy intervention took place. When a cyclist ran down a pedestrian, it was usual for a fight to break out, the intensity of which would threaten to bring half of Kingston to a halt as onlookers jostled for a good view.

If Virginia thought the East End markets in London were noisy, she found Coronation Street deafening. Apart from the sellers trying to out-sing each other, there were the boisterous greetings between fellow shoppers and the men making a nuisance of themselves shouting bawdy suggestions at women who took their fancy who, in turn, would respond with equal openness. The market was also teeming with preachers, announcing the end of the world from every street corner. These men and women told of certain judgement and hell-fire. Some of them appeared mad, but the crowd listened attentively. In fact, the more vivid the description of God's wrath, the greater the enjoyment of the sermon.

Virginia loved her weekly expeditions, always returning exhausted, greatly relieved to taste again the cool quiet of home.

At Easter the house was filled with the cries of a new Cooper — a little boy, who Gladstone named David. This tiny bundle seemed to smile as he entered the world, anxious to absorb all the excitement of his new surroundings. Grace and Gladstone were with the new mother at the nursing home when David arrived. As she took the navel cord to bury it later in the Cooper's garden, Grace looked steadily at Virginia and pronounced quietly:

"I feel this boy is going to be loved by Jamaica. He's special. Miss Virginia. I believe that God has given you this child for a purpose. He's blessed, I know it."

Gladstone, who would never take Grace's prophetic outbursts seriously, nevertheless looked closely at his son as if he were searching for a mark or a sign.

"You know, I keep thinking about my real mother, the poor woman that my father wouldn't talk about," said Gladstone. "I sometimes wish I had shown more interest in her when I was younger, maybe he would have taken me to her. After all she was David's grandmother."

As tiny David sucked at his mother's breast, Virginia felt a wonderful sense that she was holding someone who she had known for a long time. He was more than a baby, he was her friend who knew all those secrets she had shared with him in the bath. Then there had been the morning when he had wakened her with a well-aimed kick, vexed that she had neglected him for so long. He was so familiar and yet so new, and now he claimed her breast for his own.

Grace was Virginia's constant companion — a second mother to David, she did everything but suckle him. The two women had spent

104

long hours exchanging confidences but it was not until after the birth of her son that Grace allowed Virginia to know the full extent of how she had suffered at the hands of Fire-Tongue. She told of at least six other women from her area who had been similarly treated by their husbands. She spoke of a close friend who had set fire to her home after years of beatings — she and her baby perished along with the husband.

That night, Virginia decided to write to her father asking him for a loan, which in reality meant a gift. She wanted to buy a house for Jamaica's battered women so that they could have a place of refuge. Her father was generous enough with the gift, but the crafty old beggar ensured that he would hold onto the title of any property eventually purchased.

They bought a disused church hall. Gladstone managed, mostly through the Methodist Church, to raise funds for the furniture. Oliver provided cash for the paint and accessories.

"What are we going to call ourselves?" said Grace, her hands covered in paint as she finished off the bathroom door.

"What about the 'Sisters of Jezebel'?"

"You mad, Miss Virginia, people would burn us out in seconds. Why don't we call ourselves 'Lioness' because we are wounded women and that makes us dangerous."

"I like it, let's vote."

Both women raised their hands high in the air and it was carried. They hugged and kissed to celebrate their new movement.

Within a week of opening, Lioness House was full. Having given up her teaching after the birth of David, Virginia was able to attend to the organisation of the refuge. The bad cases were allowed to stay, but most of the time they simply talked to the lonely and frightened women who called at their door. Many were pregnant and just young girls themselves.

All too soon, however, Lioness hit a severe financial crisis and they took their problem to Gladstone.

"Now look you two, there's no possibility of me getting you any more money."

"What about the Church's charitable fund?" Virginia asked. "Isn't there any money available there?"

"No, they're saying they must concentrate on their African projects — they seem to think that Jamaica is a paradise where hunger and poverty is a thing of the past."

"Don't you know anyone who could help, darling?"

"Maybe there is someone. A young Anglican woman. Her father has money, he's a plantation owner in Westmoreland. But there is a complication. Our union is fighting to get more money for his cane-cutters but the old buffoon won't give an extra penny. I hear that the daughter likes to help poor people. I expect she could get some money from her church, but if the dispute comes to a strike, I can't be seen to have any association with the family."

"I promise, darling, that we'll be very discreet."

Virginia met Louise Kennedy in the foyer of the Myrtle Bank Hotel. She had objected to the venue at first as they had a policy of not allowing black people to enter. Virginia told Grace she should come anyway, but her friend thought it better that she went alone, especially as they were after money. Louise, with her jet black hair and tanned complexion, looked like a southern European. She did nothing for a living and spent her time travelling to places like London, Paris and Rome. She was kept by her father who had plans to marry her into another planter's family.

As soon as the two women had introduced themselves, Louise hugged her new acquaintance with excitement at the prospect of having something better to do than lounge on her verandah all day cursing the maid or dismissing the gardener.

"Don't worry about money," she said, when she had calmed sufficiently to talk sensibly, "I'll see that the Church provides plenty to keep your project going. But I want to be involved myself."

"That will be no problem. We are in need of a treasurer and since you obviously have a talent as a fund-raiser, the job is yours."

Grace went through a terrible labour and sadly the baby died, too weak to live. Virginia kissed nearly every tear her friend cried. If she had possessed the power to give her a child, she would have done so. All those months of carrying this miracle and then the pain of labour, only to see it end in death.

Life continued without incident for a while. Louise proved to be a reliable and indispensable partner in the project and Lioness House continued to provide comfort to many women. On the day of the Whitsun holiday, while Gladstone and Oliver were celebrating at the Jamaica Club, Virginia answered the door at home to two young girls from the refuge. Cissy, in tears, was being supported by her friend, Mitsy.

"Miss Virginia, it's Mama, them kill her at the Jamaica Club!"

"What do you mean?! What happened?!"

"The manager lick her down, Miss Virginia!!" cried Mitsy, Cissy having lost the struggle to suppress her sobs.

"She served the wrong dish to one of the guests;. When she get back to the kitchen, the manager just lick her down. Her heart was weak, Miss Virginia, and she drop dead."

"And what about the constabulary? Haven't they arrested him?"

"Arrest me backfoot!" said Mitsy, "the manager's brother is the Chief of Police."

The women drove to the refuge where everyone decided on a confrontation with the manager. So with crying babies in their arms, they made haste to the Jamaica Club, speeding past the sleeping guard at the gate and headed straight for the banqueting hall. The music came to a sudden silence as the angry women clasped hands in a circle in the centre of the room. Virginia stood in the middle trying not to look at Gladstone who had been dancing with his secretary. He looked at her, wide-eyed with shock.

"Ladies and Gentlemen, make no mistake, we are not the special Whitsun floor-show. It might have escaped your notice that a killing took place in your kitchen only two hours ago, and we have evidence that the woman who died, Miss Pearl Johnson, was struck by your manager. We are here to ensure that the man is called to answer for what he has done and we will not move from this place until we see justice."

"Yes justice, we want justice, we want justice!!" the other women echoed.

There was a rush for the door as the embarrassed and frightened guests made a quick exit, leaving their uneaten dinners on the table. Gladstone stormed across to his wife, she had never seen him so angry.

"What the hell's going on Virginia? Look what you've done!"

"What I've done? Someone has just been murdered and all you want to do is swing and dance."

"What the hell are you talking about? The matter is being investigated by the police. Miss Johnson had a heart attack. I examined her myself."

"But Missa Cooper, the manager did lick her, me did see it," said a young waitress.

"Who asked you anything?!" snapped Gladstone, then to Virginia, "Call off this protest right now and go home. I expect you there in half an hour!" He walked off haughtily.

That evening, the Coopers were alone at home, Grace having decided to stay at the refuge.

"Are you still vexed darling?" Virginia asked, serving a hot mug of chocolate. This drew no reply, so she continued. "We're not going to let this rest, you know. We'll go to the Governor if necessary."

"That's not what's on my mind."

"What is, then?"

"It's us, you know that this is one of the few times this year that we've been alone together. You seem to give all your attention to Grace and, if it's not Grace, then it's the so-called Lioness group."

107

"So are you saying that we're drawing apart? How can you think that when I love you more than I ever have?"

"No, I'm not saying that. But things seemed to have changed. You and Grace are always hugging and talking on the verandah. I only see you at bedtimes and then all you can talk about is the women's group or how you and Grace did this or went there. What about me? Where do I fit in?"

"You've never said anything before, you seemed so happy with the surgery and your union work," Virginia said rubbing his head.

"Look Virginia, don't bloody patronise me. I care about the people of this country as much as you do. I feel the union could be the basis for something big in Jamaica, even self-government. I'm bloody busy but I still make time and space for my family. I'm now going to bed, but let me tell you this, if we don't find some of the old fire, this marriage won't last long."

Gladstone left her alone in the living room. She knew he was right, they had grown apart. She now found her dashing, handsome Cambridge medical student too slow, too careful. Jamaica needed to be taken by the scruff of the neck and given a good shake. Virginia wanted to do it, she wanted the young women in the refuge to feel proud of themselves, to feel their strength.

It was Grace who wrote to the Governor about Miss Johnson's murder and after he agreed to meet the women, the manager was arrested. It all seemed a wasted effort in the end, as the killer got off without judgement.

As David grew, Grace continued to share in his mothering. She was adamant that she would never want to have another child, but she had plenty of milk for the baby who had died. Virginia didn't mind that Grace breast-fed David — in fact, she encouraged it, for her friend showed the child so much love. Gladstone, when he returned one day to find David at Grace's breast, did not feel the same way. He called out Virginia's name angrily.

"What's wrong, darling?"

"What do you mean, 'what's wrong'? Grace is breast feeding my child!"

"I know. So what's wrong? Her milk is good."

"So what happen to yours? It turn sour?"

"Don't be silly. I'm busy, the baby's hungry, so Grace is feeding him."

Grace had by now winded the baby and was on her way out to avoid further embarrassment. Gladstone grabbed her, pushed her onto the bed, and started to kiss her. Grace struggled free and ran out crying.

"Well, what's wrong with that? Grace is now the mother of my son, so she can be my wife too."

"Oh, you're so childish, Gladstone. Alright, if it suits you, Grace won't breast feed David anymore."

"She better not. You are his mother and he sucks only from your breast."

At 11, David was a bright boy attending Wolmers Boys school in Kingston. He had just returned from England where Virginia had taken him to see his grandmother. London was still the same bleak place. Now in the middle of another war, it had previously suffered chronic unemployment. Virginia felt a visitor in the land of her birth, so she was glad to once again feel the sunshine of her true home.

At weekends the Cooper's would go on picnics high in the Blue Mountains where they were refreshed by the breeze. They would stay until dusk, listening to the peadove's cry, watching crowns of coconuts swaying on their slender trunks. The hillside was covered with shrubs but occasionally a painted patch would appear signifying a zinc roof. There was an abundance of fruit trees — star apple, breadfruit, mango, jackfruit and ackee.

Virginia watched with horror as Gladstone showed David how to shoot one of the doves with a slingshot. The sling was almost too big for him. They were crouching down and had crawled near to a dove that had just landed. This poor green bird was feeding unsuspectingly in the grass, dipping and rising, then suddenly turning its head as if to check that no one was watching. David was about to aim when his mother ran towards the bird, frightening it away.

"Ginny, what are you doing?!" shouted Gladstone. "The boy had a good aim."

"I couldn't care less. I'll have no son of mine killing an innocent bird for fun."

"But Mummy, all the other boys shoot birds, some even use an air-rifle."

"I'm not interested in other boys and you should know better, Gladstone. It's illegal anyway."

"But Mummy!" cried David throwing down his sling in anger.

"But nothing, what if the police saw you shooting a bird at this time of year? They would arrest you straight away."

"Oh no Mummy, not me. Police don't arrest brown boys."

Gladstone looked at Virginia stunned by the boy's comment. He turned and walked back to the car. Virginia held David's hand and they walked slowly up the hill. She knelt down and looked at her son.

"David what is the colour of your arms?"

"It's light brown, Mummy."

"Now let me tell you something. Your grandmother was as dark as

109

the night sky and she was one of the most beautiful women in the whole of Jamaica. That is your daddy's mother. Now we don't know much about her but I believe she was strong and brave and that she loved your Daddy with all her heart. Now you were born in Jamaica, the same place as your black grandmother so that makes you black. What are you?"

"Black Mummy, I'm black," said David smiling. "But Mummy, if I'm black what are you?"

"I'm whatever you want me to be."

These were troubled times both for the poor and rich as the island was devastated with poverty. As strikes increased island-wide, the Cooper family were branded trouble makers and communists. They were dealt a serious blow when David failed to win a scholarship to study in Britain. Virginia was furious when she heard that the award had been given to the son of the Commissioner of Police, a boy who was as thick as they come. The day the news broke, David came home in silence and went straight to his room. Virginia knocked timidly on his door and barely heard his muffled voice. He was sitting on his bed, head bowed, so much like his father — proud and yet easily hurt. His mother worried that he hadn't developed a hard enough shell to protect his delicate inner being.

"Mummy, there's so much hate in Jamaica, hate and jealousy. I sometimes think we're hopelessly vengeful."

"It's not Jamaica, darling, it's politics. Your father and Uncle Oliver want to see change but of course others want to leave us in the dark ages, so we must fight for what is right."

"Even if it means losing my scholarship?"

"I know you're disappointed darling, but don't worry I have some good news for you. Uncle Oliver has agreed to pay for you to study in America."

"That's wonderful, mother, I can't believe it," said David, nearly knocking his mother over in excitement.

"Now, there is a catch to this, you know your uncle, you never get anything for nothing. When you return, you'll have to work for the union for two years."

"That's not a problem, when I get back I want to go into politics. Who knows, mother, I may well become a great revolutionary."

"You just concentrate on your studies and stop dreaming."

Two months later, Gladstone and Virginia were waving goodbye to their son, straining to see him, one of many on the dockside watching the steam ship make its slow progress towards the United States.

The offices of the Cooper Union were located near to Kingston

110

harbour. When Virginia and Gladstone arrived, Oliver was still conducting his surgery. They looked through the open window to see him talking to a distressed woman whose small son clung apprehensively to her leg.

"Siddung Miss T," said Oliver, "well, me dear, how it go?"

"Well, Marse Cooper, me have a little work as a domestic, near Hanover Street but the lady of de house want me fe wuk day and night. Me have five pickney in Admiral Pen, dem stay wid me sister ah daytime but me have not a soul fe look 'pon dem ah night."

She was a young woman but hard life had aged her. Her sagging breasts and bare feet told of years of child-rearing and miles of treading the harsh Kingston streets seeking work that was never there. Oliver looked at the woman who was now crying. He looked coldly beyond the tears, more interested in his strategy to overcome the problem, than the woman before him.

"Is what this lady name?" asked Oliver.

"Miss Cockburn."

"You mean big batty Cockburn?" said Oliver scornfully. The woman began to laugh and her son, who had been quiet up to then, shared the joke. "Me know her well. Her husband have a shop near me. I will talk to him and politely remind him that the wharf boys might accidentally drop his salt-fish delivery into the sea, if him wife nuh mend her ways."

"T'ank yuh Marse Cooper, t'ank yuh sah. Is you God send from above to save we poor black people. God sent yuh fe sure. Me jus' praise and t'ank yuh sah."

Oliver didn't look at the woman as she lavished her adulation upon him. Like a king, he expected this as a matter of duty. Instead, he turned his attention to his brother and sister-in-law, which the woman and her son took as their cue to make a quick exit from the office.

"You two have come at the right time," Oliver said confidently, "I've just finished this letter to the Governor. Let me read it to you, 'Dear Governor, with regard to the said telegram to the House of Commons. I must hasten to manifest to you that I am the person... at the cost of martyrdom it must be known... I fear nothing. I fear no one. My report can stand the acid test of investigation. I wrote from knowledge and not from hearsay as some people do. I urge you Governor, to intervene into the plight of the people or else my union, which is gaining strength every day, will reek havoc on this little colony and in the end I cannot be held responsible for the actions of the workers."

Oliver waited for Governor Hargreaves' reply, but none was forthcoming. After a week he decided to mobilise the Union members.

Soon after daybreak the city of Kingston was in the hands of the

111

working population. Groups of men and women moved from place to place, dislodging others from their stations. Street cleaners, factory workers, tram drivers, even the municipal workers, all joined the throng of people who surged through the streets. Traffic was halted, business places closed, shops were looted, passing cars stoned and roads blocked with oil drums. The authorities were taken by complete surprise as the crowd took charge. The Coopers huddled beneath a staircase outside a law firm. Most of the office workers had fled to the suburbs in fear of their lives. The people had prepared for this riot without knowing, it was a glorious release after years of unemployment and near starvation. A drunken man, a union member, stumbled past the Coopers singing in a raucous baritone.

"Build a bonfire,
Build a bonfire,
Put de white man on the top.
Put the brown man in the middle
And burn de friggin' lot."

The Coopers looked at each other, uneasy. In this orgy of violence, it wasn't clear who was friend or foe. No one could be certain, that if they rushed out to join their comrades, they wouldn't receive a machete chop in return. Virginia felt frustrated. She was not the enemy and had done so much to help the poor. She wanted to stand side by side with them. She felt she too had earned the right to throw bottles at the British troops that surrounded the city. This dilemma didn't worry Gladstone or Oliver who waited patiently, certain that they would soon be called to harness this wild energy. In the meantime, they looked on, almost indifferent to the storm about them.

The next day Gladstone called an emergency meeting, where he announced a motion that the Union form a political party, based on principles of the Labour Party in England.

"As you know comrades, we are living in troubled times. It is my fear that the present uprising will be like wild horses stampeding without direction. We need to harness that energy into a political party. A party that will ultimately work towards self-government because it has the mandate of the people."

The motion was agreed unanimously, signalling the inception of the Independent Party of Jamaica. Gladstone was elected leader. Oliver made no protest because it was the Union that had the money and he was firmly in charge of that.

Gladstone was in a buoyant mood and a few days later he called a street meeting near the wharf to formally announce the birth of the IPJ. The police had surrounded the area and many of them were armed.

112

Gladstone urged that there be no violence but as he spoke, he waved an old musket in the air.

"Comrades, this musket which I am holding was given to me by my father, Lionel Cooper. It was given to him by my mother, who was a poor woman of the people. This musket was used by my mother's great-uncle to fight in the Morant Bay rebellion of 1865. Today, as I hold it up, I don't call for violence but instead I call on you to join the real fighting power and that is the Independent Party of Jamaica, whose symbol is the musket. All of you know that I have a loving wife and a good career as a doctor, but how could I just sit down and see my people be bereft of dignity and suffering in poverty? My friend, the aim of the IPJ is self-government, we must have it. God knows it is our right. We have left the play-pen and we are all now big people ready to take care of ourselves.

"Let me tell every poor Jamaican standing here this morning, we can do it and make a better job of it than the British. I've been to their best university, got their best degree, fought for them and even got their best medal for bravery. And yet, like you, I too come from the Jamaican bush."

It would take another few years for a 'wind of change' to reach Jamaica, but when it did, the Cooper's were ready at the helm of the IPJ. Shortly after the Second World War, the Party began preparing for self-rule.

On Saturday night there was a dance at Port Royal to celebrate the birth of the IPJ manifesto. As Virginia helped serve the food, she felt for the first time part of the Cooper 'firm', it was exciting, they were on the brink of changing Jamaica.

Oliver was next in line for food and handed his plate to Virginia, winking mischievously.

"Could we have the next dance, Virginia?"

"Of course, Oliver."

He moved well across the dance floor and she felt his strong back and wonderful thighs.

"You know that you're a beautiful woman, my brother totally underestimates you. Does he ever take you out anywhere?"

"Well things have been a bit busy with the Party and meetings," Virginia said, really wanting to tell him that she was bored out of her mind with Gladstone.

"You see, sadly, my brother doesn't have a real grasp on how to make a woman happy."

"And you do?"

"What do you think? Here I am with the most beautiful woman in the colonies, giving her the time of her life."

113

Oliver was so arrogant, yet Virginia was flattered. They danced all night, while Gladstone talked politics with his boring friends. Later Oliver and Virginia walked together on the sea front with a bottle of rum between them and watched the fishermen going out for a night's work. Soon they were holding hands and Virginia was caught up in the words and charm of Oliver Cooper.

He broke the seal of a cigar, ignited the end and slowly puffed out smoke. His hair was now greying. Virginia remembered the first time they met and how raucous Oliver had been. She was curious to know why he hadn't married. Gladstone said his brother was too much in love with himself to fall for another.

"You know, Virginia, I do admire my brother. He's a brilliant doctor and he has a sweet use of English and he has a beautiful wife. That's how it's been since we were kids, David always got better than me. But I don't grudge him that because him don't understand politics. Him don't understand that when you talkin' to an ignorant man, you must talk ignorance. Mek me tell you a story... One time we were both negotiating with the management of Frome Sugar Estate for more money for the workers. Gladstone get up and him argue from every angle, the only thing left was for him fe go beg dem 'pon his knees. But the management wouldn't give way. Then him come over to me. Now all this time me ah pretend that me sleeping. He said that he didn't think we could get any more. So me said, 'A'right Gladstone, stand aside, stand aside, I'll tek over'. I went up to the managers and tell dem, 'Gentlemen, you say 1s 7d, when you reach my figure of 1s 10d wake me up — I'm going to sleep right here.' In a short time, meeting done, we get our 1s 10d!"

Oliver refilled his sister-in-law's glass, this time with neat rum.

"You think a lot of yourself, don't you, Oliver," Virginia said, a little tipsy.

"Well, put it this way, I always get what I want."

"Then why aren't you married? You're handsome and rich."

"I only have enough love for myself and poor people, not enough for a wife. Although I like women and I rarely go to bed without one."

"So what are you going to do tonight?"

"Well I might have to borrow my brother's."

"And who says she's available?" Virginia asked teasing.

"Virginia! I just can't keep my eyes from you, you're something special, I fell in love with you the moment I saw you."

She didn't know if it was the sea breeze or just mad passion but she grabbed Oliver and hugged him and they kissed passionately. They went to a room above the boat shed, which the men used when they went off fishing. It was cosy and exciting, they began making love under the gaze of the moon and ended at the same time as Gladstone finished his political debate at the dance.

In the morning Virginia lay next to her husband feeling shame and yet a wonderful sense of falling in love once again. Yet she had committed a terrible act and knew that Gladstone would be broken if he knew her sin. She cried but refused to tell her husband why. That night Gladstone insisted on going to sleep with his arms around his wife. For the first time she found it uncomfortable, he had become a stranger. Virginia was glad when morning came.

Gladstone left early for yet another meeting and Oliver arrived soon after, his face beaming and with a skip in his stride.

"How are you darling!" he said hugging her and planting a kiss on her forehead, she remained still and cold. "What's wrong Virginia?"

"What's wrong! I spent last night with my husband's brother and you ask what's wrong?!"

"Look, I know you feel bad, but we were fated to be together, let's not fight it."

"And what of Gladstone's feelings, don't they matter?" she asked, becoming impatient with Oliver's casual attitude.

"Don't worry yuh head 'bout me breddah, he need not know a thing."

Oliver pulled her close, stroking her hair and slowly kissing her neck. Once again Virginia took leave of her senses and was the victim to her passion a second time. They made love in the bed Gladstone had unknowingly kept warm for his brother. Virginia turned their marriage photograph face downwards on the bedside table, when Oliver was with her she felt no obligations. Oliver was the devil himself and oh what a joy it was to be in his hands. She was in love with his sense of adventure, his desire to take risks. He told rude jokes, he farted like a pig and yet was a gentle lover. They carried on their secret affair for a month until an unfortunate surprise ended everything.

Kingston was hot and angry. The people were hungry and the call was for independence. The big stores in Duke and King Street had pulled down their steel shutters and in every office, managers were emptying the petty-cash and going home early to their wives, rather than taking the detour to the mistress. Some of the white and brown lawyers and office workers had managed to get out of the city the previous week. They had driven at speed through the growing mob which hadn't yet reached fever pitch. Law and order was left to the Commissioner of Police who called for English troops as back-up for his officers. Kingston was sealed off and no one could get access to the rich suburbs. Gladstone and Oliver now led the movement for independence and Virginia was pregnant. But who for goodness sake was the father?

It was at a rally in May Pen that Virginia told Oliver that she was going to have a baby. They stood under a coconut tree watching Gladstone excite the people with his oratory.

"Who is the father?" Oliver asked.

"I don't know, it could be either of you," she said getting increasingly distressed.

"Now Virginia, don't worry yourself. You go on and pretend the baby is fe Gladstone. I promise I won't say a word."

Oliver was indifferent to the news. Not shocked, but cold and mechanical.

"But what if you're the father, don't you care?"

"Frankly, not as long as the baby is a Cooper, then what does it matter?"

"How could you say that, we are talking about the possibility of me carrying your son or daughter!" Virginia shouted, drawing the attention of a group in the crowd.

"You misunderstand me Virginia. What I am saying is that I will stand by you if the child is mine or not. Now please don't get yourself so agitated. I suggest you go home and get some rest."

Oliver was a patronising, arrogant bastard. He soon lost interest in the affair, now always too busy to see his brother's wife. Either there was too much Party work or he had to go to the country for weekends. Virginia wondered what had happened to her? Why was she chasing this man who didn't want her anymore? She had put her marriage in peril for him because he said he loved her. She felt a fool, she was used and now she had to face Gladstone who was joyous about the news of the baby and decided to call it Rodrigues if it was a boy and Juliet if it was a girl. Knowing that she could be carrying his brother's child, Virginia could never share fully in his joy.

Soon Oliver was making claims to the throne of the IPJ. A whole generation of troubled young Jamaicans, had been left up the creek with hungry bellies and without a messiah. Oliver Cooper was the answer to their prayers and his picture occupied the space next to Jesus on their bedroom walls. His voice bellowed with authority and he could cuss the rawest 'bad word'. He could drink any country man under the table and still stand up and hold court over a fiery political meeting. Oliver even instigated a rumour that he had one of the biggest cocks in Jamaica. Sadly, the people believed it, as they did any rumour, particularly the women. Jamaican leaders had a long tradition of spreading rumours about their sexual prowess. On street corners and in rum bars all over the island, men would discuss whether Oliver's cock was really that big and how he was able to sleep with twenty women in

116

one night. The bigger the rumours about his cock, the larger his reputation grew. In St Thomas they had him only as seven inches, whereas in Hanover and St Catherine, market women would raise a machete if you said it was less than 13 inches.

Gladstone was increasingly irritated by his brother's new popularity.

"I don't like it, I don't like it one bit, he is not educating the people, he is a rabble rouser," said Gladstone.

It was only in bed that he and his wife found time to talk, with the days being so busy.

"Don't worry Gladstone, I'm sure that his intentions are honourable."

"Listen, my brother is only after honouring himself and to hell with everyone else." He looked at his wife and smiled. "Thank God I can trust you Ginny. You know, Jamaica seems to have lost its innocence, no one seems to care about integrity anymore, everyone cheating on each other. I'm so glad that you and the baby are a world away from all this madness."

Virginia looked at her husband intensely, he was too honest, too faithful. That night she prayed to God for forgiveness, but already sensed it was too late.

Virginia had few close friends in Jamaica. She hated the pretentious middle-class which was divided into the British and the brown-skin elite who were even more arrogant. She was more or less a loner and she liked it that way. However, she needed company, someone to share this burden but the only person she could open up to was Gladstone and he was part of her problem.

David realised the change in her however, and for someone so young he was mature on matters of emotion. His mother watched him working hard at his homework, he was now 14 and she warned him that night never to enter politics.

"Daddy said that it's in the blood — we Coopers will always be political," said David confidently.

"That's not really true. You must decide what you want to do with your own life."

"Why have you been so sad lately?" David asked. "Is it the baby or is there something else on your mind?"

"It's just the harsh world of politics David, something which I really think I should have stayed away from. It's corrupt and corrupting."

She stayed silent for a moment, holding her stomach contemplatively. The only movement in the room came from the baby inside her where a kick signalled that it refused to be disciplined. She knew then that this was Oliver's child...

Gladstone chose the name Rodrigues when Virginia gave birth to a second son. It was a quirky name for a Jamaican, but then Gladstone always said he couldn't quite figure out the new baby, that there was something strange about him being so different from David. And Virginia sensed an underlying uneasiness in her husband's voice when he joked that the baby "seems to be laughing at me with that cheeky smile of his."

Gladstone tried to be fair with his sons however. Even when David returned home as an adult after completing his Masters at Harvard Law School, Gladstone made sure that he devoted as much time to his teenage son as he did to his first born. He didn't wish to make the mistake of 'favouritism' that his father was guilty of. Still, in Gladstone's mind eye, the vision of the future was clear - he would fulfil his father's dream by becoming the first Prime Minister of Jamaica and he would groom his older son to take over when the time was right.

It had to come, but it was still a shock when they heard. Oliver had split from the IPJ and decided to form his own party to fight the elections to which the British had finally conceded. His new party was called the People's Party of Jamaica. The race was now on in earnest for the first Jamaican Prime Minister. The Cooper family was split and Gladstone swore he would never speak to his brother again. Two weeks before the election Gladstone planned a rally to support the local IPJ candidate in St Thomas East. He arrived with his wife in Jamaica's Eastern parish, cutting through its hostile terrain of thick brush as their three old trucks jerked along, full of singing supporters at home in Oliver's territory.

Virginia was to address the rally in the afternoon. As she was about to mount the platform, she sensed that the crowd had become restless. Out of nowhere, a group of drunken PPJ supporters circled the platform and started screaming abuse. Then rocks and stones rained down from all sides. Virginia saw the trucks being turned over and set alight as she was hurried away from the immediate danger. A little girl came running towards her. She was barefoot, with two white ribbons in her hair, no more than five years old. She cried out that she had lost her mother. There was a moment when Virginia saw the rock coming towards the girl's head, but the warning shout was stuck in her throat. The missile tore the little girl's head open and she fell forwards into Virginia's arms. A split second earlier and the girl would have been safe. She tried to stem the flow of blood soaking the girl's clothes. Virginia wondered what dangerous force they had set into being with the IPJ and PPJ at each other's throats — poor people fighting over an argument between two brothers. David Cooper dragged his mother away from the body.

The next day's Gleaner lead with the story of the death of the little girl. Oliver was blamed for the violence. The people of Morant Bay saw that his hands were washed in blood and began tearing down his posters and swearing that they would give the IPJ their vote.

Virginia went to see Oliver later that day. She wanted to find out why he had ambushed the IPJ supporters — whatever could be said ill of him, this really wasn't his style.

Oliver received his sister-in-law with his usual charm.

"So Virginia, you come here fe cuss me over last night."

He was sitting on a low armchair. He was now 62, the same age as Gladstone, but looked in slightly better shape, his back still straight and he seemed to have a reservoir of energy.

"I can't believe that you would order those thugs to come down and injure and kill innocent people."

"No, I didn't, I never ordered such mad action. What do you think I am? The boys were drinking rum last night, them get drunk and decide fe go mash up your meeting."

"And that's it?"

"Look, what the hell you expect me fe do? Draw down dem pants and beat them?"

"If you had any decency, you would do the honourable thing and resign."

"No I'm not resigning over a few drunken buffoons."

"And what about the little girl?"

'That was unfortunate, but the Party will compensate the mother financially. I know it won't bring her daughter back but it's the least we can do."

Virginia looked at him with hate, wondering how she could have given her body to this man all those years ago and how she could have given birth to his child? For 16 years, Virginia and her brother-in-law had lived a lie. Oliver had played his part admirably, which had made it easier on Virginia. He had not mentioned one word about the child or their relationship since the day she revealed that she was pregnant. She didn't even know whether Oliver knew for certain that Rodrigues was his son. It was strange that he hadn't bothered to ask her, but that was his business. As far as Virginia and the world were concerned, Rodrigues was Gladstone Cooper's son.

"You make me sick!" Virginia yelled.

"Now before you get vex, there's a point I need to raise with you," Oliver said leaning back smugly in his chair. She wished he would fall off and break his neck. "Now Virginia, my popularity as you know is all important to me, the people need me and I need the people. After last night's fiasco the people vex with me. So I have no choice but to break the IPJ leadership."

"What do you mean?" Virginia asked, her heart pounding.

"I'm sorry Virginia, but Gladstone is the source of energy in the IPJ. With him broken, I gone clear. So I'm going to tell him about our affair and the fact that my nephew is really my son. This would finish him and the IPJ will know its place — runner up."

"You bastard!" she shouted, throwing a glass of cold water in his face. Oliver jumped up as if he had suffered an electric shock. He grabbed her arm and shoved his face in hers.

"Watch yourself, Virginia. If you mess with me I'll give you one rahtid slap that will send you all the way back to England."

"Let me go. Anyway, if you told Gladstone I would just simply deny it."

"I know you, Virginia. If he asked you, you couldn't look him in the eye and deny it. You love him too much for that. Let me concede one thing, I'll allow you to tell him in your own words. You have got 48 hours to complete your mission, otherwise I will write to him giving him all the details of our love affair."

Virginia said nothing more to Oliver but walked away, her face hot with fear and anger. Her mind was in a cocoon. There was no energy left for anger, her head was filled with a million 'if only's', but she was only a fool of time.

That night Virginia watched Gladstone undress, he talked about good coming from evil, how this little girl's death, at least brought the people to their senses. When he emerged from the bathroom, he looked at his wife, giving her a tender smile.

"What's wrong, darling? You look deep in thought," Gladstone said.

"Come and sit by me, I've got something to tell you which I hope and pray to God you'll understand," Gladstone sat down beside his wife hesitantly. "When I first came here I suppose I was looking for a new life. It was like meeting you, at first, you were this exotic West Indian amongst very plain and boring English men. I hated Cambridge and England, it was too oppressive, too stifling. With you, I have found a life where I am actually involved in changing the whole destiny of a nation. Well as you know, I have got on well with Oliver, who was even more 'foreign' and I was enchanted by his charm. I am sorry Gladstone but for some time before I became pregnant for the second time, I was having an affair with Oliver. Rodrigues is the product of that relationship."

Gladstone was silent, his face became contorted with pain.

"I'm sorry darling, it was unforgivable."

120

"Sorry, is that all you can say? You sleep with my brother, you have his child and you lie to me about it for 16 years and all you can say is sorry?! What made you do it woman?! Didn't we have enough together, didn't I show love and care?! What more did you want?!!"

"I don't know, Gladstone, at the time it was as if I had lost all control."

"Don't give me that, you knew exactly what you were doing."

"Maybe I did, but at the same time you seemed so distant, Oliver has a powerful personality and I just gave in to him."

"And Rodrigues, what happens to Rodrigues now?" Gladstone asked, getting up and looking out of the window to find an answer to this tragedy.

"I hope you will continue to accept him as your own."

"You expect me to raise my brother's son? Jesus woman, you have some front! I don't know you Virginia, you're not the same woman that I met in England or maybe I was deceived all along. I feel nothing for you. In fact I have more feelings for that cockroach over there than I do for your puny soul. I hope God never gives your soul any rest."

"I'm sorry Gladstone... I'm so sorry, please forgive me, I beg you."

"Sorry will never be enough," Gladstone swore.

As Oliver had predicted, Gladstone slumped into a depression, he even started to drink heavily. The Party collapsed around him. He was its inspiration and guide and naturally it followed him into the wilderness. With no real opposition, the death of the girl in St Thomas was quickly forgotten and Oliver became the first Prime Minister of Jamaica with a landslide victory, the PPJ winning nearly every seat.

Gladstone looked out of the window devastated, as the whole of Kingston erupted in wild celebration. He heard the PPJ brass band playing to the accompaniment of whistle-blowing, cheering supporters and exploding firecrackers. There was a stillness in the room which only the defeated know. It wasn't exactly pain, nor sadness. It was as if everything had ceased, as if no further movement was possible in the world, no going on, only a clear-cut silent realisation that his pride would not allow him to tell David that his brother was not his father's son.

BOOK THREE

...The sun had begun its late afternoon descent, as the evening breeze cooled the dying body of David Cooper. The stadium was empty. Fighting had now spread out into the ghetto areas with the news of the shooting of the IPJ leader. Spanish Town was declared a war zone and the death toll mounted as the army slowly took control of the island. But still, there was no sign of the helicopter to carry the Jamaican Prime Minister to hospital.

They say your whole life passes you by as you are about to die. David relived his life in his mind, his childhood and his rise to power - a trip down memory lane. He remembered a song that his old housekeeper would sing, out of tune, as she cleaned the family house. He began to hum it softly to himself as if the song would bring back those golden, innocent days of his youth.

Redemption's coming praise the Lord,
What a wonderful freedom,
Give joy to his name,
I'm talking of wonders
I'm talking of freedom
Redemption's coming praise His name.

Soft as it was, Marva picked up the tune and held his hand in her own and just as softly sang along with her dying husband. With the exception of Trinity, all those gathered around the fallen leader accompanied her by singing the chorus.

David felt good. He was not fanatically religious but he believed that he would get to heaven by right. After all, he had helped poor people and he stood for justice and equality.

Rodrigues was becoming restless, torn between showing respect for his dying brother and co-ordinating his troops in the field. Like Trinity and Ken Williams, he had a frown on his face. He wasn't interested in watching David Cooper die, but he couldn't leave either. Suspicion would fall on the first man to make a move. And that would be a bad card to draw. No, each player had to stay in the game to the bitter end.

David Cooper motioned to Rodrigues to come close.

"Rodrigues, who do you think set me up?" the dying man asked faintly, every word causing him to wince in pain. Even in his last minutes on earth he was determined to find out who the traitor was.

"If you ask me," Rodrigues declared loudly, smiling through a crack in his lips, "I would say is your dear wife Marva who set you up."

"Is what you mean? Rodrigues, you t'ink anyone is going to believe a stinking liar like you?!" Marva shouted, the veins in her long neck tightening. "I don't know what you doing here looking like you feel sorry for David when everyone knows how much you hate him. This was an assassination attempt ordered by yourself. You are the vilest thing that ever walked this universe — you favour patoo. All you want is power at any cost."

Ken Williams stepped forward his eyes looking at Marva. For a terrifying moment she thought he was going to back Rodrigues.

"David, it could never be Marva. There's only one gunman standing here and that's Trinity."

Everyone looked towards the accused, who quickly drew his pistol from his waist. Instantly, Williams pulled out his gun and Rodrigues was the last to draw his weapon.

"No bumba-claat soldier ah go run up them raas mouth and accuse I... don't fuck with me Brigadier, is death you ah deal with!" shouted Trinity. "Everybody knows you wanted David dead so that the Army could tek over! Is you is the culprit."

"Trinity, put down your gun!" Williams ordered, his eyes fixed on the ghetto man's gun and ignoring the fact that Rodrigues had his Magnum pointed covering the both of them.

"If you think you're bad come and tek it from me!" Trinity threatened.

David moaned in distress. There was a momentary silence. Everybody had forgotten about the Prime Minister bleeding to death on the stage. No one moved a muscle however, no one dared give way. There could be no respect for David's dying body while each man gripped his weapon tight.

David turned to his wife and squeezed her hand gently. He knew she was capable of betraying him, but kill him...? He couldn't believe, wouldn't believe, she would plot his murder.

'Well, is one of you and that's for sure,' David thought to himself as he observed the three men frozen in mid-play of the gun stalemate. He looked hard at Marva, looking for the slightest sign of treachery. Her eyes burned with venom for Rodrigues. David felt his wife's grip on his hand tighten. He looked at her as if suspicious of her intentions, but Marva simply stared daggers at Rodrigues while squeezing her husband's hand tighter and tighter. He was too weak to protest as she squeezed the last drop of life out of him. 'Could she really be cold enough to finish me off right here and now?' David wondered, frightened. He racked his brain hurriedly, trying to figure out why his wife would want him dead. What had happened? He remembered with regret how he had only married her because he knew that her good looks would be a useful accessory in Jamaican politics. 'If I survive this,' he told himself, 'and I fall in love a next time, I'll make sure the woman is a friend first.'

"You see me," said Marva, looking at herself in the mirror, "I am said to be the most beautiful woman in this island, yet at 25 and the current holder of the Miss Jamaica World title, I can't find a man. I'm not desperate and there is no shortage of suitors who would give up their lives to spend a night with me, but I'm sorry, they fall short every time.

"I have used everything God and the devil had to offer — cunning, deceit, ruthlessness and even my body to reach where I am. And I have no intention of wasting it on no dibbi-dibbi man. For in this island there is only one person more important than the Prime Minister and that is Miss Jamaica World. And that title is mine for several months yet.

"This was my first year away from school teaching. When you've had a slice of the icing of life it's hard to go back to dry biscuit. As a teacher I couldn't afford a car so I had to jump on the overloaded mini vans to and from work. It was hell on earth. The buses were always packed with nasty men whose arm pits stank, turning themselves on by rubbing-up against me. All of this, just to go to work for a pittance of a salary. In those days I dreamt of fame and fortune. When I couldn't take the teaching anymore, I realised I had two things going for me -- I looked good and I was smart."

Marva wrote a list of initials on her steamy bathroom mirror — these were the men who had tried and failed. For her they were a miserable crew, the last was Prime Minister Rodrigues Cooper, who had been her *boopsie* since college. It was an informal relationship - Rodrigues paid her bills and smoothed her path to victory. As Marva would tell her close friends, "Don't let any winner of Miss Jamaica tell you that she never once 'drop her baggy' to ease the process. If she says 'no', then she's a damn blasted liar!" Anyway, the judges' decision was unanimous in awarding Marva the beauty title.

Marva had two months left of her reign and apart from some modelling contracts, she was destined for the scrap heap of ex-beauty queens, unless she could touch a big-time move and soon. As an ex-Miss Jamaica World, the options were few — either marry a big shot, open a craft shop which never makes money on the north coast, work as a drugs courier flying to Miami and New York every week, or become a Christian.

Marva had tired of being 'the other woman', yet she couldn't think of any man she wanted to marry. It was alright having a sugar daddy, but she needed a more permanent situation for her long term security. No sugar daddy was willing to set his mistress up properly for fear that she would become too independent. What Marva needed was a way of setting herself up in a high-profile, top salary profession or something similar. As Miss Jamaica World, she was meeting all sorts of men in Jamaican high society, so it should have been easy to get some 'position' even if it was only a title. As long as it had a fat salary attached she didn't mind. She would use such a job, Head of PR or Parliamentary Private Secretary, as a launching pad to prove herself and then set up on her own as soon as she was good enough. But try as hard as she might, she wasn't getting anywhere. Men would promise all sorts of things which would all be forgotten once they realised that she had no intentions of giving away her body just like that.

No, she would never be accepted by Jamaican high society unless she became 'legitimate' by marrying an eligible bachelor. Besides, she wanted a family of her own.

One thing she knew for sure, was that Rodrigues was history. Her relationship with him had taught her to avoid politicians at any cost. It was a convention in Jamaica that the nation's leader was entitled to sleep with the island's most beautiful women and since she didn't want to rock the boat, she became his mistress. He was a real brute. His wife knew everything about the affair, but he didn't care. Marva even went to his house to make love. In fact one night, when her husband and his mistress were upstairs moaning loudly, Rodrigues' wife came up to shut the door. He just didn't give a damn about anybody else's feelings but his own and acted like he had never heard of the word 'romance'. Marva felt dirty with him. When he was finished he would always say, "I have left a little something for you on the dresser," and after that he was gone. No kiss, or romantic goodbyes, he would just leave until next time.

Rodrigues had promised to create the new minister-without-portfolio post of 'Minister of Entertainment' for his girlfriend, but since leaving college, Marva realised that he was going to make no effort to fulfil his promises. There was no reason to renege, it wouldn't have cost him anything. Marva could have done the job well and certainly Jamaica needed a government department to harness the outpouring of talent in music, theatre and literature currently conquering the world. But it was as if Rodrigues didn't want to give his girlfriend any sort of power or independence. For Marva, the only thing that made the relationship with Rodrigues worthwhile, was the brand new Mercedes he gave her on her last birthday. In the end, she told him that she had the clap and as leader of Jamaica, he should consider his own health. She never saw him again.

Get involved with politics and politicians in Jamaica and you're heading for a disaster, pure trouble. Marva lost her brother Kelvin through politics. He was only 21, walking home one night after a college dance. He walked into an IPJ area and was stopped by three gunmen. They asked which party he supported. Kelvin had no interest in politics, and he told them so, but they insisted that he choose a party. Of course, it was the wrong one, and they shot him twice in the chest. He died five days later in hospital.

As much as Marva wanted to stay away from politics, politics would always sink its claws deep into her in her role as a beauty queen. She had now got herself mixed up in politics again and right in the middle of a violent election season.

This time it all started when Rodrigues' brother David, the leader of the opposition party, asked her to read the lesson at the funeral of his father, national hero Gladstone Cooper. David was ahead of Rodrigues in the polls for the forthcoming elections and very confident of himself. This was the closest fought elections since Oliver Cooper defied all the polls by romping home to victory on the last furlong in the post-independence elections more than thirty years ago. David had planned the funeral as a star-studded affair, and the reading by Miss Jamaica World was the icing on the cake.

St Andrew's Church was packed with dignitaries from across the world, Jamaica's big shots and those who were still trying. Marva felt nervous standing in church among loyal IPJ supporters mourning the passing of their founding father. Some of the women stared at her as if she was some *streggah* who had sexed their hero to death. The coffin lay a few feet from her, draped in the Jamaican flag and flanked by four policemen unmoved by the sweltering heat.

Virginia Cooper looked a broken figure, her white hair hung ruffled and her eyes stared vacantly into space. With a look of regret in her eyes she turned to her eldest son sitting beside her on the right.

"I once did your father a great wrong," she began shakily, glancing at her younger son on the left beside her, "a wrong that will live on long after your father is buried in the grave."

"Don't distress yourself mother," David comforted. He was less interested in the great wrong than in supporting his mother.

"I know you and your brother have never been close," Virginia continued, choking slightly with every other word, "but as time goes by...before you go to your grave...try and make peace. You and Rodrigues are different spirits, your souls are from different places..."

At that moment, Virginia Cooper wanted to tell her son the secret that she had kept hidden for half a century. She had never had the courage to tell her sons that only one of them was her husband's child. They had lived a lie for too many years. For more than 30 years since she confessed to Gladstone, they had simply gone through the motions of being a happy couple with two sons, but in reality they lived their lives as two separate individuals, the chains of love having been broken by Virginia's infidelity. Partly for the sake of the children and partly for his political ambitions, Gladstone had chosen selected amnesia over

127

coming face to face with the situation. The two brothers never spoke to each other again, with Gladstone mastering the act of speaking to Oliver indirectly, even in parliament. Virginia could never understand why her husband avoided confronting his brother about the situation. He even refused to speak to his wife on the matter and simply turned his back and walked out of the room if she ever brought it up. It was as if Gladstone had decided to continue pretending to the world that Rodrigues was his own son, at the cost of any meaningful relationship with Virginia, and Oliver had agreed to say nothing more. Those last 30 years of marriage had been cold, barren and pointless, but the Coopers were like royalty in Jamaica and a public facade had to be maintained for the sake of the dynasty. Now that both Oliver and Gladstone were dead, Virginia realised that she was the last person alive who knew the secret of the Cooper's great scandal and she only hoped that she had the strength to live her days without breaking down in a sentimental confession.

Exhausted with weariness, Virginia lay her head on the shoulder of her son and both wept openly, but through the tears, David Cooper looked up and smiled at Miss Jamaica.

A private funeral reception for the immediate family was held at the Cooper family home on Hope Road. Rodrigues arrived with his four children from different mothers, all dressed in black. An hour later, David arrived. Virginia hoped that this sad occasion could bring everybody together, especially David and Rodrigues. She knew everything about her sons' rivalry, but she decided to stay out of it lest her intervention revealed anything of that secret she was now the sole guardian of.

Virginia asked Rodrigues to open the reception with a prayer.

"Heavenly father, thank you for my daddy, Gladstone Cooper, who we know is with you in heaven. Thank you for my mother Virginia, but please help my brother David who, at the age of 63, has never won an election after trying three times."

David couldn't believe his ears. He pounced on his younger brother and they began to fight, both fueled by the emotion of the day and their deep hatred for each other. Rodrigues had harboured a bitterness for his older brother since their youth when Gladstone had groomed David as the natural successor to his leadership.

The two men fought until the distressed cries of Virginia reminded them of the occasion.

"For God sake can you two show some respect, I have just buried my husband! "

Rodrigues continued arguing.

"You're so stupid David, I wonder whether mother found you under an ackee tree. Your party has become a laughing stock. Everybody's saying that David is a walking dickie. If father was alive, I'm sure he'd disown you."

"You bastard, Rodrigues!" David shouted as two of the house boys ran to restrain him. "You bastard! How would you know what my father would do, you're nothing more than a bastard yourself! You hear me?"

Gladstone Cooper had never intended to reveal the truth about Rodrigues to anyone, least of all David. He was too proud to admit to his son that Virginia had betrayed him with his own brother and for years he brought the two brothers up as if there was nothing amiss. But as Rodrigues got older, Gladstone began to notice that the youngster outshone his elder brother in every respect. While David, had returned to Jamaica a bureaucrat after his years at college in the States, Rodrigues was a real man of the people, handsome, charismatic and intelligent. By the time Rodrigues celebrated his 21st birthday, he had betrayed the family by following in Oliver's footsteps into the PPJ as their star candidate. Gladstone realised that his brother's son looked more like a future prime minister of Jamaica than his elder brother. The risk that the family dynasty would be passed down through Oliver's line, was more than Gladstone could bear and he felt compelled to tell his son the secret of why he must never allow Rodrigues to carry the family name.

"Son, we Coopers are a proud lot and I want you to know that in the fullness of time, the name of our family must rest in your hands," Gladstone had said. "Not just because you are the eldest, but because you're the only Cooper in the next generation who can genuinely carry on the family name. When I die, I want you to lead the IPJ on to victory. You are the only real Cooper in this family and you must continue the family firm. We Coopers have run things in Jamaica for almost 100 years. We are Jamaica Incorporated. We are Jamaica Inc." That was 20 years ago and until tonight, David had never mentioned the secret to anyone.

"What are you talking about?" said Rodrigues finally.

"I'll say it again, Rodrigues, Gladstone Cooper was not you father, you're nothing more than a bastard, you bastard."

"David, you're not telling me anything I didn't know already." Rodrigues had known since the day his Uncle Oliver had invited him to join the PPJ. Oliver, like Gladstone, would always favour his own flesh.

Although most women in Jamaica would give David Cooper their body for nothing, Marva never really did check for him. First, he was brown skin and she preferred her men black like the night. Second, he was too 'boasy' and she didn't want a man who loved himself more than her. However, when he looked at her, he aroused something that made her want to hold him and comfort him.

129

After the service, Marva returned home to change and soon stood naked, admiring her figure in the mirror. She loved her body and the slightest blemish on her smooth skin would send her into a deep depression. Her privacy was suddenly interrupted by the loud barking of her guard dogs outside. She slipped into a dressing gown and deftly wrapped her head with a towel.

"Hol' de dogs! Message fe Miss Marva!"cried a small boy.

Marva led the dogs around to the back and the boy ran up to her with an enormous bunch of flowers.

"Can you spare a dollar, miss?"

Marva gave him five and quickly opened the envelope. It was from David Cooper.

You read the service beautifully today and I was charmed by your presence. I would like to say thank you with these flowers and invite you to dinner on Saturday night.

Marva phoned her sister Colleen who came straight over when she heard the news.

"Go for it me girl," Colleen insisted. "David Cooper is ahead in the polls. Just think you could soon be the next Prime Minister's wife!"With a glint in her eye, Colleen began to sing the lyrics of a recent number one record, *"I'm in love with a man nearly twice my age..."*

The two sisters both had a dark complexion and they both got vexed quickly, but there their physical similarity ended. Marva was tall, but Colleen, the older by three years, was even taller and always wore high heels, which kept her head high in the clouds and made it sometimes difficult for her to distinguish between dream and reality. In reality she worked in a bank, but she acted like she was the Queen of Sheba and the men of Jamaica were only too happy to oblige her in her fantasies. Colleen never rushed for a taxi — indeed the drivers would wait patiently until she finished her long, languid stroll towards them. Both sisters were ambitious, but while Marva planned her route to financial success meticulously, Colleen expected a suitcase full of money to fall out of the sky onto her lap.

Colleen had already made herself at home in Marva's apartment, busily changing channels on the satellite television. Then like a bored schoolgirl she went into the bedroom to try on her sister's nail varnish.

"So you approve," Marva said, following her sister into the bedroom and trying to get her attention. "What about Rodrigues, they're brothers remember. I can't leave one man to have a relationship with his brother."

"David and Rodrigues may be brothers, but they hate each other like poison. I heard that David was furious when Rodrigues got elected as the youngest Prime Minister before him. And Rodrigues don't have no respect for his older brother. You keep talking about how badly Rodrigues treated you when you were together, I can't think of a better way for you to get back at him than to have an affair with David. Rodrigues would explode in anger," Colleen said.

Marva followed Colleen into the kitchen as she busily opened up the cupboards and looked in the oven, walking past her sister as if Marva didn't live in her own home.

"Borrow me yuh blender Marva, mine mash up yesterday. You wait till I go back to the mall. When I catch hold of that stinking foot Coolie man who sold me the t'ing, I'm going to cuss him yuh see. And then demand fe me money back. And him better not come tell me no foolishness."

Without waiting for a reply, Marva's blender disappeared into a paper bag ready to leave with Colleen. Trying to get her sister's attention, Marva blocked the route to the fridge, there was no way Colleen was going to 'borrow' any food.

Colleen had a point about how Rodrigues would take the relationship. Though Marva wasn't in the revenge business per se, it would fill her with pleasure to show him that he didn't own her. And unlike his brother, David Cooper at least was unmarried. Maybe it was worth breaking her vow to stay away from politicians. She followed Colleen to the wardrobe in the hallway.

"Colleen, listen nuh man! Rodrigues doesn't own me," Marva insisted. "We broke up a long time ago. Whichever man I move with is my business. Let him get angry."

"You say that he doesn't own you," Colleen countered, "but since Rodrigues became Prime Minister, he thinks the whole of Jamaica belongs to him."

"Mek me tell yuh one t'ing, no man own me, dis body belongs to me, and me alone decide what to do with it."

"Give me a wear off your shoes nuh?" said Colleen, Marva's passion washing over her like water off a duck's back.

"What about David Cooper? He must have six or seven different women already," Marva said, exasperated .

"Listen, Marva, you are a top model, no bother tek up with no ole ragamuffin. You deserve the best of the very best. An' it don't matter how many 'ooman him have a'ready, to have Cooper behind your name is like being royalty. So if one brother cyaan work, try the other."

"Anyway," Marva snapped, "I think I'm reading too much into it. He may just want to socialise."

"That's what you think!"

She followed Colleen back into the kitchen, where she helped herself to the ackee and salt fish, left over from breakfast.

"Cho, the fish too salt, thank God you won't need to cook when you reach Jamaica House."

"Colleen be serious nuh! So, would you sleep with him?"

"Anytime and anywhere. Look at the likes of me, a bank teller earning pittance. I have to find a man who has some use. A man who will take me to Miami to do shopping and give me Chinese food every week. Cho, me nuh want no man who ah go skin-up every time I want a gold chopperetta or new clothes."

"But Colleen, I'm not looking for money. I want a permanent relationship with a man that can help me achieve my full potential. I'm tired of the *boops* thing, I'm looking for love."

"Listen Princess, how long you t'ink love can keep you? Anyway, if you tek up a poor man he will suck you dry. Mind my words, them have no damn use. When David get power, dollars ah go run."

Marva gave up on Colleen and left her in the kitchen, busy finishing off the badly cooked breakfast.

If David Cooper wanted Marva, he would have to realise that she did not come easy. He wrote to her twice inviting her to dinner. On the third occasion she finally agreed to meet him. She set aside any initial apprehension of going to his house, deciding that she was tough enough to take care of herself in the house of any man.

She made her way to his house in the Mercedes Rodrigues had bought. As she waited at the junction before turning into Hope Road, a packed minibus drove past ignoring the red lights. Recognising the Mercedes, two youths called out from the bus. By the time she turned around, a small boy was busy wiping down her windscreen. He couldn't have been more than ten. When he finished he held out his hands.

"You have any small change, miss?"

"So school close today, sir?"

"No miss, me mother nuh have no money, fe buy school shoes and uniform."

Although her windscreen looked worse than before, Marva gave him 50 cents, which he clutched to his chest for safe keeping.

The Cooper residence was a huge colonial type residence on Hope Road. The policeman on duty was too busy trying to persuade one of the secretaries to go out with him to search the Mercedes. Marva was greeted by David's personal assistant, Eileen Davis. There was a strong rumour that David's ex-wife caught them in bed together. In many other countries adultery by your leader would mean immediate resignation, but David Cooper's popularity increased despite the, scandalous rumour, with IPJ men taking pride in their leader's sexual prowess. The current gossip over Kingston was about who would be

David's second wife. Eileen was hot favourite.

"How you do, Marva?" Eileen greeted her, a large smile covering her entire face. She was an interesting mix of Chinese eyes, long Indian hair and prominent red lips. "Please go straight in, Mr Cooper is expecting you."

There was a refreshing coolness from the air conditioner. David Cooper's large collection of books covered two walls and stretched to the wooden panelled ceiling. Flowers and green plants adorned every alcove. The wall behind his desk was covered with photographs of poor country people a visual reminder of his title of 'the poor people's champion'. David sat on the edge of his desk cussing one of his advisors on the telephone. When he saw Marva, his tone changed and he quickly cut the call short.

"How you do, Marva? I'm glad you could come."

Dinner was stiff and formal, but afterwards David relaxed the atmosphere by rolling a spliff of prime sensimilla from "a high ranking friend's harvest." It was the strongest herb Marva had ever smoked and within minutes her head felt light and her body relaxed as she struggled to focus on time and space. They spent hours telling their life stories to one another. David appeared to be an expert on everything, from sport to nuclear science. They stayed off politics, but argued all night about family, friends, religion and finally sex.

David acted the perfect gentleman (he was from the old school) and immediately accepted that Marva declined to "lie down and talk in the bedroom upstairs." She reminded herself that, "this pussy doesn't come cheap", even though this polite, handsome, well-read and yes, even sensitive man, had begun to intrigue her, ambition apart.

Marva drove home at 5am with her head still buzzing from that spliff and only just able to resist the call of her heart, aching to turn the car around and drive straight back to David's bedroom.

Two days without seeing David felt more painful than Marva liked to admit. She was preparing to leave early for Nassau on a modelling assignment, when she received a telegram requesting her to go to David's house as soon as possible because he was dying. When she arrived, she saw no sign of crying relatives. Instead, she was told by the housekeeper to wait in the living room. By the window was a spectacular dining-table laid with flowers and candles, then David emerged wearing a dinner jacket, with no signs of illness.

"Will you join me for lunch?" he said smiling.

"But David, the telegram said you were dying. I almost broke my neck to get here."

"Yes, I was dying to see you. And happy birthday."

"How did you know it was my birthday?"

"Well let's say with someone as beautiful as you are, a man makes it his business to know as much as possible."

David must have done his research well, because Marva lied about her age to enter the beauty competition. The whole of Jamaica thought she was only 24. Still, what's a couple of years on a beautiful woman, for a 63-year-old man like David who still looked good for his age. A good 15 years younger in fact.

A lovers' tape played softly and the waiter, who David had hired for the day, served Marva's favourite Chinese dish. After the meal they went out into the back garden where David asked her to take a seat, then he announced loudly, "In honour of Miss Jamaica World, who is sweet 26 today, we give you Jones the magician."

Out of the house came a magician who performed some wonderful tricks, even though they all had to help chase the rabbit who decided to escape from under the hat. Then the waiter wheeled out the piano from the living room and began to play some old-time ska tunes and to Marva's amazement, two of Jamaica's best dancers were introduced and performed a ballet. By now tears were falling freely from her eyes. That David went to the trouble of organising all of this to celebrate her birthday was touching. David held Marva's hand and they danced closely. It was the best birthday present she had ever had and she couldn't stop hugging and kissing him for this wonderful surprise. She decided then to hold tight to this man.

That evening they stood naked in front of the large mirror in his bedroom admiring each other's bodies. David was a fitness fanatic and his body was in supreme condition for a man his age. He stood behind her, his arms came across her shoulders. He was trim and surprisingly muscular. His skin was as soft and smooth as men half his age. Marva felt his hairy chest gently caressing her back. She turned around and he began to slowly squeeze and suck her breasts. The feeling from her nipples got her pussy wet. She looked up at him as he pushed his fingers between her legs. Marva fell back on the bed as David came inside her.

"Don't stop, push harder!" she moaned.

Her hands gripped his backside as she pushed him deeper inside her, refusing to let him go or stop, the bed rocking to their rhythm. They moved well together, but she couldn't stop herself screaming as his penis kept slipping into the wrong hole.

"Please don't stop, please oh raas, it feel nice... it feel good!" she cried. David continued unperturbed, then Marva let out one final almighty scream that seemed to go on forever. She felt no shame. This was good and she wasn't going to let go. She felt out of control, pressing her fingers deeply into his back. David was terrified that she would tear into his ribs. And finally it was there for him also, that feeling of arrival after a long journey.

David was still groaning and heaving as Marva felt his warm liquid inside her. He lay still, using a pillow to stifle his climatic grunts. She wrapped her long legs around his waist, refusing to allow him to draw away, she couldn't bare that sudden feeling of abandonment. David stayed inside and kissed Marva tenderly on her head and cheeks. Here at least was a man who understood that she didn't just want fore-play, but after-play also. He smiled and told her he loved her. She was now satisfied, certain in the belief that she had him all to herself.

They stayed in the bed for several hours listening to each other's hearts pounding, before going downstairs to his late father's study where David showed her the family album. There was a photo of Gladstone with his regiment during the Great War, and others of him receiving his degree at Cambridge and marrying Virginia Langbridge in Kingston.

"What do you think of my mother?" asked David.

"She's a remarkable woman. I really admire her," Marva lied. In truth, David's dowager mother seemed to her, to be too snooty by half.

"Yes, mother is my inspiration, I don't know what I would do if anything happened to her."

David showed Marva a copy of his grandfather's will, which instructed a certain amount of money to be paid to the two surviving children of a woman in Eden Park over in St Catherine. David explained that the woman, Mary Robinson, a poor black country woman, was his paternal grandmother, the mistress of his grandfather Lionel Cooper.

Even though the Cooper dynasty had ruled Jamaica for many years, little had been made public about its origins. David's revelations about the poor black roots of Jamaica's premier family would shock most Jamaicans who simply assumed that the Coopers had been 'redskins' and 'brownings' since they arrived on those shores as legend would have it "on the Santa Maria". Everybody believed the 'Cooper's to be the ultimate 'perfect' family with roots going back to the immaculate conception without a sniff of illegitimacy.

"What do you think your grandmother was like?" Marva asked.

"If she's my grandmother, she must have been pretty," David smiled confidently. "I don't know, I would hope she was something like you."

"Really, and what am I like?"

"You are never satisfied with what you're given, there's a hunger inside you to get more than your lot."

"Some men would say that was dangerous. They'd prefer their women safely knowing their place."

"Anything worth having is risky and sometimes dangerous," said David, caressing her hand gently.

135

"You sound like a politician, David."

"Well, that is what I am."

"And you think women are interested in politics?"

"That's how God made them. Women are always making calculations, compromises, trying to survive in a man's world. That's all politics is isn't it?"

Marva looked at him closely, studying his eyes for any sign of 'playing games,' but he looked earnest.

"So David Cooper, you seem to have studied women closely."

"It's my business. Don't you know that in a recent poll, eighty percent of Jamaican women said that they would vote for me?"

"Cho," she answered, pretending to be dismissive, "that's not because of politics, they just think you've got a nice batty and waistline. Not bad for an ole man," she smiled."

The room had the musty smell of history about it. It had been preserved by Virginia, who kept everything the way her husband left it. Although Marva never knew Mr Cooper, she could feel his dominant presence in this eerie museum. On the walls were newspaper clippings of the hero speaking at union rallies and Party conventions. His hat and stick still hung from a rack and his briefcase remained half-open as if he would be back at any time to complete his work. David looked at Marva, his face turned serious and thoughtful, and then suddenly asked her to marry him! They had barely known each other for a month, this was crazy, but Marva knew that it was the thing she wanted to do and with very little hesitation answered that she would, "but not until after the elections. If you're still serious then and willing to promise me the things I need to be an equal partner in our relationship, then we can talk business." At the back of her mind was the possibility that David might lose and she didn't want to end up marrying an "also ran." If she married him she would make an enemy of Rodrigues, she knew that. If he retained the premiership, he could make life very uncomfortable for her.

David told her that he would want everything from her, soul, body and mind, but that he would give her everything in return. He assured her that he was tired of being a bachelor and running around with a different woman every night. He wanted to get married again because he needed one woman in his life to "love and cherish." Marva had never committed herself to anyone so completely, but that was hardly going to stop her achieving her ambition.

The island was now under election fever, with voting only three months away. The radio reported an increase in shootings, with areas of Kingston divided into political territories. It was Friday afternoon. Marva gunned the gas on the Mercedes, averaging 75 mph all the way

136

to her parent's home on the North coast of the island. On the way, every main town was covered with political slogans in support of the IPJ 'David slew Goliath — 'Nuff Said!' and others championing the virtues of Prime Minister Rodrigues Cooper with the simple slogan 'PPJ — 'Nuff Respect!'. Marva's district was called Spring Head in Oracabessa. She arrived to hear her mother singing a church hymn as she chopped cabbage for the evening meal. Her father was around the back using a long stick to carefully pick the ripe ackees from the tree.

Marva wanted her parents to come to Kingston and had plans to buy them a house in Red Hills or Havendale. But they refused to move. To them, Kingston was a place of heat, evil and violence. Their only son had been killed in Kingston, for simply being in the wrong neighbourhood at the wrong time and though some time had passed since then they still saw the city as a den of iniquity, while Marva's father was not beyond holding the IPJ and David Cooper personally responsible for Kelvin's death. Anyway, as far as they were concerned, Kingston could never compete with the close-knit community of the countryside. Marva contented herself by using some of her Miss Jamaica World earnings to modernise their house. She was glad to see the back of the old pit latrine, which she replaced with a luxury bathroom. Mama would now walk proudly around what she called her "mansion". Her father didn't care one way or another. He wasn't rich, but he was well-off and he could have afforded to modernise the house years ago. But that's how country people are — he couldn't see what the point of an internal lavatory was when the old one in the yard had serviced the family for years.

Marva's father was a PPJ zealot who believed that he would be out of work for the next five years if David Cooper won the election. He was a builder by trade and did a little farming also. For him the last ten years under successive PPJ governments were prosperous, benefiting from crooked deals and kick-backs. Marva remembered her father entertaining the local MP and discussing a new tender which would be priced above the real cost so they could split the difference. He even managed to get a lucrative government contract in appreciation for his support for the PPJ in Spring Head and its environs. There was bad feeling in the district as a result, especially when Marva's father gave jobs only to known PPJ supporters.

After living many years in Kingston, Marva found country life backward. She felt no affinity to the land. For her, country was too slow, too content with itself even though life was tough in this part of St Mary, with many of the people hungry, and only able to afford the dreaded 'chicken-back'. Marva hated the pathetic rum bar with its juke-box, which played the same four tunes all day. People there were used to waiting. They waited for their crops to grow, for the government to fix their roads, for someone new to enter town, for the Lord to set them free. But most important they waited for a visa to America. If you didn't get the call, you were sentenced to the verandah, where you would sit slapping mosquitoes and re-reading the same old 'Mills and Boon'.

Marva crossed the gully opposite and entered Miss Pearl's shop where you could find out the latest gossip in the district. Although it was only two in the afternoon, the local drunk, a rugged one-legged man named Mafia, lay already sprawled over the juke-box. He had an annoying habit of stomping around on a sturdy crutch with his good foot squelching in an oversize water boot, consequently most people didn't mind him passing out wherever he chose. Mafia opened one eye suspiciously as Marva stepped into Miss Pearl's, and on seeing her stood as straight as he could without losing balance and approached, his eyes red and his breath reeking of liquor.

"So, sweetheart, dance wid an' ole man, nuh. Come mek me show you some old time moves." He began whining his waist on his one good leg.

"Ole man, yuh nearly twice my age," Marva snapped, "go home to yuh wife an' pickney!"

He got the message at once and sulked, his manhood having been chastised, and mumbled a curse in his beard.

Miss Pearl looked a formidable figure as she stood behind the counter. Her large bosoms like lethal weapons, ready and loaded to distress any man fool enough to test her. She was a frightening character in the tight jeans she always insisted on wearing, unafraid of displaying her wide hips and large buttocks.

Mafia had returned to sleep on his wooden crutch. A woman with her hair adorned with multi-coloured curlers strolled into the shop, carrying a plastic bag neatly folded under her arm. Fortunately Marva was in no hurry, for the woman conducted her affairs at a leisurely pace, ordering a piece of salt-fish, two cigarettes and a slice of cheese, in between discussing her health with Miss Pearl and then relating various domestic problems about her entire extended family. The woman's legs were scarred, testament to a life-long losing battle with mosquitoes. After ordering a tin of milk and in the middle of explaining why her youngest son was going to lead her to an early grave, Miss Pearl cut her off politely and smiled at Marva as if she knew her face but couldn't place it. Eventually she cried, "Marva! How you do me chile? Me hear yuh talkin' on the radio dis mornin'."

"I'm fine, Miss Pearl, but how are you?"

"Not as good as you. You come fe see Mama?"

"Two Craven A and a slice of cheese," interrupted a little barefoot boy who still had sleep in his eyes.

138

"Wait nuh!" Miss Pearl shouted at him. "Yuh nuh have no manners little bwoy, you nuh see big people talkin'? Cho, you head favour jancro pickney, look how yuh head so knotty-knotty, it favour pepper grain, and you have the cheek to put yuh big long mout' inna big people's conversation."

Miss Pearl winked at Marva who felt sorry for the little boy. He couldn't have been more than five years old and certainly not big enough to see over the counter. But Miss Pearl was right, Jamaican children grow fast to learn discipline and respect for their elders, without which there would be a total breakdown in social order. The boy looked bewildered, not sure if the giant size woman before him was really serious or only joking.

Marva bought two bullahs and some coconut drops and headed to the house. If she didn't see her parents before seven, it would be hard to talk to them. Her parents living room was usually crammed with an invasion of neighbours who wanted to watch soap operas on their new colour television.

When she got home, Mama cussed her for not coming earlier. Her father was embarrassed as his daughter hugged and kissed him.

"Easy nuh, you want leave some energy fe yuh husband, whenever you get married."

Marva's mother did not have a single wrinkle on her soft chubby face. Her father was the complete opposite, lighter in complexion and a skinny man who was often ill. He was never seen out of his assortment of caps — nine in all — each one carefully selected for the day by strict rotation. Her parents had worked hard and sacrificed much so Marva could go to university in Kingston. Their daughter was one of the first in the district to go to college and most of Oracabessa travelled down to Kingston in the back of two lorries to come to her graduation. The locals had subsequently followed Marva's career keenly when her upper second in chemistry got her a job teaching at a high school until she won the beauty pageant. The whole district was proud to know that Miss Jamaica World came from their area and they bore her no envy, even though they knew that the world was now Marva's oyster, while their lives would continue to plod along.

Mama had finished with her washing, and found a place in the shade where she sat down with Marva to shell a bowlful of peas. Samfie, the small puppy, sniffed around the basin. Mama produced a stick from nowhere and licked him across the back with deadly accuracy .

"Move yourself puppy — yuh too fast!"

The shelling was interrupted by the appearance of a little girl who was a mixture of Indian and black. Mama later explained that she was new in the area and had been informally adopted by Miss Bowie, a

139

neighbour, after her mother died. The barefoot little girl stared at Marva intensely as if trying to figure out who she was and how she fitted in to the whole Spring Head picture.

"Good afternoon Miss Anne, Auntie begging you some ice."

Finally assured that Marva was friend and not foe, the little girl smiled and tapped out a rhythm on the small container balanced on her head. Mama returned with the ice, drawing breath as she shuffled her huge frame across the yard. Before the girl could depart, Mama took it upon herself to start combing the girl's long ruffled hair. The girl didn't object and dutifully took her position by sitting at Mama's feet.

"Is a shame how Miss Bowie nuh mek sure your head is combed. Look how your hair tall and pretty. You must look like s'maddy. Me nah let Miss Bowie bring you up like no leggo beast and me want you fe stay far from them crusty negga bwoys, 'cause you is pickney and me nuh want you fe 'ave no big belly before time. You hear me chile?"

"Yes, Miss Anne."

Marva strolled to the front of the house, only to see Victor Powell walking down the pathway towards her. Victor was her first boyfriend. They went out until she went to university. He stayed in St Mary and took over his father's small farm where they raised pigs and goats. Victor never changed, same style of pants with his regulation flannel hanging from his back pocket and then country-boy hat which made him look ten years older than 26. Kingston men are worlds apart from those in the countryside. Town men may have all the lyrics, the fast cars and colour co-ordination, but they would never dream of cooking and doing household chores, whereas a country man like Victor would crochet, wash clothes with his hands and furthermore he could take care of a woman if she fell sick. In Kingston there are three types of men, the married man — he is a rarity, but he still can't keep his hands off the company secretary or the help. He is really of no use because if anything better comes along he's gone. The visiting man — this best sums up the attitude of many Jamaican males — don't stick around for too long. You can tell this by their famous catchphrases, "I soon come," which means you're going to have to wait three hours, "I have to see one of my bredrin," this means he's going to check his girlfriend, "easy nuh man" this is used to cool down his vexed woman after she dare ask him where he was for the last two months, "come darling, mek me tek yuh fe a Chinese dinner," this means he wants to be certain and get some pussy tonight and if you refuse him he'll tell you how much he spent on you and how he made such a sacrifice.

"How you do Marva, is long time. So me hear you turn big shot inna Town."

Marva kissed him on his cheek. It was frustrating, because as usual he declined to look her in the eyes. Why was he so sickly sweet?

"I jus' come fe say 'Howdy do' and to give you this."

He handed Marva a paper bag with five of the juiciest mangoes in St Mary inside.

"Well thank you Victor, you are so sweet," she said kissing him on the cheek.

"Tell me something Marva, is how a girl from country like you manage with the heat and crime of Kingston?" he asked.

"It's not that bad, anyway, if you want to make progress in life, you have to go where the action is,"

No matter how much she liked Victor he was no comparison to David Cooper. Life on a goat farm just couldn't compete with the opportunities to meet foreign diplomats and the world of fine wines and lavish attention that having a relationship with David afforded. It was too late for Victor, his former girlfriend had become a city woman and even there her appetite was hard to please. Marva studied Victor. Part of her despised him, the other part was jealous. She envied his contentment with his lot and his world, yet she hated his lack of ambition and his inability to see that life does exist outside of his parish.

"I can't stop Marva. I must be getting back to feed the pigs," he said.

"Yes you must hurry," Marva agreed.

"You tek care of yourself in Kingston, y'hear?!" Victor called as he closed the gate.

The radio was turned up loud (Marva sometimes wondered if Mama and her father were deaf). Marva recognised David's voice, the special guest on the afternoon phone-in show.

"Turn that raas off!" Marva's father shouted.

"I beg your pardon," she said surprised.

"I don't even want to hear that dirty communist in my house."

Marva's father had been a faithful follower of David's uncle Oliver Cooper until his death the previous year. The enormous photograph, of him shaking his leader's hand after the 1941 riots, took pride of place on the living room wall.

"Daddy, some of us would like to listen to his views. It won't harm anyone."

"No," he said, his arms at his waist. "Let me tell you one t'ing — the best man fe dis country is Rodrigues. Him understand the Americans, an' is them who ah call de tune. Look how him help you with your modelling career, is him have all the contacts fe set you up. The IPJ is full of raas communists. Is PPJ government help send you ah university. I can remember a time in dis country when a black man could never be Chief of Police or big shot banker, and is the PPJ free up the system."

"Me hear that if Missa Cooper win, then those with two goats will have to give one up," added Mama.

"Look Daddy, I'm no politician, but all I know is Jamaica dread, people ah go to bed hungry, unemployment is the highest since the thirties and nearly half the country is illiterate. David Cooper wants to change this, he wants the poor man to be self-reliant not dependent on the United States."

"You young people too fool. Jus' cause Cooper have a pretty face, everyone love him... Remember, if it wasn't for David Cooper and the raas claat IPJ, your brother would be alive today! Now, I want that radio turned off!"

Nobody moved. The old man sucked his teeth and rushed into the house, cutting David off in mid-sentence. Needless to say, his daughter kept quiet about her current affair with David Cooper during the rest of her stay at Spring Head. If needs be, Marva decided, her father could hear about it via the ghetto grapevine while the distance between country and town kept her safe from his anger.

The return trip to Kingston was always the same, with the city centre enveloping the arrivals in a blanket of smog and haze. Marva drove through the Prime Minister's constituency, which had been renamed 'Oasis'. It used to be a mountain of trash, where dust carts would dump their rubbish. For years, its residents had the worst reputation in Jamaica, and were known as the lepers of Kingston. Even the police were frightened to deal with these people who seemed to have no love for their own lives and had little respect for others'. But since Rodrigues had come to power, they had become the envy of the whole island. Their roads were fixed, water and electricity ran uninterrupted, even the air seemed fresher in Oasis. Rodrigues had certainly worked a miracle and he made sure his opponents never forgot. One of the most persistent rumours was that Oasis gunmen were behind the wholesale slaughter of IPJ supporters, which was a feature of the early build up to the elections. Marva had asked him about the rumours only once during their relationship, to which he had replied with characteristic enigma.

"Yuh t'ink seh ole man like me can control dem yardie rude bwoys? Dem is one hundred percent ragamuffin, man! Dem nuh too worry 'bout politics, more time all dem care about is dollars — U.S. style. Yuh t'ink dem will listen me?"

By the time she reached her home in Red Hills, the cool fresh breeze welcomed Marva into another world, where magnificent houses perched on the hillside encased in rows of burglar bars. Despite the excessive security, sleep was always uneasy for those who lived 'uptown'. The fear of daring robbers breaking into their houses at night was always prevalent.

Marcia, the helper, was already busy sweeping out the yard. The scent of her sister's distinct perfume wafted through the air from the verandah so Marva knew that Colleen had already arrived. On hearing her arrive, Colleen rushed out wearing one of her sister's head-wraps and her slippers and carrying the huge bunch of roses that had arrived that day for Marva from David Cooper. Colleen smiled teasingly as she handed the flowers over, reading the card out aloud:

"For the woman of my dreams... David Cooper."

Marva snatched the card from her and read the words again, her heart glowing with emotion. She asked Marcia to put the flowers in some water and tucked the card in her handbag.

"Marva, how you do?" Colleen remembered that she hadn't greeted her sister. "I thought I'd make myself at home. Me nah go a work today — me phone in sick 'cause I jus' dying to hear the latest score wid you an' David."

Colleen made herself comfortable and with a click of her finger ordered Marcia to bring her a lime drink with plenty of ice. Marcia looked at her with disgust and stormed into the kitchen to noisily make the drink.

"I don't know what you want to hear? We are good friends and we see each other regularly."

Marva had decided that it was best that she didn't mention David's proposal to her sister, particularly when marriage would depend on David's success in the elections. If Marva told her, Colleen would no doubt be unable to control her mouth and the whole of Kingston would know about it, making it difficult to cancel the wedding in the event that David lost.

"Lawd God, so you made it me chile. You came and you conquered!" cried Colleen. "Ever since I was a young girl I always fancied Gladstone Cooper's sons. I remember when David came to our high school at graduation - they had to call police when the girls went crazy. Bwoy me envy you."

Colleen began fanning herself coyly with yesterday's Gleaner while staring at her sister and smiling and singing her favourite tune of the moment:

"I'm in love with a man nearly twice my age..."

"Bwoy, the time hot," Marva said nervously. "Colleen I wish you wouldn't look at me like that. Sleeping with David Cooper doesn't exactly make me special."

Colleen finished her drink and began her annoying habit of crunching the ice at the bottom of her glass.

"Hey Marcia me dear, run mek me some tea," she commanded, rubbing her slim tummy. "Is gas you know."

143

"Is alright Marcia, I'll make it," Marva said, fearful that her quick-tempered house girl might not take too kindly to Colleen's superior attitude and might end up kicking her in that slim belly...

"Listen Marva," whispered Colleen, her over-sized gold bracelets rattling as she leaned over, "you mustn't friend-friend your helper dem — especially this one, she too renk. She too fresh Marva. Me used to friend my helper dem, but me learn good. The other day me have fe run the little dry-up foot one."

"You mean Sandra?"

"Yes the one Sandra, me catch her red-handed in me jewellry box. She turn round and have the cheek to say to me that she was cleaning my earrings. So when I see she have my rings on her finger, I said to her, 'You cleaning my rings as well or were they just drying out on your fingers?!'"

"Well Marcia is no teef — we're like sistren," Marva said firmly.

Colleen gave her a look that said, 'well I warned you,' and returned to her favourite topic of the moment.

"So tell me bout David nuh? Him can make love good? One girl tell me that him t'ing is tiny. How it stay?"

"Why don't you ask him yourself Colleen?"

"Listen girl, you hold on to that man, however small him 'oodtop. When he's Prime Minister you will be the first lady of Jamaica, an' from dat time yuh know seh dollars ah go run." Colleen had suddenly become serious, as if she had invested her own soul in Marva's future success.

That evening, Marva stayed in to watch a film on TV. She went to draw the curtains and briefly took in the magnificent view of Jamaica's capital city down in the valley. Marva's house was perched on the hillside from where the glory of Kingston was visible, unfolding right out to the sea. As Marva admired the scene, she heard Hector and Zeus barking outside. The two Alsatian guard dogs growled with anger. Marva looked out to see two men standing at the gate, one white, one black.

"Hector, Zeus, get round the back now!" she called out and then addressed the men. "Can I help you?"

"Marva, it's me Rodrigues, open the gate nuh."

She could now make out her ex-boyfriend's familiar features as he moved into the light.

"Is what you want?"

"Marva, don't leave big people outside, I jus' come to talk to you."

She wanted to send him away but somehow her tongue wouldn't utter the words. She found herself walking out into the cool night air and dragging open the gate to let them in. Rodrigues stepped in quickly, followed by his bodyguard Ferdi Douglas, Jamaica's former heavyweight boxing champion. He stood by the door keeping watch while Rodrigues and Marva went on to the verandah.

As always, Rodrigues reeked of cheap after-shave. He was lighter-skinned than his older brother and dressed from the tip of his Panama hat to his Italian loafers in his favourite all white (to give the impression to the electorate that he was a sin-free virgin) and with two huge studded rings on each hand, he cut a duppy-like figure standing on Marva's dark verandah. Rodrigues was a slim man with a pot-belly which strained the buttons on his shirt. He could never rid himself of the fixed anxious expression that always made him look frantic. As he bent down to take a seat, his bald head glistened in the moonlight night. It was the only attractive part of him, with neatly groomed hair on the side and back. He beckoned Marva to sit beside him and as she obliged, kissed her gently on the cheek and stroked her head as if she were a child.

"So how is it that you come in from New York and don't contact me? I vex wid you Marva."

"Is how you mean" she asked offended, "I'm an independent woman, y'know, I come and go as I please."

Rodrigues got up from his seat and walked to the edge of the verandah with his back to her, punching his open hand restlessly.

"I am very upset Marva because word has got to me that you're sleeping with my brother."

"I would be grateful if you didn't preach to me, thank you. What I do and who I see is my business." Marva remembered Colleen's warning that Rodrigues would get angry when he heard about the relationship with David, but now that he had she wasn't afraid of him, just determined to make clear that he didn't own her, no matter what he was thinking.

"Is that the case honey? Now you listen good. When I first met you, all you were was a poor little country girl and I taught you everything. I even taught you how to fuck. I picked you out of the Kingston gutter, I put money in your pocket and I sent you to America to learn how to become a star. I went to the stores personally and picked out the clothes that you should wear for the Miss Jamaica contest. Even your university fees it was me who paid for that. If it wasn't for me you'd still be in the Sunday choir at church. Lord Marva, I never asked for anything from you, a piece of pussy now and then but no big demands. Then you slap me in the face and jump in bed with my brother. What kind of slackness is that?! You have no gratitude. You want to humiliate me in front of all Jamaica?! An' just before the elections too! Girl, you're too fucking slack — you understand?"

Rodrigues was coarse, but that's how he generally stayed — rough. Marva wasn't impressed however. Rodrigues had only bothered to call

145

on her when he heard about her relationship with David. Rodrigues had lost interest in her and had moved on to other women. But now his pride was hurting and he was back to claim his woman before she started revealing his intimate secrets to his brother.

"Who the hell do you think you are? You come into my house, and carry on as if you own the place. You gave me some money to make a start four years ago and you made a few phone calls but that doesn't mean you own me. Now I suggest you and your bully boy take your raas out of my house now!"

Rodrigues had heard enough, he was furious. He turned to his bodyguard and ordered: "Grab her!" Before Marva could get up from the chair, her head was in a head-lock and she choked.

"Marva," Rodrigues whispered gravely, "you know that whatever happens you're my lady. You hear that? Now I don't like violence, it's a messy business, but you remember one thing: you can go and take up with David, but there's a civil war going on and out there on the streets there's only room for one don. When the fighting's done we won't be taking no prisoners. I just hope you choose right. Because no matter what, I'll remain in power and the next time you need me you'll crawl on your hands and knees and I'll throw you back in the gutter where you came from."

Ferdi released her and she collapsed to the ground holding her throat. She struggled to get up as they slowly walked away, but Ferdi turned around, pointed his finger at her and shouted: "Stay down bitch!"

"Fire to you Rodrigues!" she screamed. "You bumba claat! Fire to you!"

As Marva lay on the ground, a news flash came over the radio, reporting that top singer and deejay General Shaka and two other men had been gunned down in a car off Trafalgar Road. She got up shakily, looking down at the bright lights of Kingston and wondering when all the killing was going to end. The hilltop view of the city was so peaceful, with no bullet ridden body and no innocent blood to ruin the canvas. General Shaka happened to live in a PPJ area. Marva had heard him chat on his top ranking Warrior Sound and knew that he didn't check for politics. Her thoughts for General Shaka were mixed with fear of Rodrigues. Marva began planning her next move, as the radio played General Shaka's greatest hits, its tribute to the popular ghetto youth whose promising career had been so brutally cut short earlier that evening.

If Rodrigues had intended to frighten Marva away from David Cooper, he succeeded too well and ended up having the opposite effect. She now feared Rodrigues so much that she had no other choice than to

146

run to David for protection — he was now not only Jamaica's only hope for salvation, but also Marva's personal redeemer, who alone could protect her freedom from the clutches of his brother. And whether it was for her own protection or for the good of the people, she joined the IPJ to fight for David's installation as the next Prime Minister of Jamaica.

Driving back from Mandeville, after David had reassured the town's businessmen that the economy was safe in his hands, he pulled over into the plaza, staring ahead at the Baptist church.

"Marva, let's get married. I know the pastor of that church and he can do the ceremony right now if you like." David said anxiously.

"What's the hurry?"

"Look Marva, we're in love with each other and what better way to go before the electorate than a partnership between Miss Jamaica World and David Cooper — it's the dream ticket."

It was from that moment on that Marva got wise about this politics business. David might be in love with, her but that wasn't the issue; he needed her to secure his election, the polls only had him slightly ahead, with a pre-election marriage to Miss Jamaica World his chances of victory was assured — Jamaica loves big weddings. So that's how far David Cooper was prepared to go to serve his ambition. One of Marva's erotic fantasies had always been to go in partnership with a man that put ambition before all else. It seemed like she could fulfil that fantasy now and indeed she was tempted to tie the knot there and then also, but she couldn't help worrying about what would happen to her if David nevertheless lost and Rodrigues became Prime Minister; then -- what use is the leader of the opposition? She resolved to maintain the original plan to wait and see who won the election. If Rodrigues won, she would have to go back on her hands and knees to him, but she would do it.

"David, it's much too soon, let's wait for a month and get to know each other a bit longer," she said kissing his cheek.

"Marva, don't you love me?"

"Of course I do, but marriage is a big step and a woman must be sure that she's doing the right thing."

"Even if the man she's marrying is the Prime Minister, who will be able to give her anything she wants? When I'm the boss of this land then the good times will roll, Marva. David Cooper will be the name on everybody's lips."

"I just need time. Remember, patience is a virtue."

For the meanwhile David had to satisfy himself with her promise.

David saw to it that Marva got a job as 'special projects director' at

IPJ headquarters. After being there a week however, she got word via the office grapevine that Eileen Davis — the Party's press officer — had sacrificed a lot to become the next Mrs David Cooper and wasn't about to give up her investment easily. She was a tall, elegant Jamaican beauty described by one journalist as "the thinking man's crumpet." Hers wasn't pretty-pretty beauty, but the beauty of intellectual confidence garnered at Harvard Law School and the Massachusetts Institute of Technology. The possibility that the IPJ leader was still 'up for grabs' worried Marva. She resolved to watch Eileen closely and indeed she did seem to be after David.

Eileen had taken a two-thirds cut in salary to come and work for the party, yet she worked hard with zest and inspiration and was always willing to put in a few more hours at the slightest request from David. She didn't seem to have much of a social life, which worried Marva. She was in the office before eight in the morning and was always the last to leave. If Eileen had a man to go home to, Marva would have been less worried, but as it was, not a day went by without her tracking Eileen's movements whenever David was around.

Marva had to give it to her, Eileen was smarter than she gave her credit for. Realising that she wasn't to be given any room to manoeuvre, Eileen went on the attack against Marva personally. Not directly — to her face she was a paragon of courteousness, but the moment she was out of earshot, Eileen would spread gossip about her to the other workers and to David himself. Marva only realised this when David called her into his office one afternoon to reprimand her over an affair at a recent IPJ fundraiser.

"Marva, me hear about the madman who came to the reception last week...." David searched her eyes for an explanation.

"Yes...," Marva began, unsure of the point he was making, "and what did you hear about it exactly?"

"Me never catch all the story. All I know is that everyone ah blame you Marva."

She was astounded. The word was that she was responsible for the disruption of the event by an eccentric member of the general public.

"And who exactly is blaming me may I ask?"

"Well...'nuff people, who exactly isn't important right now. The important issue here is that we cannot have repetitions of such a display. Things like that make us look amateurish..."

"Wait a minute!" Marva raised her voice in anger. "People are accusing me of something, I want to know who!"

"Well....Eileen says that you let the man in."

"Yes, but I never knew he was a madman." Marva couldn't believe Eileen's craftiness. Sure, she happened to be present when the man entered the venue, but there was no way she could have prevented it. "I even showed him the way into the hall. I had just turned to walk outside when I heard screaming and bad words. When I came back, the madman had taken out his penis and started to piss on all the people."

"So you telling me that you can't see a madman when he's standing in front of you?"

David's self-righteous sarcasm annoyed her, but what angered her most was his unquestioning acceptance of Eileen's malicious gossip. Could this man who was asking her to marry him really be so gullible?

"Look David, it was a fundraiser. The man dressed in a rough way, but there are a lot of poor people in Jamaica. I'm sorry about how things turned out, but you asked me to organise a fundraiser and that's what I did and it was the most successful in IPJ history!"

David was surprised to see Marva angry and raising her voice.

"Look it's alright darling. It's no big deal. Just make sure security is tight next time. Anyway," he changed the subject with a half-laugh, "you should see how Rosie ah bawl all day. It seems that as the madman ah hose down everybody, she walk in and you know how short Rosie is — about waist high — well she tek a blast right in her face!"

Marva was in no mood for levity. She couldn't get the scheming IPJ Press Officer off her mind, convinced that she was being made to look incompetent to David, and Eileen had been successful. David clearly still believed her...

From that day, Marva decided that Eileen Davis was too dangerous an opponent in the fight for David Cooper to sit around waiting for her next move. She had to fight fire with fire.

When Marva next saw Eileen she bade the Press Officer keep her snooty nose out of her business. Eileen replied with her customary haughty attitude insisting, "I don't know what you're talking about I'm sure."

Marva didn't let her get away that easily however, and threatened her with physical violence if she ever interfered in her relationship with David again. Eileen replied that if David was unwise enough to take on a fiancée from the lower classes that was his business, "but being a fiancée is such a long way from being a bride..." she purred with unconvincing empathy.

Thinking about it later, Marva wondered whether it was wise declaring open war on Eileen. The Press Officer was known in Jamaica for having fought many political, business and legal battles. She seldom lost. She was smart, competent, capable and willing and eager to take on the toughest tasks put before her. But the battle was nevertheless on and there was very little Marva could do about it. It was an invisible war, which meant it was hard to attack or defend. There was little tangible to go on, but a catalogue of little incidents that followed, made sure that Marva never forgot that her betrothal to David Cooper was still under threat from the Davis camp.

Eileen may have looked good for her 40 years but she was always going on about the sun making her too black — clearly making reference to the difference between herself and her rival. Things got to a head in the headquarter's ladies' bathroom. Marva was busy putting on her lipstick, when the familiar 'click-click' sound of Eileen's high heels approached.

"I don't know why everyone in Jamaica is so upset by that deejay record *Me Love Me Browning*," Eileen began unprompted, "after all we know that Jamaican men all want a brown girl."

"So it seems; they've passed you by Eileen."

"Oh no me dear, I never will tek with any old negga man."

"That's not what I heard," Marva challenged.

Eileen then turned on the tap with such force that the water sprayed over Marva's new suit, prompting the beauty queen to reach for a small piece of wood which was lying by the sink in order to lick her right in her forehead. Fortunately God above restrained her.

"I'm sorry Marva, wrong tap," said Eileen as she turned around and strolled way.

"Eileen, yuh stockings ladder at the back," Marva cried out as the press officer left looking for a tear that she would never find. Eileen may have gone to Harvard, but Marva graduated from the Jamaica school of bitchiness.

Life at headquarters had reached fever pitch, though it had nothing to do with the coming elections. Eileen decided to start wearing revealing dress suits to work and spent each day pushing up her bosoms right into David's face. After a week Marva had decided to do the same thing, convinced that she ought to be able to look more alluring than Eileen in a revealing dress suit.

One lunch time David leaned across Marva's desk; he had that worried expression.

"Marva, hold the fort for me. I'm just going to lunch with Eileen, she's feeling a bit depressed. I think her mother is seriously ill. Oh by the way did anyone tell you that you're wearing the same suit as Eileen?"

"Yes David, I can see she's wearing the same dress as me."

They spent an hour and 23 minutes at lunch, Marva timed it and as the minutes ticked away, became more and more convinced that David and Eileen were having an affair. David had probably driven his press officer back to Hope Road and had sex during the lunch hour. For the rest of the day, Eileen went around with a smug smile of satisfaction which told Marva, "your man took my pussy!"

A few days later, Marva came across a message from Eileen on

David's desk.

David,
I'll be waiting for you in room 345 of the Pegasus Hotel at 4 p.m.
I am yours forever.
Love Eileen.

At four, Marva stormed into the lobby of the Pegasus, with fire in her eyes and made her way hurriedly to Room 345. The door was locked and instead of knocking, Marva called security, hoping to catch them in action. The guard recognised her as David's girlfriend and used his master key to open the door. Marva burst in, shouting.

"David yuh raas, I catch yuh backside!"

To Marva's astonishment, a meeting of the entire IPJ executive discussing campaign strategy, was under way. They all looked at her as if she were a deranged woman. David looked vexed, his brown face turning red with anger and shame. Of those in the room, only Eileen seemed unalarmed by the unexpected intrusion.

"Marva, please come and join us," she said, beaming with satisfaction. Marva knew then, that she had been set up.

Friday the thirteenth was billed as the 'Clash of the Titans,' this was the televised debate between David and Rodrigues. The outcome could decide who would win the election. The Pegasus Hotel was busy with journalists and cameramen, and as they entered the Negril Suite, Marva and David were greeted with the clicks and flashes of cameras. The two leaders sat either side of Leroy Palmer, the presenter of the JBC special. Marva knew him from university, where he was in Chancellor Hall while she was in Taylor. He became a pest in her final year, telling everybody that she was his woman — a complete fiction. Things came to a head after the university carnival when he forced his way into her room drunk, accompanied by a rum bottle. In the end two blue-seamed officers had to carry him away. He gave Marva an uneasy smile as she took her place at the front of the audience and then kicked off the debate.

"Mr Rodrigues Cooper, Prime Minister, what will you do to curb the increase of gun violence in Jamaica if you are re-elected?"

Leroy didn't wait for the answer before swivelling confidently in his chair and smiling at the camera to assure the audience at home that all was well.

"It is clear," Rodrigues began assuredly, "that there is a relationship between poor economic performance and gun-related crime. When we deal with the economy, gunmen will seek a new profession."

"And you Mr David Cooper?" Leroy asked, pointing his famous

accusative pencil at David to his right.

"The gun thing has become the biggest threat to hard-working Jamaicans since my grandfather Lionel Cooper began his charity work amongst the poor people of Kingston nearly one hundred years ago. We have known deprivation and hard times, but we have never known anything as evil as gunmen terrorising innocent people. This breakdown in law and order is a threat to Jamaica which must be eradicated. That is why when I get elected I will have a seven day amnesty for all illegally held guns to be turned in at any police station. After that, we shall enforce zero tolerance on any offender."

Rodrigues laughed a cool and calculated laugh. Leroy straightened his tie nervously and smiled at the camera.

"Bwoy, yuh my older brother," Rodrigues said, dropping his formal English to deploy his often used tactic of switching to patois to speak directly to his audience in the 'people's language', "so I don't mean yuh no disrespect, but you really think dat the yout' dem are going to lay down their arms just because you're talking 'bout 'zero tolerance', when he knows that the gun can be his key out of the ghetto? Bwoy, you're more naive than I thought."

"I'm not surprised that you Rodrigues, are reluctant to come down too hard on gun men," David said, deciding to fight fire with fire. "Your party has always been soft on this issue. By the same token, do you think that a better economy will make the gunmen lay down their arms to go and get a job as a welder when he can make much more money by simply tucking a pistol into his waist?"

And so the debate went on, the two brothers playing politics with one another with little resolved. A poll after the debate disclosed that 70 per cent of women felt that 63-year-old David came over sexier than his younger brother.

Debate or no debate, the gun question wasn't going away. Parts of Kingston were effectively held hostage to civil war. The army had been called out, but its ill-equipped and poorly trained soldiers were no match for the fearless youths clutching 9mm automatics and Uzis and hungry to make a name for themselves. There were rumours that local drugs barons were using the elections as a cover to mount a war about gang turf rather than political turf. But nobody seemed to know for sure. Meanwhile, the death toll was rising. The lead story on the front page the next day, announced that another ten people had been killed last night when a PPJ gunman ran into a bar off Duke Street — an IPJ stronghold — and shot it up. There was a quote from Rodrigues claiming, "It is clear that the killings are happening on both sides. I urge the IPJ to calm their supporters because, win or lose, if things continue as bad as this, we won't have a country to run."

It was a continuation of the politricks from the television

152

programme.

Election day finally came around. The army was put on 'war alert' and in the streets there was a sense of relief that the mayhem of the last few months would soon be over. The political pundits forecasted "a close run thing", but in the end David walked to a huge victory.

Once the outcome was widely known, the streets of Kingston echoed with victory celebrations. A casual observer would have been forgiven for thinking that the entire country had voted for David Cooper. Jamaicans are very good losers, because nobody wants to be on the losing side. Once the results were known, everybody wanted to share in the victory.

Late night, or rather early morning, after David's premiership was confirmed, he held a victory rally in Spanish Town market place. The crowd had gathered on some waste ground opposite the prison. The journey from the car to the rostrum was frightening. The police helped David and Marva through the crowd as if they were boxing champions on their way to the ring. Marva's heart jumped as men emptied their guns into the night sky. The platform was the back of a lorry which was ready to drive away at any sign of trouble. Reggae music pumped loudly from huge box speakers around the market place.

The IPJ colour was green, standing for the new land that would be given to the poor. The people began dancing and waving their green flags as their leader David (known as 'Solomon the wise one') looked on. The meeting was about to begin, but the music continued to vibrate through the earth. There were cries of "Turn down the music nuh, man! Turn it down, Rasta!"

More gun shots were fired into the sky as the youths honoured their leader. David motioned with his hands and began:

"Comrades of Spanish Town, there is a cry going around Jamaica -- from Morant Bay to Kingston, from Kingston to Negril, from Negril to MoBay — all over. The cry is for justice and equality. You, my friends, have named me Solomon and I take that to be an honour. But you know Solomon mek Babylon foolish, and is the wise people of Jamaica that stand firm with the IPJ. This morning I picked up my Bible and read the story of Shadrach, Meshach and Abednego — they were thrown into the burning furnace, but God spared them for an angel stood among them. Today, my friends, Jamaica faces its biggest test -- drugs and gunmen are waiting to ambush this beautiful island. Our children are not safe from the evil cocaine, which is now available in our schools and colleges, destroying our youth, while the people in Columbia are getting rich! That is why I... David Cooper, will lead this new government into a war against narcotics. This party will wipe out all those years of corruption which have turned certain areas into no-go districts. Now that the IPJ are in power, gunmen will have to go!"

There was a loud cheer from the crowd, and ironically two gun shots were fired into the air. David continued.

"When I was a child I could walk down to King Street at midnight and I knew that I would be safe. I want to bring those days back again where little children can walk the streets safe from drugs and the gun. This island needs discipline. From mini-bus driver to politician, all must be seen to have clean hands. Fellow Jamaicans, ask not what your country can do for you, ask what you can do for your country! I will do my part, you must do yours!!"

The next day, David reminded Marva of her promise to marry him once the elections were over.

"Why wait?" he asked. "We can tie the knot first thing in the morning — a simple church wedding with only a few close family members in attendance."

Marva didn't need any more time to think about it. As Prime Minister, David was now hot property and soon he would have lots of girlfriends. Marva knew she would have to compete whatever the situation, but at least as a wife, what is David's is hers and if it had to be divorce then at least she would get half of everything.

"Don't worry about that, Marva," he assured her, "when we're married my bachelor days will be over. You'll be the only woman in my life."

On their wedding eve, Marva lay upstairs in the bedroom at David's house, suffering from acute period pains and trying to read The Gleaner. Surprisingly, the front page was still carrying stories about gunmen roaming the streets of Kingston, shooting up innocent people and toughing it out with each other in Western-style gun battles. The whole nation had expected that once the election was over, much of the killings would stop. But this wasn't the case. The issue was no longer politics for these gunmen. Their existence as a constant threat to Jamaican society seemed to be the legacy of the elections. Marva threw the newspaper on the floor. She was in too much pain to give politics a fair hearing. As she lay on the bed, she heard David's voice mingled with other deep tones. There was raucous laughter. She opened the door wide enough to peep out. David was talking to three sinister looking men. Her eyes fell on the tall figure of Trinity, the heavy gold 'cargo' glistening around his neck and in his mouth. Marva recognised him from the reward posters. He was wanted in Jamaica, New York and London for murder and drug offences. Officially, he had 'disappeared', but everyone knew that he was 'running t'ings' in the Kingston ghettoes and now he was standing as bold as day in the living room.

No-one knew Trinity's real name but he was treated with the awe of a great film hero in the city ghettoes. He wore a leather cap and denim shirt with epaulets and had a ring on every finger.

Trinity pulled out a rizla and built himself a spliff. The deep 'telephone receiver' scar from earlobe to the corner of the mouth across his right cheek and a newly-healed flesh wound on his arm, told the story of earlier battles. He spread the ganja carefully on the coffee table, the gold rings on his large fingers glistening against his dark skin. Then David took out a sachet of white powder from his desk drawer and carefully mixed the two ingredients. The smoke filled the air with a foul odour. There were three other men in the room — peering hesitantly out of the windows as if they expected trouble at any moment. One of the men carried a semi-automatic pistol of a type rarely seen in Jamaica but which had featured on the television news the day before, following a bank robbery.

"Well boss, it's time for all good men to settle their dues," Trinity said casually, as he pulled a long draw from his spliff and blew the ganja smoke out of his nose. Marva noticed that despite his scar he was surprisingly good-looking, although she hated his brace of gold teeth. He had a ragga haircut, with a big 'T' cut in the side. Clearly, he wasn't bothered about being recognised.

"Trinity, wha' do yah man? Don't you see I jus' get power. Give me time nuh! We have to move all those PPJ idiots out of the harbour and airport, so that my boys can take over."

"Well boss, I hope you 'member is my men who kill an' die fe yuh in election time."

"I know you worked hard, but until we control the ports, money can't run. My Colombian contacts are already in place. It will take about four weeks," said David.

"And what about work, my men ah dead fe hungry. Dem have dem baby mother and pickney fe feed."

"Plenty of work soon, Trinity," David said, "just be patient. Plenty of work soon. Lawd boys, you don't think I've forgotten you! But let me give you a small goodwill payment." David handed Trinity a large wad of U.S. 100 dollar bills, which Trinity flicked through like a master card dealer. His expression never changed. He put the money in the pocket of his track suit trousers, not taking his eyes off David.

"Yuh know sah, me not please wid dis here pittance."

"Cool nuh man, me tell you fe have patience and the big monies will flow, 'cause from now on, ah me run t'ings, seen?! Soon, we'll be running the cocaine trade from right yah so — officially. Forget Miami, when I'm through, the streets of Trenchtown will be paved with gold, y'hear me? 'Cause all ah de ghetto yout's will get 'nuff work, man. Nuh worry yuhself. But remember dis, there's only one don, is me is de boss.

155

If it wasn't fe me all ah yuh woulda dead fe hungry. So jus' settle."

"And what about guns, sah?" Trinity asked, moving impatiently in his chair.

"Don't worry about dat. I have appointed a little fool-fool young bwoy, jus' graduate, as head of the army. I'll talk to him, he'll do what I tell him — so guns won't be a problem."

"I hope so, boss," Trinity said, exhaling a cloud of smoke from his spliff, "'cause the temperature hot in the ghetto and if man don't get pay, it will be blood and fire, believe me."

Marva thought that she should feel devastated at discovering her future husband snorting coke with wanted killers. But strangely, she felt neither shock nor outrage, just indifference. Her year as a beauty queen had taught her that cocaine was part and parcel of high society, so that didn't surprise her. She was fast learning, that success in politics means you have to be prepared to sleep with the devil.

Maybe Marva should have called the wedding off, but she had other considerations. She had become pregnant and David assured that his sacred 'Cooper dynasty' — Jamaica Inc — would continue. Marva sat on the bed alone for an hour after Trinity had gone, carefully trimming the hair around her pussy. Her thoughts were mixed. On the one hand she was thinking that she would soon be fat and puffy with thick ankles, and then the pain of labour... And on the other hand she was thinking that here she was with a new life growing inside her and about to be married to a man she didn't even know. This wasn't the David Cooper she thought she was marrying. She didn't fully understand what the meeting with Trinity meant and she didn't have any details, but she knew it boded evil. Was this really what it would mean to be Jamaica's Leading Lady?

Well, if as Mrs David Cooper she couldn't beat politics, she would play the game, she decided, and Marva would only play to win. She knew her pussy was golden and it had gotten her out of many sticky situations. It was a question of whether its value matched that of her husband's political power. She carefully cleared away the fallen hair from the bed and went to the mirror to admire her body.

They married the next day. Virginia Cooper sat in the first row in the church, as her eldest son uttered the words "I do" in front of the pastor, but Rodrigues was not invited. Marva became David's third wife. The first died with his two children in a car accident at Half-way Tree and the second was a 24-year-old who acted like a 16-year old. She became a liability and he was advised to get rid of her just before he went for the party leadership, so a hasty divorce had been arranged. The newlyweds left the church for a reception with close family members at the Pegasus Hotel. There was too much to do in the new

156

government, so the honeymoon was postponed until later. Such is the life of the wife of the Prime Minister. Her husband was public property. David promised that when he eventually managed to get away, their honeymoon would be the best.

At the end of the week when the newly-weds moved to the Prime Minister's official residence at Jamaica House, Colleen arrived at the gate. She stretched her long legs out of a Jaguar sports coupé — which then sped away, chased by some small boys enchanted by its speed and shape. Marva knew it was Colleen because one of the maids mentioned something about, "some tall *maaga* girl cussing the police guards at the gate, for not recognising her."

Marva hadn't seen her sister for a number of weeks. Colleen had given up her bank job and found herself a middle-aged sugar daddy, who she treated with contempt. Marva looked her sister up and down. She had filled out slightly around the waist and was adorned with expensive jewellry. Marva explained that security was tight at Jamaica House as a result of death threats against the new prime minister.

"Well me sister, yuh ah breed at last. Now you're truly a Cooper!" Colleen said.

"I'd rather be a woman that loved her man than be a breeding Cooper," Marva replied.

"Don't love any man," came the expected response, "the only thing you must love is him wallet."

They strolled up to the house, leaving the policeman at the gate still surly about Colleen's abuse. Colleen was in high spirits, she had got just what she wanted and was now slowly building up a mini-empire for herself based on the wealth of middle-aged men who she had truly pussy-whipped.

Colleen stayed longer than the afternoon, in fact she ended up staying the week. She sent for some of her stuff so that she could spend more time. When Marva saw that, she wasn't in the least bit surprised. This after all was her sister, a veteran 'shine eye gal' who wanted to possess everything she set her eyes on. Marva didn't mind though. She enjoyed her sister's company and Colleen got on well with David also. He said he liked her raw bluntness about things and that she had opened his mind about how the ordinary Jamaican felt about things.

It was a warm Saturday evening two months later. Marva drove the Mercedes through Kingston with its top down. The city was its usual madness. Women in stiletto-heels balanced precariously on the steps of packed mini-buses, skillfully keeping hand-made dresses from being creased, while the sound of horns, shouting conductors and reggae music bellowed from vans moving to prey on waiting passengers. A scrawny-looking goat walked across the road, and Marva thought of his fat, healthy cousins in the country, while he had to smell in the gutter for food, in constant danger of being killed by a car or stoned by school children.

She was on her way to the National Arena, her reign as Miss Jamaica World had come to an end and she had been invited to crown her successor at this year's finals later that evening. Marva looked extra special, dressed in a cream silk dress, which was figure hugging and sexy-looking even on her pregnant body. She eased her foot off the accelerator as she looked in the mirror to tidy her hair. In seconds, her open-top car was filled with black exhaust fumes. A large JOS bus had driven up beside her, packed with people and provisions from the country and belching thick clouds of dirty smoke. It drove off, leaving her spluttering at the traffic lights, her new cream dress discoloured by the fumes.

"Hey driver yuh raas, look how you ruin me dress," she cried in vain as the bus rumbled on. Fortunately, there was just enough time to go home and change.

When she got home an eerie silence awaited her. She called for David but there was no reply.

"David, you inside? David are you alright? Answer nuh man!!" she called again.

Again there was no reply. There was nobody about, only the ghostly silence answered her call with an echo. Marva became worried. She had left David twenty minutes before saying that he would spend the rest of the evening watching television. And then, there were lots of servants about... where were they all now"? Something was definitely wrong. Marva remembered the death threats and feared the worst and instinctively went to the kitchen and picked up a machete.

She called again, "David!" Then she heard a voice.

"Is who dat?!"

It was David. She rushed into the bedroom to find Colleen on top of her husband — riding him like a mad jockey!

"Lawd Jeezus Christ, Marva, I can explain!" said David, pushing Colleen off his legs.

"Explain!? I turn my back and in two-twos you're fucking my sister. Well, let me tell you this tonight — you could be Prime Minister of heaven itself, this is one negga gal yuh don't fuck with."

"Please Marva, tek it easy nuh, I didn't mean it," gushed Colleen, her naked body shivering with shock.

"You jus' shut yuh mout'... Ever since we were small you wanted everything I had, well now you have my husband. You make me sick." Colleen tried to move from the bed. "If you ever make one raas move, I'll chop yuh in yuh neck-back!" Marva screamed swinging the machete like a mad woman.

158

"Marva, I beg you don't do anything you'll regret," said David.

"Regret!? Now you tell me what I've got to lose by chopping up the two of you, tell me?"

"Marva, please put down the machete and let's talk like adults."

"You know, I hate you David, you are so friggin' reasonable. Your wife catch you red-handed and you want to talk.This is no cabinet meeting, when you choose me to play your games with, you choose the wrong kind of person."

"Marva, is not my fault, is Colleen, she mek me do it, please believe me."

"Is lie him ah tell, Marva," said Colleen, "is him seduce me. I jus' mind my own business and him come in the kitchen and start feel up my titties."

"You know how your sister stay, lie and slack!" David appealed.

Marva couldn't take any more, she raised the machete and brought it down swiftly, cutting the pillow in two and missing them by inches. Colleen, who was still naked, rushed out of the room screaming, while David managed to wrestle the machete from his wife's hands.

"Marva, please stop. Jus' listen woman, and give me a chance to explain, I beg you please, please."

"Nothing, you can say can explain this David, nothing."

"I know."

"And let me tell you one thing, you won't make me cry."

Marva sat in the chair furthest from him. David slipped on his briefs and vest. Then, thinking his wife hadn't noticed, he shamefully scooped Colleen's bra and panties under their bed. Marva felt a deep sickness, the room was like a gas chamber and she seemed to be choking. She could smell their illicit sex in every corner of the room. She could have accepted it, if it was any old *streggah*, or even a prostitute, but her sister... This was like incest. She had obviously been watching the wrong girl, keeping an eye on Eileen Davis, when she should have kept the other one on Colleen.

The Cooper style was to have no style, Marva concluded. She looked at David pitifully and wished he would just go away for ever. David sat on the bed shame-faced, looking up occasionally like a frightened schoolboy.

"David," Marva said, "why Colleen, why my sister, did you hate me that much?"

"We were fooling around in the kitchen and she was wearing just her bra and panties. Then she just came on to me, I swear I never started it."

"Oh, thanks a lot," Marva said unconvinced, "so what happened to your will-power, this was my sister and you're meant to be in love with me. You make me sick, I curse the day that my eyes ever saw you."

"I suppose you'll want a divorce."

"Just stop it! Don't ask me anything! My mind is confused."

Marva went across to the bedside table and looked at the wedding photo which was turned face down.

"I suppose it was Colleen who couldn't bear to look at me when she sat on top of you, or was it you that couldn't get a hard-on with my face smiling at you because you felt guilty? Why didn't you just tell me to jump in bed with the two of you and make it a threesome. You would have jus' loved that wouldn't you?"

David was still in his briefs, worried that his wife might pull out a gun next and shoot him dead.

Marva wanted to play the independent woman, but she was in too deep with this man. She had been so happy when she was single. He had always played it so caring and tender and now she realised she had really fallen in love with him. Husband or no husband, the thing with Colleen wouldn't have hurt so much if she didn't have strong feelings for this man, feelings that were beyond her control. If only he had just rolled off and fallen asleep every time they made love. Instead, he would gently touch her all over and cover her with sweet kisses. And why was it that he knew how to lick her pussy so she sang for joy?

"Marva, how can I make it up to you?" said David.

"Kill yourself, that would be a good start," she said walking out of the bedroom.

Marva rang her good friend Paula, who said she could stay at her place in Constant Springs. Driving there seemed to take hours when it was only ten minutes. She kept having visions of Colleen on top of David enjoying his body and her, like a fool, standing there watching them. It wasn't so much the betrayal, it was the lack of respect. She looked in the side mirror, maybe it was her own fault. Perhaps with the pregnancy, she wasn't looking as good as she should. Was it her thighs, were they too fat already? She looked again at her stunning eyes. How could she blame herself? It was David and Colleen who played the Judas. From that moment she swore that she would never again doubt herself. From now on ambition and power would be everything.

That evening, Paula's girlfriends came over to rally round, they had all experienced the pain Marva was going through. Patsy, Donna, Winsome and Carol sat around the kitchen table, listening to Marva with sympathy. The looks on their faces saying, 'yes me dear, me know exactly what you're feeling.' Marva didn't welcome this attention, after all she wasn't ill, it was just that her heart was broken in a thousand places and she was bitter about it.

While Paula busied herself refilling the wine glasses and checking on the pizza, Patsy launched into a scathing attack on her former boyfriend.

"Mark my words darling, " said Patsy, whose eyes revealed her Chinese heritage, "if I ever buck up with that son of a bitch, I'll 'cratch him eyeball. Your man was caught sleeping with your sister and you think that is bad. I used to work at the telephone company in May Pen. Simone my daughter was twelve years old and I met Derrick shortly after I split up with Simone's father. He was such a caring man, he would phone me at work twice a day and regularly buy me flowers. But most of all he would talk to me and listen to what I had to say. He made me feel important. The most I would get out of Simone's dad was, "Wha'ppen whe' me dinner deh?' Whereas Derrick was a real gentleman. He worked in insurance, but during the school holidays he would volunteer to look after Simone while I went to work, since he saw most of his clients in the evening. Now, I had noticed that Simone wasn't looking her same outgoing self, because she is a child who love run jokes. Neither was she eating and her school report was the worst she was ever given. And let me tell you, my pickney bright. Anyway, one lunch time I forget my dry cleaning, so I did come home early. Once I get in the bedroom I see him on top of my baby, and she crying 'Mommy, I'm sorry.' I must have broken every plate in my house as I tried to kill that dog. Simone will never be the same again, she's lost that spark. That raas is locked up in jail now. I jus' hope one of dem big prisoners hol' him down and tell him, 'Tonight, your name is Jane and me is Tarzan.' Listen, I don't need no man -- when I feel horny I use this..." said Patsy raising her treasured right hand, or better still I will use a vibrator."

Carol wasn't as aggressive as Patsy — she was dark-skinned with wonderful smooth skin and distinct compelling eyes, which would pick up and ask for attention.

"Well everybody thinks I'm mad staying with Dennis, but you just get use to it I suppose."

"Use to what?" asked Patsy dismayed at this weak sister's confession.

"Some of us aren't as strong-minded as you Patsy," said Paula as she served the pizza.

"It's not strong mind me dear, is call self-preservation and no man will ever abuse me again. Anyway go on Carol, is why you still with the son of a bitch," gushed Patsy.

"Dennis is a man who just can't keep one woman. I remember the day I found out he had other women, I felt used but in the end he is a man and that's the way they are. Anyway, who says a man should only have one woman? I think we put too much pressure on them. Sometimes the temptation out there is just too strong for them to handle."

161

"Now listen Carol," Marva interjected, "when I married David Cooper, I made a promise that this girl would only be for him. I expect him to act in the same way. This is no fun and games thing, what we ah deal with is serious business, me dear. Now if your man can't keep him dickie with you, then you don't have a man — you are just his mistress."

"You don't understand," moaned Carol, "the other women aren't serious, he loves me and me alone. Now if he was in love with someone else, that would be different."

"Carol, get real nuh," Marva said impatiently, "your man is taking you for a ride, he knows that you won't say anything about his other women, so he won't stop. What if he gives you a disease like herpes or AIDS?"

"I know he always wears a condom."

The other women burst out laughing, Patsy fell to her knees unable to contain herself. Yet Carol sat there motionless unable to see the joke. Marva felt sorry for Carol because everyone cussed her that night and she was too timid to defend herself.

Winsome had long, elegant legs and distinctive full lips, even the slight scar above her right eye seemed to be part of her natural beauty.

"Like Patsy, I've given men a rest. I was married for about 12 years when one day he just got up and said he was leaving me for a woman in Harbour View. I asked him why — we had three lovely children and he never complained. He simply said that he needed a change and he wanted to divorce me. I tell you, I went through hell. I lost three stones in weight and I couldn't work for a month. I had to get psychotherapy - you see, I kept on blaming myself, my self-esteem just went rock-bottom. Anyway, with the help of God I recovered and found that I didn't need a man for my life to have meaning. I found an inner-strength. It was four months later when I got a phone call from him begging to come back. He realised that he had made a mistake and that he really loved me. I tell you, he just cried and cried on the phone for about half and hour. When he finished, I had to tell him the truth. I said, 'Sorry darling, but you made your bed, now you must lie in it.' He sent me letters, flowers, presents but I didn't want a thing from him. Not even money for the children. I was too self-sufficient to go back to that kind of relationship. One day he stood outside the house and cried living eye-water, begging me for forgiveness, but it was too late. I later found out that the same woman down in Harbour View had found an American lawyer and she told my idiot husband that he must come out of her house so that she could go with her fancy man to stay in Florida. I met him one day in the supermarket and said, "What goes around comes around." The last time I heard he was in Bellevue Mental Hospital, suffering from depression."

There was a sad note in Winsome's voice, it was clear that she still

162

cared for the man. Paula told Marva later that Winsome had sent food parcels to him in hospital. "That's the problem, we can never cut that navel string to our men," she concluded. Marva agreed, she hated David, yet she still cared about him.

Donna was light-skinned; her long hair flowed from Kingston, Jamaica to Kingston in England and she knew it. She was a browning and loved the extra attention she received. Her father was Chief of Police and she enjoyed all the privileges of living uptown. Yet other women saw her as shaming the name of womankind, because she had become rich on the charity of her 'men friends' and the rumour had it that she didn't even enjoy sex.

"Well, I've been lucky with men so far, most have been gentlemen, I think you girls have been choosing the wrong type," said Donna confidently.

"So tell me Donna is which type is right fe you?" Marva asked.

"Well, my ideal man would have a stable income, he would know how to treat a woman like a lady and have a wide range of interests." "You mean a *boops*?" asked Paula.

"No, I don't need a sugar daddy because I have my own income."

"Yes, so you said Donna," replied Paula, "but you're surely not going to take up with no dry-head ragamuffin who would want to suck you dry?"

"Of course not."

"Then settle nuh. Tell the truth, is *boops* you want, don't it?"

"No."

"Yuh lie!" snapped Paula.

"Well if you're going to get personal, what about Omar?"

"What about him?"

"Well he isn't exactly a pauper and you're driving a new Audi," Donna challenged.

"Listen Donna, is me one run my hairdressing business and is my money buy my car. I don't need no money man come flash dollars inna me eye and tell me fe jump. Unlike yuhself."

"But wait, no mek me blood pressure raise tonight!"

"Is funny Donna, that when yuh get vexed yuh stop talk English and move downtown with the rest ah we."

Donna stormed off to the bathroom leaving the rest of the women to bend over with laughter. It was good talking with these women. No matter their size, shade or background they had one thing in common - men had messed up their brains. Marva resolved not to let it happen to her again."

Later that night, the women went for a 'girl's night out' to a dance at Skateland. The dance began to swing as everyone rushed to the dancefloor to wind their bodies to the latest single from Moody Ranks

163

called, 'Dickie Have Rights'.

The sound system is still the most popular form of entertainment in Jamaica, closely followed by the satellite dish. It was through these mobile discos, pumping out strong reggae bass lines through powerful, oversized speakers, that singers and deejays learned their craft and gave the people the latest domestic and international news. Marva was old enough to remember when the Rasta movement provided the lyrical content of the music. In those days, the dreadlocked deejay Longer Dread, used to be known as 'The Human Gleaner,' because his records were the ghetto newspapers. Reputedly, the first that a lot of the residents of Trenchtown heard that man had landed on the moon, was through one of Longer Dread's hit records 'Dread Outta Space'. Now, as they say, things and times have changed. The ragga deejay was now king and sexy lyrics were predominant on reggae records. Marva couldn't care what the church said; to her Jamaican women uptown and downtown loved slack music, because it was rude and allowed them to forget their troubles and inhibitions. For women in Jamaica it was freedom music, the music of liberation. And unlike the many ministers, politicians and do-gooders who preached goodness and pious morality on the one hand (only to be caught later with their pants down in the arms of a woman who wasn't their wife) slackness music was honest.

Every night, people trekked to Skateland from uptown and downtown and curbed the *puppy-show* of Kingston snobbery. This was where everyone tuned in to Moody Ranks' raucous vibes, as it ripped through the class barriers.

The group of women were dancing together when suddenly Marva got a premonition that something terrible was about to happen and her fears quickly proved to be founded. There were two loud bangs outside and three gunmen had rushed in as the music came to an abrupt halt.

"Everybody put dem bloodclaat hands in the air!" shouted the portly gunman, disguised by dark glasses. One of his accomplices was short and wiry with dreadlocks. He held an automatic gun which seemed bigger and more powerful than his tiny frame, while the third gunman was a nervous kid of no more than 13. The gunmen pushed the dancers tightly into a corner and while the other two covered, the entire mass of people were told to put their valuables in a plastic bag that the kid was carrying. Marva was wearing little jewellry, but quickly managed to take off her wedding ring and let it fall to the ground. She felt sorry for Patsy and Winsome who were carrying US dollars and some valuable gold chains. Winsome refused to give hers up because it was a birthday present.

"It's from my gran'father, it's not worth anything. He gave it to me before he died," she protested.

164

"Tek off the raasclaat chain before I tek off yuh head," the main gunman ordered. Winsome froze in fear, the gunman used his pistol to feel her breasts and then travelled down past her waist and pushed the gun between her legs. Winsome's eyes were shut tight. She quickly gave up the chain and the gunmen disappeared into the darkness. The shaken revellers quickly left, cursing the gunmen and David Cooper for the breakdown in law and order.

Marva insisted on reporting the incident at the police station, though no one else thought it would do any good. The women arrived at the station to discover it was closed.

"Please open up. Please will you help us," she shouted, banging hard on the locked door.

"You will have to knock harder, miss," said a little boy pushing a handcart. "Them is upstairs ah play domino."

After a few more minutes of banging, a vexed officer opened the door.

"At last. We would like to report a robbery at Skateland and the gunmen have fled towards the mountain region."

"I'm sorry, miss," said the officer. "I'd like to help..."

"Well what about going after them!" Donna demanded.

"Listen, I want to help but I can't — we don't have any cars at the moment."

A younger policeman — who was standing in the background busily tidying his moustache — said he would hail a taxi, and wandered casually outside. A passing truck refused to chase the criminals, and a rickety taxi which came up the road next, took off quickly, preferring no fare at all, to riding into the bush after gun-toting robbers. Donna had seen enough.

'What de bumba seed do you t'ink yuh ah do?" she said, forgetting her 'proper' English. "Are you a police officer or a Keystone Cop? There's more sense in me batty than you have inna yuh head."

"It's a matter of resources, miss, me tell yuh it dread," said the officer defensively. "This station have four police car: one of them mash-up an' the other t'ree have bald tyre. The government say them nuh have no more foreign exchange to buy any more good police car."

The policeman locked up and returned to his game of dominos leaving these high society women agreeing that things must be really bad in Jamaica when the Prime Minister's wife and the Chief of Police's daughter get robbed and there are no police cars to investigate!

The newspapers, the television news and the radio phone-in programmes all debated the shock news that the newly-married Prime Minster was to split up from his beauty queen wife. The former Miss Jamaica World came out the worse on balance, with most people concluding that whatever the differences a wife's role was to "stand by her man." The most spiteful commentators advised the Prime Minister to now find a woman from a high society background to "match the Cooper pedigree." The domestic debate offered the Prime Minister a respite from his political worries, but quelling the persistent observations that the country was disintegrating into anarchy under the new government proved more difficult.

Marva thought she had seen the last of Rodrigues but he showed up two days after the robbery. He had kept a low profile since the elections, still smarting from defeat. He arrived at Paula's flanked by his burly bodyguard Ferdi Douglas. Marva had smelt his cheap after-shave even before the knock on the door.

"How you do Marva, long time," said Rodrigues kissing her on the cheek.

"I'm fine, so how did you know I was here and my, don't you look well for a man in opposition."

Rodrigues' behaviour was unusually civil and surprised Marva who half expected some rough stuff following their last meeting. As a consequence her attitude towards him softened. Whatever he did to her, was nothing compared to what David had done. And she was interested in hearing whatever it was that Rodrigues had to say, for certainly this was no social call. They sat on the verandah while Ferdi patrolled the area in the front yard.

"Listen Marva, we go back a long way you and I. When it comes to business I believe in mutual benefit. Everyone in Kingston knows that the real reason why you and David mash up, is that you catch his raas in bed with your sister. Now Marva, I know you — you are a hurt woman desperate for the sweet taste of revenge, and since me like you, I shall tell you how you can get back at him... David and the gunman Trinity ah run a drugs racket which is one of the biggest runnings going in the Caribbean. If we could get some evidence, it would destroy him. You're his wife, you can get the evidence. David will have to resign the next day and I will become Prime Minister."

"And what do I get from all this?"

"Sweet revenge Marva, sweet revenge," said Rodrigues, a smile appearing at the corner of his mouth.

"And how do you expect me to get this evidence when I don't live with my husband."

"Cho', that's no problem... Just go back — give him some pussy the same night and all will be forgiven. You know he can't resist some hot punnany."

"Alright, I'll think about it and let you know," Marva replied thoughtfully.

"Good, that's what I want to hear," said Rodrigues.

"How come you hate your brother so much?" Marva asked. "I can't believe you're prepared to bring about his downfall just because you want to be prime minister."

Rodrigues looked at Marva long and hard before getting up to leave.

"I knew that David was just using you," he said. "Ever since we were children, I was the younger brother, but David always envied anything I had. If I had women, he had to prove that he could have more women and better women. Then when I became Prime Minister, he hated me, he cursed me saying it should have been him. So because you were my woman, David jus' greedy and jus' use you to prove that he is better than me, because ah him have my 'ooman. I don't mind all those things, but now he's ruining the country. We Coopers were born to rule Jamaica, I'm not going to allow David to destroy everything my father and grandfather built up. If I have to kill my brother, I'll make sure that the dynasty continues."

That evening Paula informed Marva that a man parked outside the gate in a criss BMW wanted to speak to her. She had no idea who he was but he said the matter was urgent. Marva was reluctant to approach, fearing that this clandestine call might spell trouble. Paula promised to keep watch from the living room window, but just to be on the safe side, went to her drawer and handed Marva a small metallic object, wrapped in a handkerchief. It was only when she got into the light that Marva saw it was a gun. She grabbed her handbag and tucked the weapon carefully inside and marched out into the cool night air. The tinted window on the driver's side of the brand new black BMW rolled down. The muscle head that appeared belonged to Trinity. Marva immediately recognised the 'T' cut boldly into the side of his head and those gleaming gold teeth.

"Miss Marva' wait nuh I just want to talk to you!" he requested as Marva turned to return to the house.

"I have nothing to say to you," she said, feeling for the gun in her handbag, as he stepped niftily out of his car. "Is what you want?"

Trinity raised his hands to show he wasn't armed and approached cautiously.

"Listen, I just want to talk... Is business I ah deal wid."

"Marva, you alright!" cried Paula from the house.

"Yes, no problem!" Marva answer realising that Trinity hadn't come to rob her.

" Can we go for a drive, I have a business proposition to put to you," she said.

It was a risk, but Marva was intrigued at what this handsome 'bad bwoy' could want with her. Soon she was lying back in the leather passenger seat of the BMW driven by Jamaica's most notorious gunman. Clean ragga sounds blasted from the stereo at deafening volume as Trinity fired the accelerator, manoeuvering expertly through the Kingston night traffic at a hair-raising speed. Trinity drove downtown towards the Oceana Hotel which was near the seafront. Marva studied him in the moonlit darkness of the car, wondering why she was attracted to the cool and confident roughness of this gangster.

"Marva — you and I were raised as poor people and the rich brown man still feel him smart," Trinity spoke slowly and determinedly. "That's why me cyaan allow David to disrespec' me, yuh understan'?"

No, that was just it, Marva didn't understand. Trinity looked at his passenger hard, wondering how she could have married the Prime Minister of Jamaica and not even know what her husband was up to. Could she really be this naive?

"David never told me any of his business," Marva admitted. "I know you and he were involved in something, but that's all."

Trinity looked at her again thoughtfully. He suddenly pulled the steering wheel all the way to the left and executed a swift U-turn across the middle of the road and pointed the car in the direction of Maxfield Avenue.

Trenchtown at night time was still filled with people on the streets, poor people who lived there. Anyone who didn't have any business in the area after work hours, had scurried home to more secure neighbourhoods.

Kingston's geography was simple and cruel. The rich lived in the hills but the poor were trapped in the shanty towns that filled the flat land between the mountains and the harbour. It was a place where not even a stray dog could walk safe. Trinity slowed the car down to a cruise, he didn't want to drive too fast, thus bringing attention to himself. This was not his domain and his eyes scanned the dark shacks — alert for any dangerous movement. Marva watched two half-naked boys who should have been in bed hours ago, wheeling a car tyre down the road with a broken stick. This was a favourite pastime for the young, another was a game called chicken when they would lie in the road and wait for a car to come close, then jump up and run for their lives. It was good training for the nerves of steel they would need to survive past childhood.

Then — like a man in a desert who had seen a mirage of a waterfall — the scene changed. They were now in IPJ territory and the apartment blocks were spanking new and well lit. Any PPJ supporter was told in no uncertain terms where he was by a road sign that was daubed, 'IPJ ZONE — PPJ ENTER IF YUH MAD'. The car stopped jerking up and down for now they were on the smooth road built for the government supporters of that neighbourhood. This was politics at its most crude.

The Kingston cake had been divided up into political sections by the two parties ever since the days of Oliver and Gladstone Cooper. These areas used to be defended by men with sticks. In those days political violence was a fist fight in a rum bar. Today, no one dared cross into the wrong sector during election time for it would be certain death — by the gun.

With every change of government there was a big change in slum clearance planning policy, politics decided who would be bulldozed out of their homes to make way for brand new housing projects for government supporters. It was people in these areas that looked the most content, they had steady work for as long as their party was in power. The politics of the slums was more than just boring slogans for these people it meant everything. It was life or 'yuh dead fe hungry'.

There were twelve main gangs in Kingston and they either fought for Trinity-who gave his allegiance to David, or the other 'top ranking' Mr Zulu who worked for Rodrigues. These areas were in essence self-governed. People didn't even use the official area or street names: Bosnia, Jungle, Angola, Berlin and Bronks were the unofficial titles.

The political gunmen were the officers. Their fathers had believed in the rasta faith and the return of the island's black people to Africa. For these youths swapping ammunition was more exciting than swapping marbles. They had grown up fast and grown out of their old ways.

Marva began to feel uneasy, she couldn't wait for Trinity to drive her back to Half Way Tree. Although that wasn't home for uptowners, that was the border between heaven and hell. Though inhabitants of both uptown and downtown found frequent cause to pass through this intersection of two main streets, they saw Half Way Tree in two different ways. The poor and working class walk through this busy chaotic square that overflows with stalls and vendors to catch one of the buses that concentrate there. While those who live in the hills can't wait to get to the safety zone.

Uptown was once in downtown. Many of the buildings that were now rented as desolate, multi-family 'yards' to the poor were originally the homes of merchants. Marva, looked out on the sun-baked, lifeless streets of another district which clearly had no government favours.

"My men risked their lives for him in the election," said Trinity, "and now he wants to cut us out of the big time deal, while him siddung inna Jamaica House and play the big don. But what vex me the worse and my men ready fe kill, is that David promise to pay us after him win the election. When I went to check him, the man say the shipment never come through, now I find out he used the same old PPJ people to trans-ship the cocaine. Well is time fe me play the don. David Cooper is interested in one thing and that's the money he can get by controlling the coke from Columbia. If you want to get back at David for dealing with your sister then shut down his earnings."

"And how do I do that?"

"Easy, find out for me who his Colombian contacts are. I plan to deal with them direct and make 100 percent profit. David Cooper must learn that slavery days done."

They arrived back at Paula's house, Trinity looked at Marva, his bloodshot eyes worn down by ganja.

"Trinity, how do you know that me and David haven't split fe good."

"I know for a fact that he'll have you back tomorrow if you decide to go back. So the ball is in your court."

"Well check me next week and I'll let you know."

"Remember Marva, you and I raise in the same ghetto!"

David Cooper had only been in power a few months, but already the country was going to pot. Cooper seemed less interested in the running of the island than in his repeated constant long-distance calls to Columbia, Miami and London. The one thing he had achieved in his short term, was to increase taxes universally, a move that hurt poor and rich alike. But while the poor had no choice but to turn to hustling to survive during these unpopular austerity measures, those who could afford it were buying up every available seat on Jamaica Airways hourly flights to Miami, hoping for a better life in the United States. Marva heard that her old college mate Karen Sinclair was emigrating to Miami in the morning. Karen was married to one of Jamaica's biggest hoteliers, Jeffrey Sinclair. When Marva arrived, there was a large removal van in front of the house and a flustered Karen directed operations. Marva had arrived just in time, because it looked like her friend would burst a blood vessel if she continued shouting at the removal men. The two women cooled down in the kitchen where Karen untied her scarf and her long brown hair fell down to her shoulders. She had dropped out of university after her second year to take up modelling. She was Marva's predecessor with the title of Miss Jamaica World. Karen won under controversial circumstances. It was said that her husband Jeffrey Sinclair bribed the judges and paid for the massive pre-competition promotion campaign of his then young girlfriend. Karen was virtually white in complexion and worked hard to tone down her country accent but with Marva she was truly herself.

"So Karen how you stay so? You mean you would have just left Jamaica without a word?"

"Well I would write you me dear. But to tell you the truth, is shame me did shame. What with you married to David, and Jeffrey being PPJ, I didn't know what to say to you. I know you are my friend Marva, but Jeffrey says David Cooper ah mash up the country, so we leave.

Whatever happens I love Jamaica and here is my home. But Marva, me can't tek the killing no more. Only last night dem kill a police gal on a mini bus in Havendale. Three gunmen jumped on the bus and tell everybody fe lie down. When dem search the bags and see the gal police uniform, dem beat her. I tell you Marva, Jamaica turn sour and evil."

Though one of the richest women in Jamaica, Karen was still vexed that she had sold her car for half what it was worth, but she wanted a quick sale. She gave Marva her new blender, which made up for the one that Colleen had 'liberated' from her sister's house, and also a teasmade.

Marva had had a few days to think about the two proposals by Rodrigues and Trinity. Clearly, they were both determined to destroy David Cooper's power. The last few days had taught her more about the man she had married — she couldn't bring herself to call David 'husband' any longer. The sharp twinge inside her stomach reminded her that come what may there was a Cooper on the way inside her. She held the key card, because only she could get close enough to David to bring him down, but at the same time she didn't want to play the card for either Trinity or Rodrigues' benefit. If either of them profited from David's downfall, the country would still need a miracle to save it.

David's newly appointed Brigadier-General Ken Williams had invited Marva to his place for a late breakfast. Although ten years older than Marva, they had graduated the same year from university. He had fancied her at the time but she chose to remain 'just good friends'.

Ken lived at Jacks Hill, on a treacherous road 15 minutes from New Kingston. He had been officer material from the word go and after college had become the youngest Jamaican to attend the military academy at Sandhurst. The Mercedes screeched to a halt outside Ken's pad and Marva stepped out to find the young soldier having a late breakfast as he read the editorial of that morning's Gleaner calling for, "discipline and manners in Jamaica." That was exactly what Ken believed in and he hated the inefficiency and slackness which was a part of the country around him. This didn't stop him from having one of the finest physiques in Kingston and he was unmarried to boot.

Ken was dressed simply in a dressing gown. Marva admired his powerful naked legs and the hairless chest which were partly exposed. He seemed more muscular than he had been at university and all the better for it. Marva was also impressed by her former college mate's newly-acquired pinstripe moustache.

"You look good, Marva," Ken beamed, "will you join me."

"No thanks, Ken, I have to watch my weight, you know,"obviously

171

Williams had not noticed that Marva had gained weight with her pregnancy.

"Oh yes, yes of course, Marva... Well, whatever you look like, you'll still be my favourite beauty queen."

They exchanged pleasantries and memories from college, but sex was on both their minds. Marva wanted Ken badly his uniform and good looks made her curious as to what he was like in bed. Ken wasn't so hungry, but he couldn't resist a good dish and Marva looked irresistible. It took them an hour of small chat before Ken made the move, and took Marva in his arms and kissed her, gently at first, then more passionately. She responded with equal passion. Within seconds, Ken's robes had fallen in a pile on the floor, and Marva got her first full view of that renowned behind. Soon, Ken's curiosities were also being answered as the two stumbled from living room to kitchen to, finally, bedroom in a wild, inhibited sexual display. His time in the army had kept Ken fit and Marva gladly took in all the benefits of his muscle-toning.

Lying exhausted in bed afterwards, Williams admitted that he had not asked Marva over just to make love to her.

"So Marva, look what David is doing to the country." He picked up the daily paper and waved the headlines at her with a frown, "We need some firm leadership."

"I know, the violence is getting out of hand."

"Is more than that, I love my country and when politicians like your husband use this place as a trading post for drugs and guns, then serious questions must be asked," said Ken as if he were giving the men a pep talk before sending them out into the ghetto streets to maintain law and order.

"You sound like you could do better," Marva suggested. She caressed Ken's strong biceps almost incredulously. 'He is a real man fe true,' she thought.

"Well that's my point Marva I know I can. Jamaica is in danger of becoming a floating crack house if we let David continue with this madness. Rodrigues is just the same. The people need a break from corrupt politicians. It is time for the army to seize control before the country degenerates into civil-war or anarchy."

"You want to have a military coup?"

"This island is on the brink of collapse. How much more can we take?! The streets are filthy with garbage everywhere, while everywhere one looks there are young people lounging around with nothing to do and nowhere to go. There is no electricity because the government can't control a handful of striking workers in an essential service. Last night a bus driver was stabbed in his chest and as a result there were no buses running this morning. Everywhere you go, people no longer have confidence in the government to keep them safe from violence and death!"

"Ken, why don't you wait for the next election?"

Ken looked hard at the woman who had just enabled him to enjoy her wonderful body. He had dreamt about Marva since college and he couldn't believe that he was finally lying in bed with her. Unfortunately, he had to spend the time talking politics.

"No, we must have change now! I have an idea that needs your help. I know you may want revenge on David, but I want more than that. I want to arrest Rodrigues, David and even Trinity and put them on trial for smuggling cocaine; but we have to arrest them together so they can't mobilise their men. At the moment, they are evenly balanced in firepower. If we only took one or two of them out, whoever else was left would clean up. If we are to rid Jamaica of this guns and drugs thing forever, we must arrest all of them together. And here's my idea... I want you to go back with David and persuade him to call a truce to all violence. The highlight of this truce will be a Peace Concert at the National Stadium which you will organise, using all your celebrity contacts to find artists to appear. If David agrees to it, Rodrigues and Trinity will feel obliged to also lend their support in the name of peace. Then we will spread a rumour amongst the people that David, Rodrigues and Trinity will meet on stage at the Stadium and shake hands. With all three of them up on stage, my boys will get a golden opportunity to make the arrests and we can cleanse our country once and for all of the scum that is making our lives a misery."

Marva listened to the whole plot silently. Once again, it seemed that she was the key player in the move. She suspected that Ken might be doing all this for his own ambitions of political power, but at least his hands didn't seem dirty. Of the options presented to her, Ken Williams was not only the handsomest, but the only one who didn't seem to be motivated by money and greed.

"Tell me one thing — why is the whole of Jamaica so convinced that I'll easily go back with David," she said finally.

"Come off it Marva you're no longer Miss Jamaica. This way, you get to help your country, the other way you get to be married to the man who fucked up your country! If you play your part in this, I'll make sure that you are rewarded when the military takes over."

"Is that a pass Ken?"

"Let's call it a promise to a beautiful woman."

Ken hugged her in his large, naked frame and as they kissed Marva's hands reached out to clench the best bum in Kingston.

Though everybody had heard that David was running around town having affairs since his wife left home, he was still pleased to see her when she returned.

"Marva, how you do? I knew you would come back."

"Is how you reckon that?"

"Let's put it down to instinct," he said. "So have you forgiven me?"

"Forgiven yes, forget no. So, I've got you to myself now, have I ?"
Marva said icily as she looked about the bedroom, expecting to find a
mistress hiding somewhere. David gave Marva a letter from Colleen
who was now in Miami.

"The bitch!" she said opening the envelope.

Dear Marva,

*I know you must be vex with me but I'm really sorry. If it's any
consolation, I didn't really enjoy sex with David, I was just pretending that I
liked it. So since I didn't enjoy it please don't hold anything against me.*

*I don't know when I'll be back in Jamaica but it might be a few months.
Remember what it says in the Bible, Marva — don't let the sun go down on
your anger.*

Please forgive me.

Colleen

Marva tore up the letter in disgust.

At dinner later on that evening, David acted as if nothing had
happened. He confided in Marva as if she was still the same old
innocent woman he had married. She listened silently as he told her of
all his great ambitions. He had no one to share these dreams with since
Marva walked out. He had changed, she could see that, but she couldn't
put her finger on what it was about him that was different.

"You know Marva, I was speaking at a rally in Old Harbour the
other day and a man called me a 'pretend black man,' can you believe
it?"

"People call me names every day," Marva said impatiently, "you
must be strong. How can you let some fool-fool man bother you?"

"I don't know, sometimes they are never grateful. After all, the
things I have done for the people and this is all they can say. If it wasn't
for me, over half the people in this country would be illiterate, many
would be homeless. Look how I make sure they get a minimum wage.
Cho' these people are never grateful."

Marva brought up the Peace Concert and to her surprise, David
jumped at the idea saying that it would help his ratings in the polls if it
could be seen that he had 'initiated' the idea. Marva was happy to let
him take all the credit.

Within hours of the media getting the press release, the news had
carried all over Jamaica that a Peace Concert starring ghetto superstar
Moody Ranks was to be held two days after Christmas. It was to be the

biggest musical gathering in the history of Jamaica. Soon, the country was calling on the leaders of the three factions: David, Rodrigues and Trinity should come out with one love and one heart and shake hands on the stage as a sign of their goodwill.

Marva expected to be overcome with a feeling of revulsion making love to her husband after she returned, but fortunately for her, with David's world crumbling around him he was having difficulty getting an erection and sex was a lengthy bedroom struggle. David avoided any attempt at intercourse for it simply caused him to droop. Now, the only thing that got him excited, was a walk on the wild side.

"Come nuh Marva, I want to lick you all over from head to toe," he kept saying, repeating the same words like a rehearsed play.

"David I feel tired, leave it for tonight, nuh."

"Cho' Marva, you know you like me to turn you on. Just lay back and enjoy me."

She took off her blouse and David jumped up like a puss and began sucking her nipples — hard. Then he struggled to take off her jeans, nearly tearing off her panties in the process.

"Easy nuh man, mek me do it."

Marva lay legs apart, smiling and winding her waist, to turn David on. She had decided to do whatever it took to play her part in the army's plot to wrestle power from her husband. As she smiled alluringly at him, licking her lips, he simply knelt in front of her, watching her show and smiling manically. Then he jumped up and rushed to the bedside table and pulled out the small packet containing rock cocaine from the drawer. He flashed an expectant smile at his wife lying in the bed with a look of surprise.

"It's alright, it's alright, Marva," David explained, "it's strictly for recreational use only. I've discovered that this stuff is a wicked aphrodisiac."

After smoking the coke quickly from an ornamental wooden pipe, David turned to his wife, bloodshot eyes glaring and declared, "It's time for the action." Without further ado, he pounced on his wife, totally ignoring her pussy but digging his teeth into her nipple. Marva screamed with pain, but David only bit harder. Panicking, she managed to get her hands on one of his balls and squeezed it tight. He yelled and came quickly, flopping over on the other side of the bed with exaggerated ecstacy.

"Yuh feel good darling?" he asked after a while.

Marva couldn't believe what she was hearing. Her breast throbbed with pain; that was a price she was unable to pay for any reason. David explained that intercourse didn't do anything for him anymore.

"I'm not past it," he insisted. "I might be past 60, but I feel like I'm in

175

the prime of my sexual ability. So I don't know why dickie is acting up like this, but I know a man who can help.

"The same person who has been protecting me from my enemies," he said mysteriously and turned over to go to sleep. Soon he was snoring. Marva heard the loud crickets outside getting excited as the day closed down. She switched on the bedroom TV to watch the late night talk show. The topic was appropriate: 'How do you live with a man you hate?'

The next morning David asked his wife to follow him to St Catherine, where he was going to see a 'special man'. It didn't surprise Marva that her husband was now seeing an 'obeah' man. Nothing he did surprised her now. Though she didn't want to have anything to do with the occult, she went along to humour him.

They drove by night to the Golden Pen area of St Catherine, David at the wheel, alongside them the bank of the Rio Cobre river, once a mighty river but now little more than a dried-up stream.

They arrived at Bro-Gideon's yard shortly after midnight. In front of his house was a Naseberry tree hanging over the broken down fence. Marva loved Naseberry, pulpy and thick, and when you finished with the richness, you rolled the seeds inside your mouth making them click against your teeth. Bro-Gideon's house was perched precariously on a small hill and chickens, poorly kept pigs and goats roamed freely about the house, while a tired dog slept on the steps of the house. David entered as if he owned the place. Inside, he and Bro-Gideon hugged each other like brothers.

"This is my wife Marva, who will be with me during the ceremony," David announced.

Bro-Gideon was wrapped in white and wearing a blue turban. He was an old man but his cheek-bones were high not saggy, which told of a handsome youth. He was very dark and his gold teeth sparkled under the shaking light of the kerosine lamp.

The front room of his house was really a small church, where cheap paintings of a blue-eyed Jesus stood next to a carving of a black Madonna. They were led through the house into the back yard, which was surprisingly big, and towards some thick bush at the bottom and they climbed down a small gradient to be met by about a dozen women dressed in white. Two of them led David away to a small hut, while Bro-Gideon said he would bless the ground before the ceremony. In the middle of this small clearing was a large disused bath.

"What is in the bath?" Marva asked.

"Oh, it's goat's blood my dear, said Bro-Gideon casually as if he was revealing a recipe. "It will give Marse Cooper power to defeat his enemies, and it will make his seed strong again."

David came from the small hut naked like the day he was born. The women led him to the bath, where he was covered with salt and some herbs, before being lowered into the sticky red liquid. The women encircled the bath and began to sing.

We must chase the devil out of the land,
We must clean our sins with the blood of the lamb.

Bro-Gideon suddenly grabbed Marva's hand and pulled her reluctantly to the bath.

"We must both lay our hands on God's servant for you are his woman, and you are the sea that carries his seed. We must not only make the seed strong, but we must calm the waters. Come rest your hand on his head and let me pray."

The Prime Minister of Jamaica sat there shivering in the goat's blood, his eyes closed, while Bro-Gideon's face contorted, jerking up and down as if a snake was inside him.

"Oh Lord, save thy people and mercifully hear us when we call upon thee Oh Lord. We pray to thee so that your spirit may touch your servant on this holy ground. Give him power blessed father, Give him power."

Bro-Gideon's eyes stared manically at the sky and then he burst out into language that sounded like a mixture of Greek and West African. He then pushed David's head under the goat's blood. Marva had seen enough and tore away from Bro-Gideon's grip and ran screaming back to the car.

That Sunday, Marva went to a service at her uncle's Pentecostal church, hoping to exorcise the paganism of Bro-Gideon's ceremony right out of her hair. Marva's uncle was a preacher who hated politics with a vengeance and it was always worth going to hear his oratory. When he got going the congregation would end up rolling with laughter.

Waterford Pentecostal Church was a large building that serviced mainly the poor ghetto people. However, on Sundays in Jamaica, rich and poor look alike as the best dresses and smartest suits are proudly worn. Marva arrived late and missed most of the early singing and dancing. Inside, women were fanning themselves with anything that could generate a cool breeze. The female choir marched unto the rostrum and sang two numbers which sounded badly out of tune, then the tall figure of Pastor MacIntyre climbed onto the platform. He was Marva's father's brother, a middle-aged man who had kept his good looks — no doubt inspired by a predominantly female congregation or vice versa! The preacher wore a white leather suit and a stunning gold sovereign shone on his finger. He opened up his large bible which seemed the size of a suitcase and the congregation looked up with high expectation...

"God is the abiding, never-changing one," he began dramatically. "Independent of all things that exist. God is before all and is absolute creator and controller of all! Everyman in Waterford tonight with an M16 - God is your boss! "

The congregation shouted 'Amen!' tambourines were rattled and feet stamped the floor in agreement.

"He controls you. And is soon going to let you know who is the bigger boss. The Bible says, 'Jesus Christ is the same, yesterday today and forever.' To use the phrase 'Our God' would suggest that there are other gods. Amen! In fact Jamaica tonight is filled with gods...gods made of wood and stone — some people worship dem car, some dere house some worship dem family, some worship politician..." he said looking across to his niece in the back row. "To many of you, David Cooper is a god, to many of you Rodrigues Cooper is your god. And to some of you even Trinity, that gunman, is a god... But our God...Our God...!! The Christian God, is Jehova. Let somebody say amen...The Lord reigns. He has created a people to worship Him. Even the beasts of the field worship Him. Ev'ry mahning, the donkey gets up and say 'T'ank God!' The very dogs when dem bark, dem seh 'T'ank yuh God'. Only man is vile, only man. There is some men more devoted to deejay Moody Ranks than to Jesus Christ. Some are more devoted to Major Mackerel, you can call him a salt-salt mackerel tonight... I don't think you like me tonight church... Every year they have Sunsplash when they promote the reigning reggae artists — when it's not yellowman, it's black man, when it's not rastaman, it's bongo dread, when it's not bongo dread, it's natty dread. Church, our God reigns. No one can ever dethrone Him, No one ever takes away His crown. He never gets old, He never sleeps. The Bible says that the Lord that I serve 'never slumbers or sleeps', an' Him nevah wear pajama yet! Hallelujah, somebody shout 'yes'! Now, I was in an establishment the other day, in the presence of a man — well, you could call him a man. He looked funny, him speak like a sophisticated lady, him walk funny, him have a funny attitude — Lord, him funny! Some of you don't like this type of preaching. When God made Adam, him mek Eve, him nevah mek Steve! He does not change his plans, he says a man shall leave his mother and father and cleave to his wife — Amen! In the name of Jesus, God reigns, God reigns. Somebody here may not like the way I cut it raw, but let me tell you, you must stop fe yuh foolishness! You don't give a man a position for what he has... Listen to me, there's a little preacher man up the road. He says we must leave each to his own, because God mek dem. God nuh mek dem! This man gets on the radio and talks of liberation theology — come out of Zion with yuh nonsense

— Amen! Bredrin, did you call me here to preach? Then, what we must do then?"

The congregation shouted, "Preach!"

The preacher surveyed his congregation and was getting ready for the altar call. He spread his arms wide.

"I sense that there are some troubled souls here this morning. They need the Lord to restrain them from evil. Come to my altar my children, and humble yourselves. Don't be like Satan who was the Angel who wanted power. Let God be your ambition, because it is he that reigns."

Marva sensed that her uncle was speaking directly to her. She went to the altar expecting God to judge her or give her power. At the altar she felt the preacher's heavy hand on her head. He then came closer and whispered, "Don't let Rodrigues down Marva, he is the man that give the money fe build this church."

Marva got up and stormed out of the Lord's house or was it, she wondered?

The run up to Christmas was stressful. Kingston was hot and every day reports came in of gang warfare. The city was now cut into two, with the IPJ to the West and the PPJ to the East and with Trinity and his men forming a third column. For David it was getting tough, even though it was only a matter of days before the Peace Concert, his men were taking heavy losses. The battle for control of Kingston looked like it would go on, peace concert or not, straight through the Christmas period and into the new year.

Back at the Cooper residence, the rest of the Christmas party were gathered around the television as a festive programme was interrupted by an important news flash. Ken Williams had called a press conference. David sat tense as he watched, biting his nails and unable to keep still. Williams already looked like the man in charge. In a matter of weeks he had matured and grown in confidence. Marva noticed he was wearing a row of medals which he must have picked up in Miami, since he was hardly a war veteran. Williams had informed David about the press conference but nobody knew the scale of what he would say with the eyes of the world's media on him.

"I have called this conference," Ken addressed the cameras somberly, trying to look older than his age, "to give you an update on the present security situation here in Jamaica. Sadly armed thugs have decided to reek anarchy on our beautiful island. There can be no doubt that they are drugs-motivated. I refuse to leave the ghetto districts to the will of gunmen. If they do not put down their arms from tomorrow when the Peace Concert takes place, they will feel the force of the Jamaican Army."

Back at home, David was boiling over with anger.

179

"That raas, you wait till I see him tomorrow, I'm going to strip him bear. When I finish with him he won't even get a job as a foot soldier. Who gave him permission to say all those things. He's trying to cause panic in the country. That bastard! I'll fix Ken Williams, by God I will."

The Peace Concert had Jamaica in high spirits. Never in the history of the island had so many musical greats performed on the same bill. There was the great expectation that the Prime Minister, his brother the leader of the opposition and the notorious 'community leader' (as he was now being called) Trinity, would appear on stage in an act of unity. The National Stadium was packed to capacity and surrounded by the army — who were out in a discreetly higher profile than usual. Helicopters flew across the stadium as the whole of Jamaica seemed to be corked into the venue. The atmosphere reminded Marva of her proudest moment at the National Stadium, the previous year, when she was crowned Miss Jamaica World — the first dark-skinned winner since the competition began. The year before that a riot broke out as Karen Sinclair, yet another virtually white woman, went on stage to be acknowledged as the most beautiful woman in Jamaica. People were vexed. To make it worse the tune which the orchestra played to bring the contestants was the *Ring- Game Song*:

There's a brown girl in the ring - tralalalala
There's a brown girl in the ring - tralala
There's a brown girl in the ring - tralalalala
She look sugar in a plum....

When Marva won the following year, everybody sang "There's a black girl in the ring..."

Back at the Peace Concert, deejay Zack Grind was already on stage telling us about *Pussy Too Sweet*. The crowd moved to the rhythm; a vibrant sea of different colours, everyone believing that they were a star.

The finale of the concert came when an 11-year-old deejay jumped on stage. He ended his set to a fanatical response. He stood there, proud, dressed all in white with a massive gold chain which seemed to weigh him down and a bow-tie in the national colours — green, yellow and black. He looked like a pint-sized Rodrigues and announced with a confidence beyond his years.

"Now as you know, Jamaica people, this is a dread time we are living in. Gun men and bad bwoys won't give peace and unity a chance. I call upon the stage the Prime Minister, Mister David Cooper and the leader of the opposition Rodrigues Cooper and Trinity, the community leader, to come on stage and hold hands in unity. I represent the future of this island — I beg you to give peace a chance."

There was an expectant silence which rippled through the crowd as they wondered who would come on stage first, if anybody at all. David looked at his wife his eyes intense with fear.

"You t'ink I should go up first or not?" he asked her.

"You're David Cooper, the Prime Minister of Jamaica, go and show them how to dance," Marva said.

"You're right. And anyway, Bro-Gideon has given me this," he opened his palm to reveal a flat, smooth grey stone. "With this, no harm can come to me. I'll be back soon darling," he said throwing the stone in the air and catching it as if he were tossing a coin.

David rose and so did Jamaica. The deejay played the 'Cool Down' rhythm and the crowd went wild as the Prime Minister flexed his way across the stage, looking like a champion boxer making his way to the ring, shadow-boxing and weaving in time to the latest reggae rhythms. Once on stage David, although an old man, showed any youth man how to move, his hands cocked-up like pistols, bubbling to the classic rhythm.

David took the mike from the deejay and in that moment the stadium fell silent. It was then that David Cooper realised that Rodrigues wasn't joining him on stage.

"Come on Rodrigues, if you're a man enough to call yourself a leader, come on the stage and make peace!" cried David, "Rodrigues, come nuh man!"

David's call had a tinge of desperation about it. He reached into his pocket and felt the comforting dull coldness of the stone. He pulled it out and tossed it into the air with confidence.

"Come on stage Rodrigues, if you think that you is a bad man. Come test me nuh!"

David looked like a fool on the stage. He bent down momentarily to pick up Bro-Gideon's stone which had fallen out of his hand as he tossed it.

There were only two shots. They came rapidly and echoed deafeningly around the stadium. They came from different directions. One hitting David in his chest, the second in his head. David glared at the crowd, his eyes wide-opened as if asking 'why me?' He fell to the ground and all Jamaica went silent. Marva rushed towards the stage her passage was suddenly blocked by Ken Williams.

"Marva, leave it be, the power is now with the forces of law and order. Justice has been done."

"Lawd Jesus, you had David shot didn't you?"

Ken Williams was silent and avoided her gaze.

Later that evening David Cooper was officially certified dead of gun shot wounds by doctors at the University Hospital.

181

LICK SHOT

PETER KALU

Another Hit From The X Press.
Out on the streets November 15.

DATELINE: A FEW YEARS FROM NOW...

'White Power' terrorists are holding the black population of Manchester to ransom with the world's first race-specific bomb.

As the vital seconds tick away, there's only one man who can deal with the threat and that's Chief Inspector Ambrose Patterson, a black cop with a gun to match his attitude.

YARDIE

By The Number One Black Author In The UK
VICTOR HEADLEY

**At Heathrow Airport's busy Immigration desk, a
newly-arrived Jamaican strolls through with a kilo
of top-grade cocaine strapped to his body. And
keeps on walking...**
By the time the syndicate get to hear about the missing
consignment, D. is in business — for himself — as the
Front Line's newest don.
But D.'s treachery will never be forgotten — or forgiven.
The message filters down from the Yardie crime lords
to their soldiers on the streets:
**Find D. Find the merchandise. And make him pay
for his sins...**

'A book which everyone should read, and soon'
THE VOICE
'Who said you need a review in the quality Sundays to
have a hit?
CITY LIMITS
'The black Godfather... quite simply, Headley knows
what time it is'
THE JOURNAL
'It's the ruffest, the tuffest and the boo-yacka of all
gangster novels'
CARIBBEAN TIMES

Also by
The Number One Black Author In The UK

Victor Headley

EXCESS

THE SEQUEL TO YARDIE

Things got really hot after D.'s arrest. The police virtually closed down Hackney for business. The posses have had to take stock and regroup. But the shaky truce that followed their turf war, is getting shakier as Sticks, a 9mm 'matic in his waist, dips deeper and deeper into his own supply of crack...

Jenny meanwhile has given birth to D.'s son and Donna has given him a daughter. But the battle of the sexes was one war The Don hadn't figured on having to fight.

"Headley <u>knows</u> what he's talking about."
THE OBSERVER

" 'Excess' makes 'Yardie' look like Noddy's day out."
TOUCH MAGAZINE

"Victor Headley is a breath of fresh air on the stale literary scene."
THE FACE

Coming very soon...

COP
KILLER

"A young nigga on the warpath and when he's finished there's going to be a blood bath of cops dying..."

After his mother is shot by the police, he swears vengeance on the officers concerned. In the orgy of violence that follows there's only one question remaining... Can they stop him before he takes them out?